BLADE

OF THE

SIREN

BLADE

OF THE

SIREN

AMBER GRIFFEY

THE FAE REALMS
Harpy Rock
Island Realm
Telaria
Northern Realm
Eastern Realm
Western Realm
Southern Realm
Neutral Territory
Mortal Realm
THE FAE REALMS

CONTENT WARNING

*For those who fought their way out of the darkness,
and to those who are still finding their way.*

CHAPTER

ONE

Emira has been a slave her entire life.

The weight of the empty, golden plates made her frail bones shake as she loaded one after another in her trembling arms. She rounded the massive, mahogany table, belly grousing at the delectable smells that still clung to the air—fresh meats, steamed vegetables seasoned with fine spices from lands beyond her knowledge, sweet blackberry pies and faerie wine. This meal, like all that were served to her master, had been exquisite. Jealousy gnawed at her chest as she continued piling the empty dishes, practically licked clean by her king and his cronies.

Meanwhile, Emira looked forward to devouring the broth and bread meal that awaited her, before she fell asleep on a rotting cotton mat, and resumed her grueling tasks in the morning.

Upon her birth to a siren mother and fae father twenty-five years prior, both of whom had also been slaves, Emira was claimed as property by her master, King Vyrion. She lived and served in his kingdom of the Eastern Realm, one of the five territories of the Fae Lands, since her birth.

She had once been told her mother's name by another slave who was now long deceased; but it was an empty name, for it held no memories or meaning to her now. As for her father, she had no memory of a face, or a name, nor had she been told the over embellished story of a gentleman who loved and cared for his wife and child. It was as if he never existed at all.

Children were rarely born in the Eastern Realm, like Emira had been. Most women could not maintain a pregnancy for longer than a few months, due to the harsh conditions under which they lived. Any child that did survive its time in the womb was born small and frail, if not already eternally sleeping.

But King Vyrion replenished his supply of slaves via abduction and trade. New slaves were regularly brought to the realm from all over the land. Many came from the Mortal Realm; sold by those who were so desperate for food or fae riches. Few came from the Fae Lands, usually weak travelers or runaway youth that roamed too far from home and too close to the eastern borders. Emira had seen all kinds of species pass through—fae, mortals, shifters—and most of them ended with the same predictable fate as her parents.

Emira managed to stay alive by keeping her eyes cast downwards and speaking as few words as possible. The scars upon her wrists and ankles from various sizes of shackles used over the years were mere blemishes compared to the injuries sustained by most; missing limbs, scarred backsides, tongues cut from between too talkative teeth. Her master did not shy away from suffering.

He basked in it.

As a domestic slave, Emira was assigned to work inside the castle and complete the chores that fell under the category of housemaid. Each day, she scrubbed lavish, colossally sized rooms that were constructed with high ceilings, white walls trimmed in gold, and decorated with luxurious, velvet covered furnishings. She then laundered the linens made from the rarest sea silk, all harvested and hand spun by the slaves that worked and resided in the villages beyond the castle walls. After that, Emira spent hours polishing the alabaster statues that depicted the previous line of masters, which adorned the grand corridors. She bit back cries as the blisters on her knuckles cracked and bled as she scrubbed the moonstone floors. And every evening, she cleared the mahogany dining table after an extravagant meal had been served and devoured.

Her stomach curled painfully with hunger as she continued her chores. The vacant dining hall echoed with every clang of cutlery, and every grouse of her empty belly. Her senses were penetrated again by the smell of roasted potatoes, slathered with gravy and bread soaked with oil and garlic.

With an exhausted huff of breath, Emira slammed the pile of plates onto the surface of the mahogany table. The prang of gold on gold echoed through the hall, louder than she had anticipated. Rubbing her sore arm, she rolled her neck, cracking the aching bones in her shoulders as she did so. The promise of bread and broth was not enough to urge her forward like it did most nights.

It wasn't due to a lack of resources that the meals of slaves were barren. The land was fruitful, producing hundreds of acres of beautiful gardens and large, healthy trees. The castle was constructed entirely from grand, expensive stone, and was decorated with extravagant furnishings and art from places beyond Emira's knowledge. The royal stables housed beautiful horses, all of which were powerfully muscular and well fed. Emira's master was exquisitely clothed, always adorned with rare jewels and armed with weapons made for a king. The Eastern Realm was prosperous.

However, King Vyrion would have sooner seen the bounty fed to his dogs before his many slaves.

Emira's stomach roiled again, and she winced at the pain. Nausea crept up her throat, and her weak muscles cramped as she made to press on. As she reached her trembling hands again toward the fine dishes, an untouched, red apple caught her eye.

It was like one of the rare paintings she had become accustomed to dusting day in and day out. The vibrant, shining red skin of the fruit was stark against the deep wood upon which it sat. It was entirely spotless, not a bruise or blemish upon it, and completely untouched as if it had rolled from the fruit platter and in her direction willingly.

Emira's gaze darted between the fruit and the closed entry doors as she considered the rare opportunity that had presented itself. Theft was punishable by slow, torturous death in Vyrion's realm. But as her stomach ached again, begging for mercy, Emira stepped forward and acted on survival instinct, in lieu of logical thought.

She swiftly grasped the apple, and hesitation be damned, bit into it. The sweet juice flowed over her tongue and kissed the insides of her cheeks. She swallowed the mouthful and released a sigh of heavenly relief as the food dropped into her aching belly.

"What the hell are you doing?"

The enraged voice of King Vyrion suddenly grated at her ears. She spun on her heel as the fae king swiftly grabbed her by the wrist, crushing down on the bone like a snake squeezing the life from its prey. With his incredible fae strength, Vyrion twisted the fruit from her grasp. It fell to the floor, landing with a *thump*, and rolled away, taking with it any courage she'd had when she'd decided to quell her hunger.

Vyrion's emerald eyes swirled murderously as he stared down at her. A pathetic whimper passed her trembling lips.

"P-please," Emira stuttered, legs buckling as he stared back menacingly. His thin lips curved downwards with disgust at her supplication.

Suddenly, their surroundings spun rapidly as they tumbled through space and time.

Transference.

It was an ancient form of transportation, a skill possessed only by fae royalty and nobility. Emira had witnessed Vyrion do it many times before, vanishing into thin air with a thunderous *crack*, only to reappear somewhere else in the realm. Their surroundings became like that of a black hole, squeezing her from the inside out. Emira's stomach lurched, threatening to empty the bit of bile that tumbled within it.

And just as quickly as the universe spun, it stopped.

The slave glanced around frantically. Vyrion had transferred the both of them into an overgrown forest with no trail and no sign of a nearby village or town. The treetops towered above, creating a massive, green canopy that blocked out the last few rays of light from the evening sun, and the only sound she heard came from the stomping of her master's boots over the foliage.

Vyrion's strong hand gripped the collar of Emira's linen apron as he hauled her through the underbrush, as easily as if she had been nothing but a limp corpse. His expression was still that of evil, unholy hatred.

"Please!" she sobbed, grasping at the rough fabric as it tightened around her slender throat. "Mercy, please!"

But without a doubt, Emira knew that pleading would do nothing to save her life. Her master did not have a reputation for compassion, or even pity. He had butchered countless other slaves for far less than stealing an apple. She only hoped that her execution would be swift.

"You slaves sicken me," he growled. "Greedy, pathetic, vile things."

With a swift wrench of his muscular arm, the fae king lifted her frail frame off of the ground and threw her against the rotten trunk of a tree.

Pain clawed at Emira's spine as her body hit the wood. The back of her head scraped against the crumbling bark, and her dull, blonde hair caught on its ridges as she slid down the trunk and tumbled onto the forest floor.

Pointed ears ringing from the blow, Emira tried to push herself up, but the pain that radiated through her shoulder and down into her hand forced a scream to unleash from her cracked lips, and she fell back to the decaying, moss covered ground. Emira's arm was broken. She turned to face her master.

Vyrion stalked closer, rage contorting his features. His high cheekbones were caressed by his shoulder length, blonde locks. Malice swirled in his green eyes, and disgust furrowed his thick brows. He looked down on the slave like she was no better than a sewer rat.

Emira braced herself for another blow, sucking in a sharp breath and squeezing her eyes closed. The sound of Vyrion unsheathing the curved dagger from his side cut through the silence of the forest, and rang in her ears as she trembled at his feet.

Emira's mind fogged over, and she thought of nothing at all as she held her eyes closed and waited for death. The slave had no family or friends to consider, no unachieved dreams to mourn. King Vyrion would be the one to end her life; this she knew. It was a fact that she had accepted in her earliest years, and it still held true in this moment now.

But all at once, the ground beneath them rumbled and the overhead branches shook as a fierce wind blew its way through the forest. Her master stopped and sneered over his shoulder as the ground trembled around his steady feet. Emira opened her eyes to witness rocks and twigs quaking upon the dirt around her as spiders and centipedes crawled out from their underground burrows, disturbed by the vibration in the dirt.

She sat upright, gripping at her painful, disfigured arm, and craned her neck to peer around her master's large frame. When he didn't turn back to her, and continued staring into the darkness that swirled before them, she knew.

Something was coming.

CHAPTER

TWO

"This does not concern you, harpy!" the king of the Eastern Realm called into the powerful wind. Still craning her neck to see around her master, Emira squinted through the darkness as the winged silhouette of a muscularly framed male came raining through the forest's canopy. He landed on the ground, sending a burst of thunderous sound waves in every direction, and throwing her weak body onto the hard ground again. The slave cried out as pain seared through her arm, but she forced her gaze up to the silhouette as it moved closer to her master.

Vyrion's expression calloused further, and he turned the rest of his body away from his prey as the male came into view. The stranger was incredibly tall and broad from what Emira could see through the looming darkness. Large, feathered wings of black and gold stretched out wide behind him, casting menacing shadows over his hard facial features. His dark hair lay in lengthy, thick waves that blew about his sculpted face in the swirling wind. And even in the dark, she could make out the ocean blue of his eyes, glinting with beautiful ferocity. He was clothed in black, leather armor and fitted with various weapons that he made no effort to hide, including daggers, a sword at his back, and a whip that was rolled up and attached to his side. It writhed and hissed and slithered, as if it were alive and anxious to be cut free.

"Fly back to that *child* you call king. This slave is mine to deal with," Vyrion continued, now fully facing the harpy.

"You don't have slaves," the winged male replied sinisterly. His voice was deep and dripping with lethal malevolence. Fear clutched Emira's chest as the harpy spoke. His words hit her ears like the edge of a blade hits flesh, quick and sharp. "The treaty made sure of that centuries ago."

Never once in her life had Emira heard her master spoken to with such a cool disregard. The harpy's defiance shook her to her core. She clutched her arm and forced her frail body upright again, leaning her trembling frame against the tree trunk.

Vyrion will end him quickly, Emira thought.

And then his rage will be amplified, making her death even more torturous than he'd already planned. The thought squeezed at Emira's already labored lungs, and a wail escaped her lips.

"*Silence, girl!*" her master hissed. She choked back her cries, chest heaving and broken arm throbbing.

"Have you already forgotten, Vyrion?" came another voice from behind them as a second male appeared. If the stealth of his arrival had not already done so, then his pointed ears gave away any secret to his heritage as fae. He had auburn hair, cut short at the sides while the lengthy top was pulled back into a sleek bun. His build was that of a warrior, as were his clothes, and his amber eyes glinted with mischief.

"Forgotten what?" Vyrion seethed, turning himself towards the newcomer.

The fae male smirked and responded, "When King Valinor handed you your own ass at the Meeting of Kings a thousand years ago."

The air thickened with Vyrion's rage, and the slave instinctively shrunk away from him. The harpy's oceanic eyes glanced at her briefly as she did so before landing back on her master.

"Enough!" Vyrion roared, raising the curved dagger he held at his side and storming toward the fae male. Emira shuffled out of his way, crawling haphazardly over the raised roots and mossy overgrowth beneath them, and clawing at the dirt in an attempt to avoid Vyrion's unforgiving boot.

With a hiss, the harpy's wings spread out wide behind him, shuttering the trees once more. Gripping the black whip at his side, he pulled it free and shook it loose. With an earth shattering *crack*, Vyrion was pulled backwards and onto the ground as the whip wrapped around his throat. Emira yelped at the speed of the attack, clasping her uninjured hand over her open mouth.

"I wouldn't do that," the harpy hissed at her master, pulling the sentient whip tighter.

"This girl is *mine!*" Vyrion choked, writhing, and pulling at the slithering whip as it snaked tightly around his neck. "You have no right to intervene!"

As she clumsily shuffled farther away from her squirming master, Emira's sore back collided with the boots of the red headed fae male. The swiftness of his movement had been unseen to her hybrid siren and fae eyes.

He knelt down beside the shivering girl, flashing a soft smile, and gently lifted her from the ground, cradling her broken arm as he pulled her body against his own. She winced, but the dark, leather armor that he wore across his chest was cool against her battered face, and for a moment, she leaned into the relief, too exhausted to consider fighting him off. The male looked down at her master as the king struggled to free himself.

"You brought her to neutral territory," the fae warrior said, gesturing to the surrounding forest. His stern voice rumbled against Emira's weak body. "We have *every* right."

With a sudden jolt, a pair of tremendous, translucent bat-like wings burst from the back of the fae male. Procuring wings on demand was a quality of the fae, although Emira had never seen it done before. She had not anticipated them to appear so quickly. His were the same amber shade of his eyes and lethally tipped with a long, curved claw. Emira yelped from the shock as well as the pain that the jolt had sent through her injured arm. His golden eyes shifted to her and softened, in what appeared to be repentance. He extended the impressive wings out wide behind him, as if needing to stretch after a long sleep.

"Our king will be interested to hear that you are keeping slaves," the harpy said threateningly, slowly retracting the whip from around the eastern king's throat.

"I am not afraid of *Alicus*," Vyrion spat, still rolling on the ground. "I am not afraid of the Southern Realm!"

With a swift flick of his arm, the harpy retrieved the whip entirely and sinisterly replied, "You should be."

With that, he launched into the sky before Vyrion could stand to his full height. The motion of the harpy's powerful wings sent a gust of wind through the forest, kicking up dust and temporarily blinding the struggling eastern king. The fae male followed his comrade quickly after, his grip on Emira tightening as he pumped his wings and lifted into the air. With a roll of her gut, Emira gave in to her body's weakness, and as they flew through the night sky, she fainted.

CHAPTER
THREE

Emira awoke, propped up in a bed that, despite her injuries, felt like heaven. The thick, luxurious mattress cradled her bruised body like a mother cradling a newborn babe, and her tired eyes fluttered as she forced herself awake, taking in her new surroundings with caution.

She was in a large but cozy bedroom, decorated with exquisite furnishings, plush carpeting, and massive open windows. The early morning sunlight poured in through the sheer curtains, warming the room and casting shadows against the light gray walls. Across from the bed, a white stone fireplace was alight with flames, and two plush, oversized chairs were placed near the hearth. In the center of the vaulted ceiling hung a bronze chandelier, artistically bent into the shape of leaves and branches that cascaded downwards as it delicately held dozens of low lit candles. The smell of fresh air and fresh linens warmly encompassed Emira's senses.

Her attention snapped to an old woman who stood at the bedside, digging through a wicker basket. The stranger turned and smiled kindly, easing Emira's startled breathing. She was a short, plump woman, with a round face and kind, brightly shining, brown eyes. Underneath an apron, her long gray skirts were old and patched. She wore her frizzy, silver streaked hair haphazardly in a low bun, and topped with a white, lightly laced bonnet.

"It's alright," the woman said softly. Her voice was as gentle as her face. "My name is Sarolina. I'm a healer." Turning back to the nearby side table, she reached into the basket and pulled out a vial of white, glimmering liquid. With a pop of the cork, she opened the container and poured a single drop into a cup of water and held it out to Emira.

"Your arm is broken," she said softly, "but it will heal."

"You're a witch?" Emira croaked, remaining still. Her throat was dry and screamed with pain as she spoke, but her eyes remained warily pinned on the potion that Sarolina held before her. Witches were natural born healers, and many of them made a living using their gifts. But some were not to be trusted as power easily received could be easily misused. Witches were also assassins, spellcasters and evil doers for those who were willing to pay the price.

Sarolina smiled and nodded in response. She lifted the small vial of shimmering liquid to be more easily within Emira's view and said, "Essence of Quartz. Added to water, it creates a tonic that will help you to heal more quickly." She lowered the vial and gestured to the cup she still held out.

For a moment, Emira hesitated. But her injured arm, which was now meticulously set and wrapped, throbbed in protest. Accepting the tonic, she peered into the cup curiously. The water was clear, as if Sarolina had not mixed it into a potion only seconds ago. Tipping the cup back swiftly, Emira downed the drink in one gulp. It was light and cool and tasted sweet, like rose water, before dropping into her empty stomach.

"Thank you," she said shakily, handing the empty cup back to the witch. Silence lingered between them for a moment as Sarolina tidied her items: linen gauze, cotton cloth, potions and herbs among them. The only sound came from the clinking of her jars and vials, and the soft brushing of cotton on linen, like sea grass in an ocean breeze.

Emira cleared her throat and finally choked out, "Where am I?"

Sarolina tilted her head as she answered, "The Southern Realm, my dear."

"South," Emira repeated quietly. Sarolina nodded, smiling kindly again. "How far south?"

The witch's expression grew serious and she leaned closer. "You're safe, if that's what you mean. We are quite far south."

Emira was startled then, by the sound of a knock at the door.

"Yes?" called Sarolina cheerfully, standing upright again. "Come in."

The door opened and a tall, fae male stood at the threshold. He had waist length, forest green hair that was braided away from his face and adorned with a golden headdress. His white tunic was trimmed with gold, and his stance was regal—his head held high and his shoulders and back as straight as a pin. The gaze from his dark gray eyes was penetrating, highly contrasted against his paper white skin.

"Your Grace," Sarolina said, bowing her head respectfully as he entered the room.

Your Grace.

This male was royalty. Perhaps even king. And Emira was in his realm without permission. Why had he, himself, come? Why not send a messenger or a servant to do his bidding? Perhaps he and her master had spoken, and this ruler was prepared to hand her over to the eastern king in exchange for hefty compensation. Vyrion was likely in the adjoining room, waiting, planning, smirking at what was to come.

He stepped forward, and Emira's gut twisted. She withdrew into the pillows, her throat bobbing as she choked back the sob threatening to rise.

The male's gray eyes roamed over her, and as if sensing her discomfort, stopped his intrusion and began to speak from midway across the room.

"How are you feeling?" he asked. His baritone voice was as smooth and fluid as melted caramel.

Emira did not respond, but kept her head down and her gaze averted. Truthfully, she did not feel well. Her broken arm continued to throb, and there was a stinging pain on her backside, likely from the tree trunk she had been thrown against. And aside from the physical pain, the fear that crept through her bones roiled her stomach and made her nauseated.

With a softened expression, the witch healer placed a withered hand on Emira's shoulder and said, "It's alright, dear." She looked back at the fae male and answered in Emira's stead, "She will heal nicely." She reached for her wicker basket, closing the crooked lid on top and finished, "I'm done here, for now."

"Thank you, Sarolina," the male said. He turned to Emira once again and spoke gently. "I am King Alicus. I would like to ask you some questions."

Emira gulped fearfully, wringing her sweaty hands together underneath the cover of the lush blanket. She had no reason to believe this king was any different than her previous master. Was she to be commanded here as well? Or perhaps, Vyrion was on his way to retrieve her. He would be breaking down the door at any moment.

The king continued, breaking Emira's chaotic train of thought. "Tallen and Xemile heard your screaming while they patrolled our borders last night. That's how they came to find you."

Chin still touching her chest subserviently, Emira thought back to the night before. Images of the dark forest flashed in her memory, alongside the fear she had felt at the hands of her master. She remembered the harpy, raining down from the canopy like Death himself. And she remembered the fae warrior who had lifted her broken body from the ground and flew her away from Vyrion's clutches.

"My lord," Sarolina cut in as she picked up her basket and rounded the end of the bed. "Perhaps some food and rest for the young lady? I'm sure she is exhausted after such a night, and she is quite malnourished."

Emira's cheeks flushed at the witch's statement. She tucked her uninjured arm across her thin body and pulled her knees up, attempting to shrink away even further.

King Alicus sighed sympathetically.

"Yes, of course." He bowed slightly to Emira and said, "You are a guest of the Southern Realm, and you are safe here, Miss…?"

She shifted her gaze to his for a moment as the word registered.

Safe.

"Emira," she answered cautiously. "My name is Emira."

CHAPTER

FOUR

Emira remained in her room for the remainder of the day, sleeping in between treatments from Sarolina. In the evening, the witch bid Emira bathe, showing her the adjoining bathing room, and running the water for her patient before moving on to other tasks.

The white stone floors of the bathing room glistened while luscious, green vines climbed the inside walls. The tub was equipped with a modern plumbing system, a luxury that even Emira's eastern master did not possess, and was aligned next to another massive window, similar to the one in her room. She gazed out through the clear glass to see that the stoney castle was built along the plateaus of a monumental cliffside that overlooked an expansive forest of thick, salubrious trees. The sun had set, and a heavy layer of mist began to settle over the wood's canopy.

Emira soaked in the oversized basin while her pale skin turned pruney, and her mind wandered.

The scent of the fresh lavender oils that Sarolina had added to the hot water before departing for the evening rose into the air and enveloped Emira in its calming embrace. She rested her head against the cool, porcelain edge of the tub basin and allowed her mind to reel, remembering as much information as she could about the events that had taken place in the last twenty four hours.

According to Tallen and Xemile, the border scouts who had found her in those dreadful woods, Vyrion was not supposed to have slaves.

But Vyrion *did* have slaves; Emira had been one for her entire twenty-five years.

King Alicus had also called her something. *Guest. Safe.*

Emira could not believe that her master would give up his search for her. He'd made a promise to end her life, and Vyrion, as vile a man there ever was, had always been true to his word in that aspect.

Emira picked up a body brush from the edge of the tub and began gently scrubbing the mud and dried blood from underneath her fingernails, careful to not hurt her arm more than it already did. Sarolina had given her a medicine for the pain, but it only slightly eased the throbbing.

Then, bringing the brush to her scalp, she scrubbed at her hair, rinsing away the blood and dirt that was matted into it. The water, that had started clear, became a revolting brown. She stood, quickly wrapping her frail body in a clean towel, and toeing the plug away from the piping, appalled at the amount of filth that had been clinging to her skin.

She looked again out the massive window as the water drained. Far below, the entirety of the Southern Realm was safely tucked away in the forest's embrace. It was an entire world that Emira had known to exist but had never dreamed she would ever see.

A strong knock sounded on the door, reverberating through the silent bathroom. Startled, Emira slipped on the water that had dripped onto the tub floor from her hair and body, and she barely managed to catch herself on one of the many thick vines climbing the walls.

"Miss?" came a familiar male voice from the other side of the door.

The harpy.

"It's Tallen," he continued. "The hour grows late. Are you alright?"

"Yes," she answered quickly, stumbling over the edge of the tub, careful to not slip again. "I'm alright."

He continued from the other side of the door, "I'm stationed outside your room for tonight. King Alicus' orders."

He was a spy, then. And she, not a guest but a prisoner.

"I'm at your service should you need anything," he continued, his voice no longer that of the menacing harpy vigilante from the previous evening but soft and laced with what sounded like concern.

"Okay," Emira answered timidly. She took a cautious step toward the door and checked the handle.

Locked.

Although, she had seen how easily Tallen apprehended her master in the woods the night before, using only a whip—albeit, a whip that slithered as if alive. A locked door likely wouldn't do much to stop the harpy if he had malicious intent.

"You are safe here," Tallen said, as if reading her mind. "Try to get some rest."

Emira did not reply but rested her forehead against the locked door while listening to the harpy's footsteps grow quieter as he left the bedroom to stand at his post.

CHAPTER

FIVE

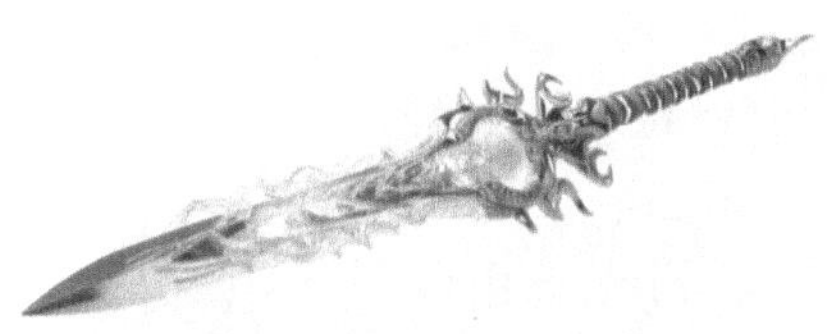

"You will not say a word to that child *they call king.*"

Vyrion's malicious voice crept through Emira's mind, like a snake slithering through weeds. Her neck twisted as she tried to turn about, begging her eyes to spear through the surrounding darkness, and search for his emerald glare. She tried to speak, tried to scream, but she could not move, could not open her eyes. She was held by invisible bonds, unable to move or sit up.

"You will tell him nothing."

Emira writhed, weakly fighting against the bindings that held her as still as stone.

His wretched voice continued, vicious and malevolent, "I will find you, Emira. I will find you and I will finish you."

Emira squirmed, trying to move away from the sound of her master's voice but to no avail. Everything around her was black. Darkness swallowed her body, and she gasped for air as if drowning in the unending midnight.

"You belong to me," Vyrion hissed. Emira tried to beg, but no sound came from her parted, trembling lips.

She thrashed violently at the feeling of warm breath suddenly caressing her ear.

"I'm coming for you, Emira," her master promised, the feeling of his lips almost close enough to kiss the delicate points into which he rasped.

But then, all at once, his voice and her chains were gone.

EMIRA SHOT UPRIGHT FROM HER PLACE ON THE BED AND RELEASED A glass-shattering scream. Sweat drenched her skin, cooling her body as the southern breeze blew in from the open window. Her hair was plastered to her face, and the dry skin on her lips cracked and bled as they parted.

Tallen sprinted through the bedroom door, a bolt of white hot lightning cracking across the sky as he did. With a dagger wielded in one hand, his slithering whip in the other, and massive, feathered wings spread wide behind him, the harpy was prepared to defend.

"He's coming!" Emira screeched. "He's coming to find me!"

Tallen's ocean eyes scanned the room. They shone brightly, like a predator searching for prey in the dark. He took in his surroundings as Emira wailed, listening to, looking at, and scenting the space. When he resolved that there was no palpable threat, he repealed both of his weapons and stalked to Emira's side, as she writhed beneath the sheets.

"Miss," he started, grasping her shoulders firmly and kneeling beside the bed. "It's alright."

Emira thrashed side to side against his grip, squinting through the darkness in the room, looking for signs of her master's arrival.

The window, surely he will come through the open window. Or the door, now unguarded. He'll use his fae wings to—

"Miss Emira," the harpy said again, this time more firmly than before. "It was a *nightmare*."

Emira slowed at the sound of her name and focused on the face of the harpy. Stark against the once again clear sky beyond the window, his black curls were tousled chaotically, and his face was sprinkled with black stubble. His lips were pressed into a thin, worried line as he loosened, but did not relinquish, his firm grip on her.

"It was no nightmare," Emira breathed, voice barely above a whisper. Her heart was racing and her stomach was twisted. Her chest heaved erratically as she rambled, "It's my life. It's every day. He'll find me, I know he will, and when he does, he'll—"

"Vyrion will not find you," Tallen cut in, voice like stone. "This realm is warded against intruders. He cannot come near you." Emira sucked in a breath and nodded, but her stomach remained in a tight knot. Beads of cool sweat speckled her face, and her bloodshot eyes remained as wide as the moon that shone through the curtains.

Tallen studied the fear on the girl's face before promising, "He cannot harm you anymore, Miss Emira."

Emira turned away when the harpy spoke. She could not be a part of that promise. Not after her dream, not after everything she knew about her master and how his realm was ruthlessly commanded. She would wait, silently, for him to retrieve her and hope that he showed mercy if she kept her knowledge of the east to herself as he commanded.

The harpy released his grip on Emira's frame.

"What can I do for you?" he asked, rising from his knee and standing tall.

Emira had not realized how massive he truly was, but as he stood over her now, it was clear that he was easily over six and a half feet tall, every inch of his broad frame covered in muscle. She cowered slightly, withdrawing into the pillows and bringing her knees to her chest. He stepped back, curling his black and gold feathered wings closely inwards—an attempt to look less intimidating. But even tucked tightly behind him, his wings were twice the width of his body.

Emira's breathing hitched, and Tallen stood quietly waiting for an answer. When after a moment, one didn't come, he spoke.

"I'll be back with some water."

He left the room silently, and Emira was grateful to be alone. She sat up tall, flung her legs over the side of the bed, and made her way to the large, open window. She pushed back the sheer curtains, letting the light from the moon shine into the dark bedroom. It was full, like a pearl in the sky, and the night was all but clear, save for a sprinkling of stars. She scanned the forest below but saw no signs of hordes of eastern guards. No flickering lights, no sounds of hoof steps, no clinking of armor or weapons. It was only still, calm darkness.

As she continued to stare out the window for any sign of Vyrion or his legionaries, her body grew cold from the nighttime chill. The fireplace that had been alight earlier that day with roaring flames, was now only embers that dusted the ashes. The shadow of an owl flickered past the window, causing her breath to catch in her throat. Like a frightened child, she flew back into the bed, and pulled the covers to her chest.

Tallen soon re-entered the room with a crystal decanter of fresh water. He cautiously approached and poured the clear liquid into a glass. It looked laughably small in his grip as he held it out to her silently.

Emira's eyes met his for a moment, but she looked away quickly as she accepted the drink.

"Thank you," she murmured, keeping her gaze down. She lifted the glass to her cracked lips and tipped the cool drink into her mouth. It soothed her burning throat, and she downed the rest eagerly.

"Will you try to sleep?" the harpy asked.

Emira shook her head, placing the empty cup on the bedside table and drawing the blankets up around her shivering body. Tallen eyed her movements before walking across the room to a large, wooden chest. He opened it swiftly and withdrew a heavy, white quilt. Approaching the bed with slow, prudent steps, he held the blanket up, offering it silently. Emira nodded her acceptance, and he gently placed it over her lap.

Emira said nothing, and kept her eyes down. His icy blue gaze through the dark bedroom was beautiful, but unsettling.

"You must try to rest," the harpy insisted, stepping back slowly. He made his way to the door, and Emira appreciated the distance.

She nestled against the pillow and admitted, "I will not be able to."

Every word felt like the slice of a blade against her strained vocal chords.

"I assure that you are safe, Miss Emira," Tallen replied. But she could not believe him. One night as a… *guest*… in the Southern Realm would not undo a lifetime of fear and torment at the hands of Vyrion.

When she didn't respond, Tallen straightened and left the room quietly, returning to his post outside of the bedroom door. Emira's eyes remained fixed on the window, and she watched the moon disappear as it was slowly replaced by the blazing sun.

CHAPTER

SIX

Sarolina knocked gently at Emira's bedroom door the following morning. She entered cheerfully, carrying her aged wicker basket, and smiling when she saw her patient alert and sitting upright.

"Well, your color is already looking healthier," Sarolina said, placing the basket on the end of the bed. She plopped herself onto the mattress and took Emira's chin in her hand, tilting her patient's face upwards towards the sunlight. Emira's eyes snapped shut at the brightness, and Sarolina asked, "But you didn't sleep, did you?"

"Nightmares," Emira answered quietly. As she had predicted, she did not fall back into sleep, but spent the remainder of the night scanning the room, her eyes shifting between the window and the door.

"To be expected," the witch responded, as she stood and turned her attention to her patient's arm, gently lifting the injured limb for examination. Emira winced, but noticed that the pain had significantly eased since the evening before.

"Splendid," the witch said matter-of-factly, gently flexing Emira's arm at the elbow, and then again at the wrist.

"How has it healed so quickly?" Emira asked as the healer prodded the tender bone.

"The quartz tonic, no doubt," the old woman replied. "But your fae healing abilities will pick up soon enough."

"Healing abilities?"

The fae were blessed with immortality and gifted with the ability to procure wings, but Emira had never done so. Could they also heal themselves of injuries and illness? Could she?

Sarolina froze and eyed her patient, a puzzled look spreading over her wrinkled face. She gently placed Emira's arm back down and said, "You *are* fae, correct?"

Emira nodded. "Half. And half siren," she clarified.

"But you have never healed on your own?" the witch continued, placing her fisted hands on her wide hips. "Not even simple scratches as a child?"

Emira shook her head, feeling doltish.

"Have you always been so..." the witch said, pausing for a moment, looking along Emira's emaciated figure, "...thin?"

When Emira did not answer, Sarolina sighed in frustration although it was blatantly obvious that her ire was not with her patient, but with those who had kept her skeletal.

"You will heal rapidly," she continued, standing, "as the fae do, once I get you healthy. Come." She padded to the oversized wardrobe and pulled the doors open. "There must be something in here to fit you."

Emira swung her legs over the edge of the bed and let them dangle above the cool floor, noticing that the scars from her shackles had started to fade, before stepping down and slowly walking up behind the witch. Sarolina shuffled through the various fabrics before pulling a petite, emerald dress from its hanger.

The fabric was thin and silken. The neckline of the dress dipped sharply, and the sleeves were loose and long, ending in golden wristbands to keep from sliding. The lengthy skirts flowed and shimmered as Sarolina shook the gown about, holding it up against Emira's sickly frame.

"This will do," she said, holding the dress out for her patient to take. She pulled a pair of gold, slipper-like shoes from the wardrobe and laid them on the floor. "Breakfast is being served soon. I want to see you eat three large meals a day." The witch eyed Emira impatiently, her brown eyes sparkling until the girl nodded her head in response.

"Good," she finally said. "I'll give you a moment." Sarolina snatched up her wicker basket, and headed to the door, making to wait in the corridor. As she did, Emira peeked into the hallway beyond, expecting to see Tallen standing at his post. But there was no sign of him. No oversized shadow, or feathered wing around the door frame.

"Don't be too long!" Sarolina called as she closed the bedroom door. "King Alicus is expecting you!"

Emira inhaled deeply, holding her breath within her lungs, fearful that if she exhaled, she would lose the contents of her stomach. She had met the king the day before, briefly. He had wanted to ask her questions. About what, Emira was sure, but she couldn't tell him anything.

Vyrion will know, he'll find me, and he'll make me suffer. He'll—

"Did you hear me, my dear?" Sarolina called again.

"Y-yes," Emira stammered, quickly shedding her sleeping gown and reaching for the emerald dress. "Yes, I'm coming!"

The siren dressed quickly. The gown was loose and felt more like a bathrobe than a dress. Her collarbones and sternum jutted from her lackluster skin, an ugly contrast, she thought, against the silken dress. She swept her mousy, blonde hair back into a quick braid before washing her face and brushing her teeth. Then, quickly sliding on the shimmery, golden shoes that Sarolina had left out, Emira slipped from the bedroom and into the hall, where the witch was waiting.

"Lovely," she said, admiring the gown. "Follow me."

Sarolina led Emira through the massive corridors of the castle. The impressive keep was made mostly of pale stone that created tall, vaulted ceilings. Along many of the halls, were arched, paneless windows, completely open to the elements as well as balconies that were free of railings. Emira considered that the people of the Southern Realm must be fair natured for the home of its king to be so exposed. Perhaps Tallen and Xemile had a fierce reputation, one that the citizens of this realm knew was not to be tested. That seemed a more likely conclusion to Emira.

This realm is warded against intruders, Tallen had said.

"What does it mean," Emira started, "that the realm is *warded?*"

Sarolina continued forward, answering without looking back. "It's about intention," the old woman began. "Those who enter our realm must have an innocent objective, or they cannot cross the borderlines."

"At all?" Emira asked, disbelief lining her voice.

"At all."

As she followed the witch, Emira occasionally slowed her pace to peer over the window ledges, and saw how close to some of the treetops the castle was built. She could easily reach out her hand and touch the branches and vines that begged to grow inwards. A warm breeze blew through, bringing with it leaves and flowers, gifts from those same trees.

It was as if the forest was grateful to King Alicus for allowing them to be a part of his realm at all.

"I'll leave you to it, then." Sarolina smiled when they reached the entrance of the dining hall. "Remember what I've said. Three meals *every day.*"

Emira nodded inelegantly as the witch turned to leave then turned her attention back to the dining hall.

Her heart raced as she stared up at the pale, arched doors. The golden handles were shaped like vines, and the only sound from the other side was that of rushing water. Sarolina didn't tell her what to expect. She already knew. The king was awaiting her entry, and he was going to ask her about the Eastern Realm, about her master.

If she betrayed Vyrion, he would kill her. What would this fae ruler do if she refused to answer?

Emira pushed open the oversized doors and cautiously entered. The room was massive on its own, but it gave the illusion of even more expansive size due to the open balcony that hugged two of the four walls. It overlooked the lush forest as well as a great waterfall that surged nearby, causing clear, icy droplets to speckle onto the shining, white floors of the hall.

In the center of the room, and taking up a majority of the space, sat a circular, white wooden table. It was surrounded by multiple chairs, all the same ashy color, and made up of branches that twisted and embraced each other to form the tall, decorative backsides.

King Alicus sat at the table, his gray eyes fixed on Emira as she entered. His long, green hair was French braided back in two, and his headdress created the illusion of deer antlers protruding from his skull.

To his right, sat an unfamiliar female.

She was undoubtedly fae, with exquisite olive skin, deep brown eyes lined with kohl, and full red lips, quirked up in a kind smile. Her pointed ears protruded from behind her black hair, which hung in long, straight strands around her face. She wore a simple gown of silver, and sipped from a delicate mug as King Alicus began to speak.

"Hello Emira. Please, sit."

Emira slowly stepped forward, also recognizing Xemile and Tallen, who sat to the left of the king. Tallen's expression was unreadable as he watched Emira move across the room. Xemile, the red headed fae warrior, leaned back carelessly in his chair.

He wore a friendly smirk and said cheerfully, "You made it through the night! I hope Tallen didn't unnerve you too much." He chuckled, giving the harpy a playful jab in the arm.

Emira sat in the empty chair between Tallen and the unfamiliar female, who spoke with a mellifluous voice.

"The real test will be how well she can sit through a meal with the three of you!" She turned to Emira and placed a warm hand on her arm. "Truly, I'm not sure how I've survived this long surrounded by them."

Emira did not respond but looked down at the female's softly bronzed hand and sat frozen by the affectionate gesture

"What do you mean?" Xemile continued, his small smile becoming a mischievous grin. "We're a delightful bunch." The female rolled her eyes and the group chuckled, but Emira kept her gaze on the hand still resting on her arm.

"My wife," Alicus began, gray eyes back on Emira, "Queen Zuriel."

"Zuri is fine," she added, gently patting Emira's arm. Emira finally looked up at the queen's face. She wore a kind smile, her dark eyes slightly upturned with the action.

"And you recall Xemile?" Alicus added as the fae warrior gave an impudent salute in her direction.

"Yes," Emira finally said, remembering he who had lifted her from the forest floor and flew her away from Vyrion's reach.

"I'm sorry to hear that you did not sleep well," Alicus continued. "Tallen reported that you had nightmares."

Emira tried to swallow, but her throat was dry.

"Yes," she said again, her gaze trailing from Xemile to the harpy. His eyes were still pinned on her, his face still indecipherable. Emira wondered if he had looked away at all. And she wondered what else had been said about her before she arrived for breakfast.

"I hope you were able to sleep at least a little," Zuri added, moving her hand from Emira's arm to the handle of the teacup in front of her.

Emira only smiled shyly in response.

The dining hall doors opened and a line of fae servants trailed in, holding silver platters of steaming, hot food. They were dressed to work—brown pants, clean linen tops, tall boots, and long hair swept back from their faces—but they held their heads high and dignified, something Emira was unfamiliar with seeing and found curious. Sarolina, and these servers, were all under the employ of the Southern Realm, but none were treated with disregard or dressed in rags, or hunched over in exhaustion. Emira straightened, slightly eased by the sight.

Her eyes scanned the spread as it was set on the table. The silver platters were placed in front of her like gifts. Each one was filled with something delectable. There were piles of steaming scrambled eggs, sticky, maple covered buns, fried meats and fresh, colorful fruits. A carafe of aromatic coffee was placed in the center of the table, swiftly snatched by Xemile. Finally, a delicate and intricately painted kettle of tea was placed near the queen. The servants bowed to their rulers before they took their leave.

"Please, eat," Alicus said as the doors to the dining hall closed, leaving the five of them alone again.

Emira did as he asked, gladly and without hesitation. She had not realized how famished she felt until the array of breakfast foods were served, and truthfully, she had not eaten since the midday before.

Except for a bite of apple.

She ate her fill, and then ate some more. Food had never been so readily available, and so she took the opportunity while it was presented. She foolishly didn't think to consider if the food was poisoned or enchanted. The grousing of her empty belly eased with each bite, a feeling that made the risk of poison almost irrelevant.

The others sitting around the table didn't seem to notice her appetite. They made conversation amongst themselves, Xemile occasionally tossing in a sarcastic comment at his king's expense. Emira studied the group as she ate, noting the informal dynamics between them. It was like nothing she had ever seen in the Eastern Realm.

Vyrion ate with his appointed court, made up of a few males who had a similar taste for blood and a desperation to remain alive. They were vicious, and cruel, and carried out Vyrion's wishes with an all too eager hand. They trained his armies, beat his slaves, and complimented him endlessly on a realm well ruled. But they were not his friends. They feared him, his quick to anger mind, and his enjoyment for torture. These men were often killed and easily replaced.

Tallen and Xemile did not fear their rulers but loved them. Their relationship appeared friendly first and political second. No such relationship existed in the Eastern Realm. Vyrion was sure to squash alliances before they were made, and caring for others made you a target of his wrath.

Emira knew this truth too well. She had experienced it firsthand, many years ago.

She remembered Rocas, the stable hand, fondly. He'd had curly, blonde hair and dark eyes that took up most of his thin face. He'd been tall and scrawny, and understood horses better than people. But he had also treated Emira more kindly than anyone else ever did.

They had met by chance in the kitchens. Rocas was gathering a fruit pail for the horses, and Emira was refilling water pitchers. They had exchanged quick glances before Rocas eventually smiled at her. She had not expected the gesture, and it caused her naive heart to flutter and her face to heat. She remembered feeling so flustered by the unexpected formality that she had almost dropped one of the pitchers onto the stone floor. Her palms would have been whipped or scalded for such a mistake.

After that, they met frequently in secret, or under the guise of chores. Rocas would enter the kitchens, feigning the need for water or horse feed, and Emira would venture to the stables after twilight.

From there, their relationship grew into something like romance although Emira now supposed that they had both craved companionship and intimacy more than anything else. Rocas did not speak much, nor did he know how to read or write, a skill Emira had picked up from working within the castle walls for so long. They had nothing in common, other than their interest in one another, and the cruel life they both endured.

One evening, after one of many intimate encounters between them, Rocas told Emira that he loved her. But he was just as naive as she, and Emira did not return the sentiment. He never said it again.

They continued to meet in secret for over a year before the consequences arrived. Perhaps Vyrion had known all along, allowing for them to feel confident enough that they wouldn't be caught before distributing his punishment. Their master enjoyed inflicting emotional pain just as much as physical pain.

His soldiers did eventually come late one night. They stormed into the stables, waking Emira from a deep sleep and ripping her from Rocas' arms. She was dragged outside to the nearest courtyard and forced to watch as all four of the stable hand's limbs were tied to separate horses. Emira remembered how she had screamed and cried and begged that his life be spared; that hers be taken in his place. She remembered his wide eyes, and the sound of his shaking voice as he, too, pleaded for mercy.

With barely a word, the soldiers carried out their task and whipped the backsides of the beasts. The horses had reared up before galloping, all four in different directions. Rocas hardly had time to scream before his body was ripped apart.

Emira remembered the cracking of his bones as the joints were torn apart, and the hot spray of blood and flesh pelted her face. She remembered the firm hand of an eastern guard, grasping her head and holding it in place, forcing her to watch the execution. There was a crimson stain on the cobblestones that remained for weeks after Rocas' death. King Vyrion ordered that it not be cleaned, so as to remind his other slaves what would come of alliances. Emira remembered the sound of crows and vultures, cawing and cackling at all hours of the day and night for weeks after Rocas was killed. It was as if they were laughing at her, taunting her for being so foolish.

She had cried for months afterward and from then on had refused any invite to friendship from another. She would not be the cause of someone's demise ever again.

The sound of her name pulled Emira from the wretched memory.

"Emira?" It came again. She looked up to see the group staring back at her. King Alicus had been the one to speak, his gray eyes unblinking. "I would like to ask you some questions if you would be prepared to answer them."

Emira heaved a nervous sigh and nodded her head as anxiety clawed at her gut.

King Alicus continued, "Is Vyrion keeping slaves in the Eastern Realm?"

Emira looked between Alicus, Zuri, Xemile and Tallen, but her master's words rang in her mind.

Tell him nothing. You belong to me. I will finish you.

She knew it to be a promise and not a threat.

"Miss Emira," came Tallen's stern voice. "You must answer my king."

Fear squeezed her bones as the harpy's eyes remained on her. His electrifying gaze pierced her own, and Emira was sure he could read her thoughts. As he held his unblinking stare, her heart thundered beneath her chest. Her eyes darted between the southern fae around her, and her lips tightened against each other, as if creating a firm seal would keep the secrets from spilling out like liquid.

Tears welled in Emira's eyes and her stomach flipped. Bile crept up her throat as the group before her stared, waiting for an answer she couldn't give. As she parted her lips to defend the east, Queen Zuri stood.

"It's too soon for this." She looked to her husband, who remained seated. He raised a curious brow as his queen moved away from her chair and closer to Emira's. "It's barely been a day," she continued. "Come, Emira. Let's get some fresh air."

CHAPTER

SEVEN

Queen Zuri moved through the halls with grace, her silver gown trailing behind her like a glittering river. Emira followed cautiously as Zuri led her to one of the many balconies off of the castle. It was then that she noticed the queen wore no shoes as her feet crumpled over the dried leaves that had blown in from the treetops. How strange that the queen of the Southern Realm would choose to be barefoot. King Vyrion refused to be dressed in any manner other than that of royalty, yet this queen had just dined without shoes. Zuri leaned up against an alabaster pillar, and Emira stepped alongside her. The sun was already high in the clear sky, and a dusting of reds and golds began to sprinkle the tops of the trees as autumn approached.

"You truly are safe here," Queen Zuri started.

However hard she tried, Emira found herself unable to look at the fae queen.

"I know you're frightened," Zuri continued. "There probably isn't a word to properly describe what you are feeling." The queen reached out her hand and placed it on Emira's bony shoulder. "But it's going to be alright."

Emira nodded, still unable to look at the queen. Her kindness set Emira on edge; it was too good to be true.

Queen Zuriel continued, retracting her touch. "Tallen will be posted outside your bedroom indefinitely. He's a skilled warrior. And he's a good friend; he's like a brother to us. He will keep you safe." There was a yearning in her voice, a plea for Emira to believe her words. "He'll rest during the day, but Xemile and Alicus and I will be here. And Sarolina too. You're surrounded by friends."

Guilt crept up Emira's throat. Queen Zuri was desperately trying to connect. King Alicus was providing her with a bedroom, something she had never dreamed to have in the Eastern Realm while Sarolina nursed her poor health. Xemile had carried her away from the forest and away from Vyrion. And Tallen would spend his days resting so that he could spend his nights guarding and protecting her. Perhaps he would be spying as well, but Emira had to dismiss her suspicions and show appreciation. The alternative was likely a dungeon.

Or worse.

She looked at the queen and forced a smile.

"Thank you," she finally responded. "I'm sorry. I think I'm still tired. I will have to remember to thank Tallen for his protection."

Zuri chuckled. "He won't accept. That's just Tallen. Xemile, however, would *love* to be told how *amazing* and *wonderful* he is." She laughed brightly, and Emira gave a smile in return.

"How long have you known Xemile?" Emira asked, forcing the words from her lips. If Zuri noticed her unease, she didn't show it.

"For as long as I can remember," she answered. "We grew up together, here in the Southern Realm. Alicus too. The three of us used to play in the forests and swim in the rivers together as children. He was a boastful child, but I'm sure being named the Head of Military Command for the Southern Realm hasn't helped." She laughed again, brushing her bare feet distractedly over the cool stone floor. "He's a good male, Xemile."

"And Tallen?" Emira asked cautiously.

Zuri's smile faded slightly. "Tallen is a fierce warrior and a solemn soul. He's half harpy, you know, so I think that's where his seriousness comes from. He's been through a lot, but I think he's finally finding some peace here after a few decades."

Emira nodded, noting that she called him 'half' harpy.

But Zuri quickly stood tall and smiled brightly again, changing the subject.

"Let me give you a tour. You are not a prisoner. You are free to roam about as you please. May as well know the route."

"Why?" The question slipped from Emira's mouth harshly, and she immediately cast her eyes downwards subserviently. She had just questioned royalty. A *queen*. Punishment was sure to follow.

"Why, what?" Zuri asked, her voice atypically calm after being spoken to in such a way.

"I'm sorry," Emira responded quickly, eyes still looking down at the stone floor. "I should have said nothing. You have done so much for me, and I am grateful."

Zuri's bronzed fingers found their way to Emira's chin. As she lifted her face to her own, Emira kept her eyes averted, looking any way she could that was not directly at the queen.

"You are not a prisoner," Zuri repeated. "You must not act like one."

Emira finally met the queen's deep brown eyes. They were wide and sparkling, but also... begging. The queen had raw beseechment in her gaze.

"Why?" Emira breathed, her voice barely above a whisper. Her heart pounded, and her throat bobbed as she continued. "Why am I not a prisoner here?"

Zuri's gaze softened, and she lowered her hand. "You are not a threat to our realm, Emira. You are not our enemy, and we are not yours. You are a guest of the Southern Realm and will be treated as such."

With a smile, and eyes that implored Emira to believe her, Queen Zuri turned and began speaking of the stone used to build the castle walls, and the vines that grew upon them. Emira listened as well as she could while she followed the barefooted queen who called her guest.

CHAPTER

EIGHT

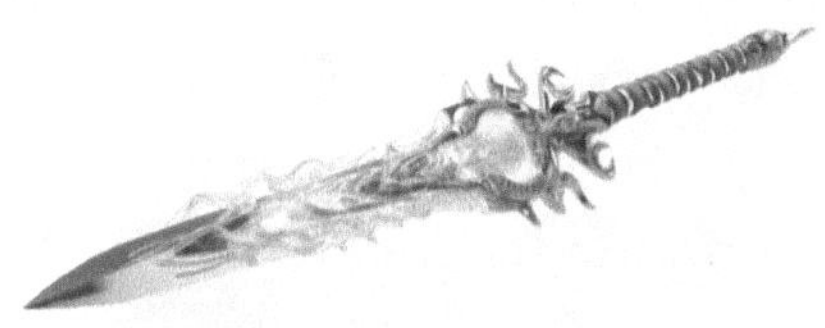

Emira spent most of the remaining morning in her bedroom, and after taking a bath, studying herself in a wall length mirror that hung in the bathing room. Its golden edges were shaped like vines and flowers, twisting one upon another, carefully crafted and intricately detailed. Everything here was art.

Sarolina's words from the night before echoed in her memory as she stared at her naked body.

She is quite malnourished.

Emira would rarely see her reflection in the Eastern Realm, save for her passing a freshly washed window. Slaves were not permitted personal items, like mirrors.

But she saw it now, and the reflection of her naked body was sickening.

Her skin was sallow, and her cheeks were gaunt. Her yellow hair resembled the straw that was fed to horses. It was dry and coarse and unkempt, even in the braid that currently held it away from her face. Her green eyes were dull, and even her dry lips looked pale. She ran a single, bony finger down her torso, starting at her collarbones, and bumping down along every protruding rib, landing on her prominent hip bones.

The witch had told her to eat at least three meals a day as part of her care routine. Emira could hardly believe she was allowed to eat one meal each day, let alone three or more, and at her own discretion. It was a small freedom with which she did not feel familiar but did not intend to refuse.

As midday came, she cautiously left her room and slowly padded down the long hallway, trying to recall her way to the kitchen. Queen Zuriel had shown her the route only hours ago. She recognized the vines that crept along the wall, flowering with beautiful heart shaped, purple buds. She followed the lianas to the end of the hall and turned when she reached a large, flowing fountain, decorated with a stone nymph pouring water from a gemstone vase. As she did so, she entered the massive galley.

The kitchen, like most rooms in the castle, had vaulted ceilings and stone floors. There was an oversized fireplace that took up almost the entirety of one wall. Moss and vines climbed up the chimney sides, and various sizes of pots and pans hung above the low lit flames, the iron heating upon the glowing embers. In the center of the room sat an enormous, wooden island that held various bowls of fruits and nuts. Behind it, lay a large, white cooler, draped with more greenery.

Pride swelled in Emira's chest at the small victory of remembering her way.

Before she could enjoy the sensation for too long, she was startled by Tallen's presence. He was leaning on his forearms against the island countertop, eyes fixed on her, so stoically still that she had not seen him in plain sight.

He tilted his head slowly in acknowledgement and said, "Miss Emira."

"Tallen," she gasped. "Sorry, I—"

The siren turned to leave, but Tallen's deep voice stopped her midstride.

"You are not intruding."

"I was just coming for something to eat," she answered, facing him again and trying to keep her words steady.

Tallen gestured to a full plate that sat in front of him. "Looks like we had the same idea."

Emira's lips quirked up into a weak smile as she reached towards a fruit bowl and placed her hand on an apple.

The memory of Vyrion twisting her arm flashed into her mind. She saw the apple roll onto the floor as Vyrion squeezed her wrist. Her gut twisted as she remembered the sound of his voice, and fear squeezed at her throat as dread pooled in her gut.

Emira released the apple and picked up a pear instead, shaking off the image of her master's hateful gaze. Tallen must have sensed her shift as his feathered wings shuddered slightly and he shifted his weight. Emira turned her attention back to the harpy, who had not broken his intense gaze.

Zuri had called him something.

Warrior. Friend. Brother.

"Thank you," Emira started, "for, you know..."

Her hands trembled around the fruit as she forced herself to maintain eye contact with the intimidating figure before her.

"You don't have to thank me," he answered. "I'm honored to follow orders given by my king and queen."

Emira nodded, unsure how to respond. Zuri had told her to expect such an answer from him.

"Sarolina reported that you are undernourished," the harpy said. Emira felt her cheeks heat. "She won't be pleased to hear that you chose to eat a single pear."

Tallen pulled a clean plate from the nearest cabinet, stalked to the cooler, and opened the door. He moved swiftly, his large wings moving with him, following him like massive shadows. He loaded the plate with cheese, yogurt, fresh vegetables, and a sandwich that had been previously made and wrapped in wax paper.

Tallen stepped in Emira's direction, his intense gaze back on her, eyes hovering for a moment over her jutting collarbones.

He held the out plate. "Here. Eat."

She accepted, and the foreign sensation of a smile curved her lips.

"Thank you, Tallen," she said once more.

"An honor, Miss Emira."

CHAPTER

NINE

"I told you I would end you."

Vyrion's voice slithered into Emira's mind. Unlike the night before, when she was unable to move, she was standing. There was nothingness around her, again, the same endless black void as before. She could not see her master, but she knew from the malice dripping off of his words that his expression was contorted with rage.

"I said nothing!" Emira cried, spinning around frantically, searching for his brilliant, emerald eyes in the darkness. "I said nothing! They know nothing! Please!"

Blunt force knocked her to the ground. Her left ear rang loudly, and she rolled to her side, holding her hand over the rattled eardrum, trying to stop the deafening sound. Her mind buzzed, and she squeezed her eyes closed.

"Master, please!" she begged.

Tears spilled from her eyes as she remained on her side in a fetal position, with her hand still covering her ear.

"You will suffer, Emira," her master hissed. "And your disobedience will be the cause of many deaths in the Eastern Realm."

"I didn't," Emira cried. "I didn't disobey. I said nothing. Please! Please!"

Heat curled around her ear as Vyrion's breath whispered menacingly, "Of course, you remember what happens to those who take me for a fool."

There was a scream. Rocas' scream.

It rang in Emira's head, as if he were standing right in front of her. A warm spray covered her face, and dripped onto her lips. She could taste it. Blood.

Rocas' blood.

Vyrion was forcing her to relive his death.

She scrambled to stand and wiped at her face, only smearing the blood and dirtying her hands.

She looked up and glanced around. Everything around her was still black. She could only see her crimson soaked palms, as if candlelight shone directly on them.

Emira wailed and pressed her hands to her ears as Rocas screamed within her mind. The sickening snap of his bones came next, and Emira cried out, balling her fists and pounding them on either side of her head.

"So much blood on your hands already, Emira," Vyrion taunted. She looked at her trembling hands, both as red as poisonous poppies.

"Please," she begged again, voice cracking. "Make it stop."

"Lower your gaze, Emira," her master commanded. She did, defeatedly and tear soaked.

The sight that laid before her violently twisted her gut. Emira gagged and choked as she emptied her stomach into the black void around her. She screamed and looked again, sour bile in her mouth threatening to make her sick over and over.

Rocas' broken body was at Emira's feet. His limbs were torn off, and his dark eyes were wide open with terror. His mouth was agape, frozen in the scream that she still heard in her head. Blood oozed from his torso, his flesh lying around him in heaps.

Emira covered her eyes with her blood covered hands and screamed again, before she awoke suddenly with a jolt.

EMIRA BOLTED UPRIGHT, SHRIEKING, AND LAUNCHED HERSELF FROM the bed. Eyes still squeezed shut, she scrambled for the door, and tripped over her nightgown. Her body hit the floor with a *smack* as Tallen bounded inside. Her bones groaned from the fall, but she made to push herself upright. She needed to run, needed to escape. She needed to go somewhere, far from wherever she was, from what she had just witnessed.

Again.

At her side in an instant, the harpy made to lift Emira off of the ground, but she thrashed violently against his touch.

"No!" she begged. "Please! No!"

"Miss Emira!" Tallen bellowed. "Open your eyes!"

He gripped her frail shoulders in his powerful hands and held her still against the darkness. Emira sobbed and wailed, letting loose another glass shattering scream before slowly opening her eyes and frantically looking around the room, allowing her sight to adjust.

Emira's gaze landed on Tallen, whose hands still held onto her trembling frame.

She tried to speak, but when she parted her lips, she could only weep. She released a deep, guttural cry of grief as Tallen's sharp, blue eyes sternly searched her face.

"You've hurt yourself," he said, lifting Emira's quivering body from the floor.

He strode to the edge of the bed, and set her down gently. She gripped the heaps of blankets in her sweaty palms as she sucked in short, frantic breaths. Her toes curled into the plush carpeting as she tried to feel a sense of grounding, getting a grip on the real, tangible world around her.

"Breathe deeply," Tallen ordered as her chest heaved.

Xemile, who had heard Emira's screams from his own nearby apartments, came sprinting into the room, a dagger in his grasp and a grave expression on his face. He was ready for a fight. Tallen held up a single hand to the commander, stopping him in his tracks.

"Get Sarolina," Tallen ordered. Xemile sheathed the dagger, scanned the room with his amber eyes, and left without question.

"Look at me, Miss Emira," the harpy said gently.

The siren pulled her eyes away from the shadows in the bedroom and looked at Tallen's steely face. He was kneeling at her feet, holding her trembling hands. His wings were spread out, instinctively providing a protective shield from the invisible danger.

"I'm… sorry…" Emira heaved the words as she tried to regulate her breathing. Her heart raced and her adrenaline pumped as she continued to focus on the harpy's face; his tanned skin, his icy blue eyes, his sharp, stubbled jaw.

"Don't speak," he answered. "Just breathe. Slowly."

Emira did as he commanded, allowing her lungs to fill and empty, fill and empty. The harpy's wings remained outstretched and he continued to watch her, clutching her hands in his own. As her breathing slowed, he nodded his head slowly.

"Better," he murmured. "Good, keep breathing."

As the minutes passed, Emira's breathing returned to normal, and the tears that had stained her cheeks dried. Tallen released her hands and stood, folding his wings closer to his body once more.

"Have you always had these dreams?" Tallen finally asked.

Emira shook her head. "Never. Only since I was brought here."

Tallen's jaw ticked, but he said nothing.

Xemile soon returned with Sarolina. King Alicus and Queen Zuriel followed closely behind them, both dressed in magnificent, emerald, silken night robes. They too had heard Emira's screams, and followed the commander and the witch on their way to the siren's chambers.

The harpy stepped back, allowing Sarolina to kneel and examine Emira's face. He told her briefly what had happened—the nightmare, the fall, the thrashing. Heat crept along the skin of Emira's throat and shame encompassed her. She could not look at the harpy as he explained what happened. She had been nothing but a burden since her arrival.

"A superficial laceration from the fall," Sarolina stated, examining Emira's temple, "and a bitten lip." Emira tasted the blood upon her mouth, and she quietly reminded herself that the blood was her own, and did not belong to Rocas. The witch squinted as she swept away a lock of Emira's hair, exposing a purpling of bruises along her hairline. "These bruises," she continued, squinting. "Were you hit?"

"I think…" Emira replied softly, remembering her own balled hands striking her skull. "I think I hit myself."

The witch let Emira's hair fall back into place as she stood and turned to her rulers. "All will heal without intervention."

"Thank you, Sarolina," Alicus said from the doorway.

"And the nightmares?" Tallen cut in. His arms were crossed and any expression of sympathy that he had previously worn was now gone. His face was stone, a trained warrior once again.

"I have a nighttime tonic that may help," Sarolina answered as she began flexing Emira's joints gently, searching for sprains or breaks. She looked at her patient and continued, "It tastes like tea, but it will put you into a deep sleep for the duration of the night."

"And it will help these nightmares?" Zuri asked.

Sarolina smiled at her queen. "She'll sleep so soundly that she won't remember anything she dreams, good or bad. With your leave, I'll head to the kitchens and make a batch now." The witch bowed to her king and queen, and left the room.

Stale silence followed her.

"Emira," Alicus started gently, with a quick glance at Zuri, "do you want to tell us what happened?"

"No!" Emira snapped. She straightened her posture and corrected her tone, one fit to speak to a king. "No, I mean... I'm sorry."

"Take your time," Zuri added.

"I mean I can't. I can't tell you."

Zuri's shoulders sagged and Alicus placed his hand on her back. Xemile was leaning against the wall, lips tightly pressed together as he observed. Tallen remained nearby, arms still crossed and face unreadable.

"Alright," Alicus finally said. "Tallen, be sure Emira receives the tonic before sleep takes her again. We will speak more tomorrow."

Tallen nodded once. The king and queen filed out, followed by Xemile. Once they left, the harpy's arms relaxed at his sides.

"I'm sorry," Emira repeated.

She was ashamed that she had acted so fearfully, but afraid that the nightmares would persist. Seeing and hearing and feeling Rocas' execution all over again had been excruciating.

"Will it help," Tallen started, still standing, "if I stay with you?"

His voice was deep, but there was no agitation behind it. Emira's cheeks flushed as he spoke. She pulled her legs up into the bed and hoisted the heavy blankets over herself. Before Emira could assume the worst of his offer, the harpy added, "I will sit on the other side of the room." He gestured to the white stone fireplace and walked to one of the chairs surrounding it.

Emira watched him as he stepped away. His wings glimmered against the penetrating moonlight, the feathers dark but still iridescent. He turned and sat, the oversized chair cradling his large body, and his wings dropping along the plush backside.

Emira nodded her acceptance of the harpy's proposition.

"Remember to breathe deeply," he said calmly. "I will not leave unless you order me away."

Order.

He expected her to command him?

Emira nestled against the pillow and admitted, "I will not be able to sleep."

"You don't have to sleep if you do not want to."

"Will you sleep?"

"No."

Her brows furrowed, but she remained nestled in the pillows, keeping her eyes on the windows. "Do half harpy warriors not need sleep?"

She heard Tallen chuckle at the question before answering, "Yes, I require sleep. But I am on duty, and I will not rest until I am relieved of the job."

"What is the other half of your lineage?" Emira questioned.

"Fae," Tallen answered. "My mother was a harpy."

"Tell me about her?" Emira requested. She needed a distraction, something to keep her mind free from the echoing of her master's promise, and of Rocas' scream. And Tallen must have known, because he gave the information freely.

"She lives at Harpy Rock with the rest of the flock. She is fierce and callous, like most harpies."

"But you do not also live with the flock?" Emira questioned.

"I did as a child, but harpy males migrate away from home when they mature, and only return in spring to mate. They say that's why we have a rainy season as the fae main lands become relieved of harpy population."

"Really?"

"It's only ancient lore, but male harpies do have some control over the weather. If the sky is clear, but a bolt of lightning appears suddenly, it's likely that there may be a harpy nearby."

Emira nodded, "So, you go back often? In the spring?"

Tallen smirked through the darkness, and continued, "A half harpy is no desirable mate, so I spent my adolescent years with my father."

"Oh," Emira said, blushing.

She would never have considered Tallen to be ruled as undesirable. His strength and ferocity all seemed to be qualities a harpy female would want in a mate if they were as harsh of a people as Tallen claimed.

"And then?" Emira pressed.

The conversation was keeping her mind busy, and she couldn't bear another moment of silence. Emira sat upright again, facing the harpy as she searched for answers, which he continued to provide willingly.

"I trained," he responded. "But my time with my father came to an end. I left when I was of age. I made my way here, befriended Alicus, and I've been in his employ since."

"You trained?" Emira repeated.

"Weaponry, hand to hand combat, espionage…" he listed. "I am second in military command to the Southern Realm, after Xemile. Among other things."

"What… other things?"

"Anything my king demands of me. I have lived a long life. I have been a spy, an assassin, a soldier…" His voice trailed off, as if trying to remember the many titles he had held over the years.

"A guard?" Emira added, gesturing to herself and the room, and surprising herself with the light hearted comment.

"Yes," Tallen said with a smirk. "Although these accommodations are more desirable than most to which I am assigned."

"Oh?"

"I am well acquainted with the dungeons below the castle."

Emira shivered as she remembered the dungeons in the east. They were dark, with not a single window to allow a streak of sunlight through. The stone walls were always wet, as moisture collected and dripped down the cracked edges. Infestations of rats and roaches were normal, and Emira had the bites and sores to prove it so.

"And why have I been given a room?" the siren questioned.

Tallen chuckled again. "An odd question. Would you prefer a cell?"

"No," she responded quickly. "It's just… you don't know me. None of you do."

"My king and queen do not believe you pose any threat to our realm, and therefore, you have been given a room." He spoke so matter-of-factly, his allegiance to the southern rulers unquestionable.

Emira allowed the silence to stretch between them. His king and queen were right, she was not a threat. And even if she were, there would be no getting past Tallen.

"And you?" the harpy suddenly asked.

Emira straightened. "Me?"

Tallen tilted his head and said, "Your lineage. Are you fae?"

Emira's hands instinctively went to her ears, caressing the point they both had. She presented as fae, so it was a question she was used to being asked.

"Also, half," she responded. Tallen was silent, waiting for her to reveal more. "My mother was a siren. She and my father are both dead." And before Tallen could respond, she finished, "It was a long time ago. I don't remember them."

The harpy nodded his understanding. "Were they also… *residents* in the Eastern Realm?" he asked cautiously.

"Yes. They were both—" She paused, choosing her words carefully so as to not reveal the secret that she was compelled to keep about the east, "—they lived there. And I know my mother's name, but that's all." Tallen continued to stare at her, his ocean blue eyes spearing through the darkness like stars. Emira recoiled slightly and said, "You don't believe me."

"I believe you," he responded, never breaking his gaze.

"You don't know me. How could you possibly believe a word I say?"

"I have spent a fair amount of time as a spy, Miss Emira," Tallen answered impassively. "You are not a threat to my home, and you are not a liar."

Sarolina suddenly entered with a brief knock, holding a mug of her freshly brewed tonic. The witch instructed Emira to drink its entirety before sleep took her, and Emira obliged as the witch left once again. It tasted sweet, like peppermint, and Emira was lulled into a deep sleep only moments after consuming it. She slept through the rest of the night with a mind as dark and still as the midnight sky.

CHAPTER

TEN

The sun began to rise, and as the early rays peeked through the sheer curtains, Emira dragged her sore body from the bed and padded to the wardrobe. She rifled through the many gowns, each one made from delicate material and adorned in finery to befit royalty. The sparkle on each gem and crystal flickered as she pushed past the dresses, each one far too lavish and valuable for someone like her. The exquisiteness of them was an unearned commodity, and she was unfit to be given such upscale items.

Her eyes caught on a sage green set of linen pants with a matching, flowy top. She lifted them from the bin in which they had been stuffed at the bottom of the closet and shook them from their folded state, squinting through the dark shadows of her room. The waist of the pants didn't look as if they would stay in place on her fragile frame, but the drawstring was functional and would help to keep them upright.

Tallen stood from the armchair where he sat, his shuffling startling Emira as she closed the wardrobe door.

"Gods!" she cried out, sucking in an alarmed breath. He had been as silent as a shadow.

The harpy froze, becoming unnaturally still as he looked down upon Emira, who now had a hand held over her racing heart.

"Apologies," he said gruffly. "I'll wait in the corridor." The harpy made for the door as he finished, "We are both to attend a meeting this morning. Before breakfast."

Emira stood still, watching him pass by. His feathered wing lightly brushed her shoulder, causing a shiver to trail down her spine. Tallen stopped briefly at the sensation of their touch but soon quickened his pace and left the room.

Emira dressed, avoiding looking into the mirror. She did not care to see the bruises on her face from the night before. The sensitivity around her eye told her well enough that it looked horrendous.

When she entered the hall, Tallen was waiting.

The harpy's eyes landed on her face, scanning the wounds that she had inflicted upon herself. His expression was unreadable, but he stared for long enough that Emira thought he had asked a question that she did not hear.

"What?" she asked quickly.

Tallen blinked and turned away, striding down the hall.

"Follow me," he ordered.

She did.

The route through which he led Emira was unfamiliar, but so was the security she felt with the harpy. He had come to her aid more than once in the past three days, more than anyone ever had in her short lifetime. Her heart thundered beneath her chest as she followed him through the castle with credence.

Emira stood behind Tallen as they walked. Her eyes lingered on his dark hair that fell in tousled, curled heaps, swaying with each step he took. They then trailed to the feathers of his massive wings that shimmered against the rays of sunlight pouring in through the open castle walls. Emira wondered if they felt heavy. They certainly looked like it. He kept them tucked in tightly, his tanned hands peeking slightly from beneath them. Emira's eyes scanned the muscular cords beneath his skin, then down his powerful back and across his trimmed waist. As her eyes dipped lower, to the sculpted curve of his backside, heat pooled low in her stomach.

His wings shuddered, and Emira's head snapped upright. Even though he had not seen her wandering eye, Emira's ears warmed with embarrassment.

"We're here," Tallen said over his shoulder. His hands were placed upon two white double doors, and he pushed them open effortlessly.

The doors led into an enormous library. The high, vaulted ceilings had domed glass windows built into them, and the walls were lined with ashy, white bookshelves. Like every other room in the castle, the shelves were caressed with green vines that climbed upwards, reaching for the beams of light that came through the above windows. Emira looked around in awe as Tallen led her through the library and passed what was easily thousands of books.

"Is this...?" Emira breathed, awe pressing down on her shoulders.

"The ancient library of the Southern Realm," Tallen responded at her astonishment.

Emira had heard of the ancient libraries that existed, one within each realm, that held books and scrolls and records of the histories of the Fae Lands. The east had one as well, but Emira never ventured there, and even though she carried a love for books in her heart, she did not wish to trade her life for a glimpse at it.

They continued walking through the maze of books and scrolls, all neatly tucked away on the white shelving. How one would not become lost among so many tomes, Emira could not fathom.

"There are thousands of books here," she said to herself, although aloud.

"Four hundred seventy thousand," Tallen added over his shoulder, still walking ahead of her.

Emira stilled at the unfathomable number, although Tallen did not seem to notice. She glanced up once more at the massive domed window above the library, before taking three steps at a time to catch up to the harpy's long strides.

He led her to the furthest wall of the athenaeum, to a semi-circle of high backed, mossy green lounge chairs. Awaiting their arrival, sat King Alicus, Queen Zuriel, and Xemile. Emira gave a half smile to the group, embarrassed by the unsightly state of her wounds, and the events of the previous night. But when her eyes landed on a new, unfamiliar face, her embarrassment faded and was replaced with caution.

Sitting beside Xemile, was a woman of extraordinary beauty. She had skin like midnight, and her waist length, black hair was braided into the curves of her silver headdress. Her gown was an exquisite silver to match, with lengthy bell sleeves and high cleaves up either side of her legs. Her slitted, silver eyes watched Emira, her red lips unsmiling. In her lap, the woman held a leather-bound notebook and a stylographic pen.

"Emira," began the king, gesturing to the woman. "This is our emissary, Lady Vyla, a shifter from our realm." Vyla did not speak but kept her cat-like eyes on Emira, as if she were prey to be hunted.

"E-emissary?" Emira stammered. She remained a cautious distance from the group, still shaken by the presence of the beautiful, intimidating shifter.

"Loosen up, kitty," Xemile said to Vyla brazenly before turning to Emira. "Whatever I can't fix with brawn, she'll fix with brains."

Vyla's gaze moved away from Emira and shot to the fae commander before she spoke, her voice a low, rumbling growl. "This is no joke. If what we suspect is true, King Vyrion has committed treason."

Tallen took one of the last two chairs, motioning for Emira to sit beside him, his eyes fixed on the exchange between the fae and the shifter. There was an inkling of a smirk on his lips, hinting that the ire between Xemile and Vyla was not unusual, and Emira relaxed slightly.

"You and Tallen claim that Vyrion is keeping *slaves* in the Eastern Realm," Vyla continued, her voice smeared with urgency.

"Yes," Xemile answered surely.

"What makes you so conclusive?" the shifter questioned.

"Vyla, the bastard admitted it himself when we found him ready to murder Emira," Xemile responded exasperatedly. "Isn't that enough?"

Vyla's silver eyes, as sharp as knives, darted between him and the harpy.

"We must be sure," she stated. "The Southern Realm cannot go to war over a misunderstanding."

"It's not a misunderstanding," Tallen interjected sternly.

Vyla's voice lowered as she hissed, "*Let the siren explain.*"

All eyes fell on Emira and she shrank in her seat.

"I-I cannot say," she admitted after a long pause of silence.

"Because you are unsure?" the shifter asked, scribbling in her notebook as she spoke.

"No," Emira responded. "No, I..." Her voice trailed off.

Your disobedience will be the cause of many deaths in the Eastern Realm.

Rocas' mangled body flashed in her mind, as did his screaming, and the spray of his blood.

Her voice shook as she finished, "I am not permitted to speak on behalf of King Vyrion."

"And why must you require permission?" Alicus started, his voice sterner than Emira had ever heard it. He was surely hopeful that today would be the day Emira gave away all of her secrets.

"He is my mast—" Emira paused and corrected herself, "He is my king."

Zuri placed her hand on the king's forearm, and took over the questioning. "Emira... Tallen and Xemile found you in the woods."

The siren nodded her confirmation.

"And when they did, Vyrion was hurting you."

The queen's voice was calm and soft, and her questioning made Emira's eyes well up with tears.

She blinked them back as she responded, "Yes, he was."

"Why?" the queen asked carefully. "Why was he hurting you?"

Emira's breathing hitched as she tried to answer. Her heart raced, and her palms grew sweaty. She would not speak ill of Vyrion. She would not make others pay for her defiance. But she knew she couldn't remain comfortably in the south for much longer if she continued her silence.

"I stole from him," she finally choked out, wringing her hands in her lap.

"What did you steal?" Vyla asked, still scribbling in her book.

"An apple," Emira responded slowly, biting her lip and blinking her eyes rapidly. They stung as they filled with tears, and her heart continued to race. She was treading too close to the line of disobeying her master. She had to stop the questioning. She couldn't answer any further.

"You mean to go to war with the east?" she asked, voice cracking nervously, in an attempt to change the subject.

Vyla's spine straightened, and she stopped writing. Her lethal stare lifted to Emira once more as she said, "Treason must be punished."

"What treason?" Emira asked. "Can a king not do as he pleases?"

Alicus turned to her, his expression soft. "You are familiar with the Shifter Genocide that occurred one thousand years before our time?"

Emira's eyes darted between him and Vyla, embarrassed to admit that she was not educated in the history of their world.

"Sorry, no."

Zuri sat up taller in her chair. "The previous lines of kings believed all shifters to be an… *inadequate* species."

"A parasite upon the lands of the ever-powerful fae," Vyla corrected resentfully.

"Civil war followed," Zuri continued, "after one hundred years of murder at the hands of the previous kings."

One hundred years of death was unfathomable.

"Why?" Emira balked.

"Shifters, besides immortality, do not have abilities beyond that of their animal counterpart," Vyla answered. "A bird may fly, a fish may swim, but we do nothing more than a mortal when unshifted. My people were massacred for being deemed unexceptional."

Emira's breathing hitched as she listened.

"That's…" What could she say to describe such a thing as genocide? "What does the genocide have to do with the east?"

"When the war ended, the previous line of kings also ended, and new lines were appointed," Alicus continued, "for no ruler, but one, would surrender."

Silence stretched between them as the group waited for Emira to understand, but her green eyes remained wide as she anticipated more.

"Which king surrendered?" she finally asked.

Xemile answered, his eyes darkening as he did so. "Vyrion."

Emira's heart pounded rapidly, and she remained frozen in place as the information registered, but Alicus continued.

"My father, Valinor, became the newly appointed King of the Southern Realm, and after some… *persuading-*"

"And a few blows to that rat's head," Xemile added quickly.

"—Vyrion entered into a magically bound agreement with the other realms that he would not participate in a degrading class system within his kingdom, which included the keeping of slaves. This was done in reparation of the genocide, so that it would never happen again. Vyrion was able to keep his kingdom and allow his line to continue, but he cannot physically break that treaty."

Emira's mind reeled as her eyes darted, letting the information settle. Vyrion had been part of a one hundred yearlong massacre, and then he had surrendered to keep his realm. But this magical agreement—that couldn't be true because Vyrion *did* keep slaves.

"What happens if he breaks the agreement?" Emira asked, voice shaking slightly.

"He dies," Tallen answered. "Instantly."

Emira's brows furrowed as she tried to piece the information together. There couldn't be truth to this.

"So, you see," Vyla added, throwing a glare in Xemile's direction, "we must be sure of these accusations before we proceed."

"Could there be another way?" Zuri asked her husband. "Could he find a way to breach the contract and keep his life?"

"A loophole," Emira murmured to herself.

Eyes landed on the siren and she gasped aloud, realizing that she had crossed Vyrion's boundary of silence.

"I'm-I'm sorry," she stuttered, standing quickly and straightening the fabric of her pants. "I've said too much. With your leave…"

She bowed her head in the direction of the southern rulers. Alicus and Zuri solemnly nodded their agreement to her dismissal, and Emira turned on her heel, speed walking in the direction she came. Tallen stood from his chair and followed closely behind, but Emira kept her gaze forward, focusing on the unfamiliar route and on keeping her shuddering, panicked breaths silent.

The surplus of information sat in her mind heavily, like dense bread. She could not pick it apart while she scurried from the library and back into the corridor, Tallen taking the lead and guiding her out. She could say no more. She could no longer risk giving Vyrion more reason to find her—and end her.

CHAPTER

ELEVEN

The next morning was cool and crisp. A dusting of reds and golds sprinkled over the tops of the trees beyond the castle walls, as autumn knocked on the door of summer. Emira had been awake for hours, gazing out the vast, open windows of her bedroom watching the sun rise. Tallen had departed when she awoke before the light touched the sky, granting her privacy to replay the meeting from the day before in her mind.

She ate breakfast alone. An assortment of golden eggs with cheese, buttery toasted rolls, and juicy elk sausages adorned her silver plate, complemented with an herbal tea of chamomile and honey. Seated at a bistro table on the balcony off of her bedroom, Emira looked out over the realm.

Most of the land was covered with trees, each one growing ever closer to the next. The forest below was like a vast ocean, with waves made of branches and a tide of billowing leaves. Beyond the forest, and hugging along the Western Realm's border, was a thick mountain range. The clay cliff sides were jagged and unruly, an intimidating boundary if Emira had ever seen one. She knew nothing of the land, or of the realms it made up. She thought then that she could search the library and find the information she craved.

But when she turned to the east, Emira's stomach twisted. She could not see Vyrion's realm, but she knew it lay there, beyond the lush forest of the south. It crossed her mind for a moment to return. She was not a prisoner here, as was said many times before, and perhaps her master would show mercy upon her loyalty to him. Perhaps he would spare her, and she could go back to the life she knew, however back breaking it had been.

Emira scoffed aloud at the thought. She was no fool. Vyrion had never shown clemency to anyone. He was a vicious male with a thirst for suffering, and she was a replaceable piece of meat.

Vyrion had always been a murderer. Centuries before her existence, he had participated in mass genocide, one hundred years of bloodshed and discrimination, which spiraled into a civil war among the Fae Realms. And he had since continued ruling with fear and dishonesty. Emira's stomach knotted as she considered how many more lives had been taken at the hands of her master than she had previously thought.

When Vyrion found her, he would kill her, but for now, she decided that she was safe in the Southern Realm.

A powerful gust of wind rolled through the room, pulling her from within her troubled mind. She forced her tired body up to dress and slipped on a simple, blue dress and matching pair of shoes before she left the room and entered the corridor.

Aside from the shuffling of leaves upon the ground with every breeze that blew throughout the castle, the halls were silent. Emira took her time, strolling past the vine covered walls and large balconies at every turn. The cool air on her face felt clean and exhilarating, and she relished each flurry as it came.

As she continued on, the silence was slowly replaced by muffled shouts and laughter, as well as clangs of metal on metal, and metal on stone. Emira followed the sounds cautiously, until she came to a narrow set of crooked, stone steps that led down to a balcony turned training arena.

It was a massive space, with no railings to provide protection against the lengthy drop off the cliffside, and only the questionable stone steps to provide entrance or exit. A scattering of weapons were laid upon the cobblestone-like ground, and in the center, Xemile and Tallen were sparring.

Emira stood at the top of the steps, anxiously peering down at them. Xemile had a glinting sword in one hand, his other motioning for the harpy to come closer. The fae warrior smirked as he dared Tallen to strike. Tallen grinned in response, and his slithering whip unraveled in his grip, vibrating with anticipation.

The harpy attacked, and in a flash, the two warriors were entangled in a dance of fists and weapons. Xemile swung his sword, but Tallen blocked it, using armored plates that he wore on his forearms as a shield. The sentient whip wrapped itself around Xemile's ankle, taking him to the ground. But the fae general quickly recovered, flipped to his side and kicked behind the harpy's ankles. Tallen hit the stone, his black and gold feathered wings splaying out behind him as he fell. Xemile stood upright again, pulling a dagger that had been sheathed within his brown, leather boot. He went to strike the harpy, but his target rolled swiftly to the side and became airborne, whip still in hand.

"That's how you wanna play it then, eh?" yelled Xemile into the wind.

His amber hued, bat-like wings exploded from his back and he leapt into the sky after Tallen. They continued their brawl, darting through the air as they threw punches and flung their weapons. Tallen shoved Xemile, causing him to tumble through the air at breakneck speeds.

Suddenly, Tallen's icy blue eyes landed on Emira, and he stopped midair, hovering as his wings beat against the autumn currents. He lowered his head in acknowledgement and held a hand out to the arena below, silently inviting her to join. As she took a step down the stone stairs, Xemile burst through the sky, plowing into Tallen with a thunderous *crack*, dragging him down onto the hard ground of the arena and slamming him onto the stone.

Emira gasped at the sudden assault, but the warriors below laughed deeply and stood easily.

Xemile brushed the dust from his pants while Tallen rolled up his whip and stretched his massive wings.

"First rule of combat," Xemile said in Emira's direction as she continued her descent, "never get distracted."

"Are you not hurt?" she questioned the harpy although neither of them looked injured. There were no bruises or wounds to be seen, despite the violent clash between them.

"Only my pride," Tallen answered with a chuckle.

"I'd say I won that one," Xemile added smartly. "How about another go?" He turned and made his way to the center of the arena.

"You are welcome to stay," Tallen told Emira gently. "The air is fresh today; it would be good for you."

"Alright," she responded with a half-smile, her chest swelling at the kind thought. "I will try to avoid being a distraction."

"You are welcome here, Miss Emira," Tallen started. He was cut short as Xemile hollered from behind him impatiently. The whip at the harpy's side slithered and hissed in response, and the siren's eyes darted to it.

"A gift from my father," Tallen said, noticing her curiosity and placing his hand upon the leather of the handle, "many years ago."

"Is it… alive?" Emira asked apprehensively.

"No," he replied "The whip can sense the surroundings and respond, but it answers only to me. It cannot think or act on its own. I would call it enchanted before I would call it alive." Emira nodded as she continued to stare at the whip that vibrated beneath the harpy's resting hand.

"Tallen!" Xemile called, picking up his sword that had earlier fallen to the ground and skillfully rotating the blade in one hand. Emira shuffled hurriedly back to the stairs and sat on the lowest step. Tallen remained as still as stone as she did, watching her frail body lower to the ground before finally turning to engage with Xemile.

"Be careful!" Emira blurted.

Tallen threw a smirk over his shoulder in her direction as Xemile hollered playfully, "You haven't seen a damn thing yet, mermaid."

CHAPTER
TWELVE

As the days passed, Emira spent her time exploring the fantastical forest castle. She became more curious each day, taking new routes and learning the layout of the keep. She occupied her early mornings in the library, exploring the ancient tomes, or by watching Tallen and Xemile spar on the rocky balcony arena, sometimes with their weapons and sometimes with their fists. They were equal opponents each day, and the victor was unforeseeable.

She also made sure to visit the kitchens frequently. The anxiety of helping herself had dissipated as quickly as some of her meals had. After a lifelong diet of broth and molded bread, every new meal was exciting. She found the different smells and textures to be almost as mouthwatering as the taste of the food itself.

And Sarolina had been pleasantly surprised with Emira's health at her most recent visit. Her wounds had completely healed, and her figure had started to fill out. She no longer had jutting collarbones or protruding ribs, but had started to develop a pear shape at her hips and some muscle tone along her arms. She was *healthy*. She had never felt so strong, so energetic, so alive and like herself. It was an extraordinary sensation.

In the evenings, Emira lay by the fireplace in her room, watching the flames crackle on the hearth. The warmth on her skin was heavenly; nothing like the biting cold where she had slept in the Eastern Realm.

And while Sarolina's sleep tonic tamed her nightmares, Tallen continued as her overnight guard, staying within the bedroom walls, instead of outside the door.

Tonight, Emira sat on the floor by the hearth of the fireplace while Tallen sat nearby on his usual arm chair. The warmth of the flames crawled up her back and heated her wavy hair as she flipped through the pages of a geography book she had chosen from the library earlier that day. Her arms and legs were exposed in a short, summertime nightgown, but she enjoyed the warm lick of the flames on her bare skin. Tallen, however, only watched, the flickering of the flames dancing upon his stubbled face and lighting up his blue eyes.

Emira peered up at him from over the book.

"Geography?" the harpy questioned. Emira closed the heavy cover so that they could both look upon the title.

"Only the Fae Realm," she answered. "I didn't know there were mountains nearby until I came here."

"The Caseli Mountains," Tallen confirmed. "They border the west. The mountains produce a violet gem that can be found nowhere else. They have made the Western Realms very prosperous."

"I can't imagine how beautiful they must look in person," Emira said, eyes drifting to the strong flames warming her skin.

There was a beat of silence between them, nothing but the sound of the crackling embers in the hearth.

"Where did you learn to read?" the harpy finally asked. "I didn't think your previous circumstances allowed for such an education."

Emira stroked the cover of the book as she answered. "It didn't, but I lived mostly within the castle walls. You pick up on some things after a time. I can't say I'm a strong reader, but at least functional."

There was another stretch of silence before Tallen asked curiously, "There must be other things that you... *picked up*... while in the Eastern Realm?"

Emira opened her mouth to speak, but when no sound came, she snapped it closed. Oddly, she trusted Tallen, and the thought of telling him something - anything, *everything* - about her time in the Eastern Realm was deeply enticing. But visions of her nightmares and Vyrion's voice replayed in her mind, and she couldn't make the words come forth.

And the trust she felt for Tallen was equally as terrifying.

"It's alright," Tallen said softly. She looked up at him, his gaze gentle and his feathered wings relaxed. "When you're ready, Miss Emira. If you ever are."

Her chest heaved as emotion crawled up her throat and threatened tears.

"I believe the restitution for my being a guest in this realm will be a detailed admission of my life in the east. A time will come when I will have no choice but to speak of it," she responded shakily. "I just wish..."

Emira pulled her gaze off of the harpy and turned towards the flames, attempting to hide the welling in her eyes.

As her voice trailed off, Tallen leaned forward, resting his massive arms on his knees.

"What do you wish, Miss Emira?"

A tear fell from her cheek, splashing onto the cover of the book. She wiped it clean with a swipe of her hand before grasping at either side of her face and giving in to the emotion that held her in a chokehold. She began to sob.

Tallen slid from the chair and onto the floor. As he moved closer, he timidly placed a hand on Emira's shoulder, brushing her hair back as he did so. She continued to weep while Tallen sat silently beside her, running his calloused hand along her shuddering backside.

"It's alright," he said gently.

She looked up through puffy eyes. The harpy was only inches away from her.

"You are not expected to reveal anything. My king and queen know Vyrion hurt you without you needing to say so. *I* know he hurt you. You are not expected to be okay. Not yet."

As his words settled, Emira heaved a breath and leaned into the harpy's shoulder. He wrapped his arm around her frame, his massive feathered wing following to cradle her trembling body.

Emira had not been held in the way that the harpy held her now since the night Rocas had been executed.

But this was different.

The feeling of warmth and protection that Tallen was providing, whether he realized it or not, was one Emira had never felt before. At his touch, she wailed, releasing twenty-five years of raw anguish.

Her body trembled against his sturdy physique. She brought her knees to her chest and clawed at Tallen's clothes, desperately searching for grip, for grounding.

Flashes of Vyrion's face entered her mind, and a soundtrack of his wretched voice played in her ears. She could hear him ordering an execution, followed by the cry of a helpless slave. She heard the rattle of shackles, the crack of a whip, the whirring of a blade slicing through the air, and the sickening squelch of steel coming down on bare flesh.

Emira released another cry, her voice turning raspy. The harpy continued to sit by her side, allowing her to rake her fingers against his armor and squirm beneath his wing. She needed this,

this release. Her trauma had been pent up, buried, for so long. Without a word, Tallen held her tighter and allowed her to cry into the late hours of the night.

CHAPTER

THIRTEEN

It was barely light out when Emira awoke from the best sleep she'd had since arriving in the Southern Realm. Early dawn light trickled in through the sheer curtains. She turned away from it, burying her face into the luxurious pillows.

The events of the night before flashed in her mind, and she realized that she had not remembered going to bed. Had she fallen asleep in Tallen's arms?

Emira whispered into the dark edges of the bedroom. "Tallen?"

The rustle of his wings came as the harpy stood from his usual armchair, which remained cloaked in shadows. He emerged, the pink light from the rising sun illuminating his chiseled face as he walked to the foot of the bed.

"Good morning," he started.

Emira sat up with a groan and rubbed the sleep from her eyes. The autumn air chilled her bedroom and she shivered against the cold. Tallen grasped a silken, white robe that had been slung over the footboard of the bed and held it out in her direction.

"Thank you," she said, accepting the garment gratefully. "What time did—"

"Late."

"And you… put me to bed?"

"Yes."

Emira bit her lip, embarrassed by her previous show of inelegant emotion.

"I'm sorry," she said.

"You owe no such apology," Tallen responded calmly.

Emira only nodded, knowing the harpy meant what he said.

"I…" the harpy hesitated, still standing at the foot of Emira's bed. "I wanted to propose a change in our typical morning routine."

"Oh?" Emira answered, straightening her back and flinging the robe around her shoulders.

"Just for today," Tallen amended.

Emira stood, putting her arms through the silky sleeves and tying the knot just above her waist. "What did you have in mind?"

The harpy rounded the end of the bed and stepped closer to Emira.

"The Caseli Mountains," he answered. "Will you allow me to show them to you?"

"The mountains," Emira repeated, arms glued to her sides. "You mean, outside the castle walls?"

"Yes," Tallen replied matter-of-factly, still holding out his hand. "And then, west."

Emira smirked at his attempt to make a joke but still did not accept his outstretched grasp.

Tallen's voice deepened and his gaze softened as he took a small step forward.

"You'll be safe with me," he promised.

His icy eyes bore into hers, pleading that she would believe him, trust him.

Emira lifted a trembling hand slowly and placed it in his calloused grip. He entwined his fingers in her own, and Emira's stomach knotted with emotion. Happiness, fear, and caution consumed her, leaving the siren to only gulp down the lump in her throat. As she did, the harpy's shoulders relaxed. It was a small tell that he, too, was riding an emotional wave.

"We'll have to fly," he prefaced.

Emira bit her bottom lip and nodded, "I trust you."

Tallen's mouth quirked up into a half smile at the confession.

"My clothes?" Emira asked, looking down at her robe.

"It will be only us," Tallen replied. Emira nodded, and he chuckled. "Hold on then."

Tallen swiftly lifted Emira from the ground, cradling her body gently, easily, as if she were weightless. She wrapped her arms around his neck, gripping as tightly as she could. His scent of dark chocolate and cedar penetrated her senses. Tallen walked out onto one of the many balconies off of the castle and stepped up onto the edge of the railing. The sky was pink with the beginning of the sunrise, and the city below still slept, cradled in the forest's embrace.

"Ready?" he asked quietly, looking upon Emira's sunrise-stained face.

She peered down over the balcony edge. They were hundreds of feet above the ground, with nothing but the rocky mountainside below and the forest canopy beyond that to painfully break the fall that Tallen knew she was expecting.

"You're not going to jump, are you?" she asked incredulously as her gaze snapped back to Tallen, whose eyes remained unblinking.

His lips were pressed together tightly, trying to hide his answer, *yes*, and he began to beat his feathered wings.

As the air currents around them swirled in response to each rap, Tallen repeated clearly, "Are you ready, Miss Emira?"

She buried her face against the leather of his tunic. "Yes," she mumbled against him. "Yes, I trust you."

Tallen's grip tightened around her, and as swiftly as he unfurled his feathered wings, he leapt into the air.

CHAPTER
FOURTEEN

Tallen stretched his massive wings wider and flapped them harder. They caused a swift change in air pressure that had Emira gasping for breath as her hair began to fly about wildly. Tallen leapt from the balcony, dropping slightly lower before the beat of his wings propelled them upwards and into the air. Emira yelped at the sudden lurch and kept her face buried. She had never flown before, aside from when Xemile had rescued her, but she had been unconscious then.

Moments later, when their movement evened out, Tallen's voice coaxed her.

"Have a look, Miss Emira…"

She glanced up at him from the feigned safety of the harpy's chest. The light from the rising sun shone upon his hard features, and his dark curls fluttered around his handsome face. His wings beat powerfully behind him, fighting against the air currents and pushing them upwards. For a moment, Emira thought Tallen looked otherworldly.

He cocked his head to the side, urging her to glance down. She peered over the edge of the harpy's shoulder to see the sharp rocks of the mountainside below them. He rushed past each plateau with a swift beat of his wings, their shadow chasing after them. They climbed higher and higher into the air until the cool mist of the low hanging clouds tickled her skin.

"You alright?" Tallen asked, his voice slightly raised to be heard over the rushing wind.

Emira turned her gaze forward, eyes wide at the scattering of pink tinted clouds that engulfed them. She sucked in a breath as the varying currents fought for a place within her lungs and released a laugh—the purest one that had ever come from her own lips.

"This is unreal!" Emira exclaimed.

She glanced down again, spying a flock of geese below them that flew in perfect form. But the harpy's speed was unmatched, and they quickly passed the birds, cutting through the air with ease.

As they began their descent downwards, and as they whipped through the chilly mist of clouds, the forest canopy came into view, like a river of green racing by. Emira chuckled as they glided, and the cool morning air tickled at her reddened cheeks.

Tallen tightened his grip as the Caseli Mountains came into view. Emira peered over Tallen's arm, taking in the magnificent sight before her. The mountains were indeed vast, stretching further than she could see. The rocky faces of the mountainsides were steep and unforgiving. Atop each peak sat a white dusting of snow.

The harpy's wings shifted as they made their descent. Emira felt her stomach drop as they landed, the air pressure making her ears pop. Tallen carefully set Emira on her feet.

"Be careful," he warned, "it can be icy."

"Where is the snow coming from?" Emira asked, eyes fixed on the sky, searching for a gray cloud.

"The west," Tallen answered. "It always snows there. If we were to cross over these peaks, the Western Realm would be in view."

"It's so close," Emira stated.

"The wards keep the cold weather in its own realm. That's why we don't feel it in the south."

Emira stepped closer to the gray stone that made up the mountain border. As she looked closer, she saw a faint glinting within the rocky material. She placed her hand upon it, the surface like ice beneath her touch.

As the clouds moved across the sky, sunlight poured upon the mountain's surface, which shimmered like diamonds beneath the rays.

"Western gems," Tallen said from behind Emira. "There are vast tunnels and housing beneath the mountains for western miners."

Emira's eyes moved from the mountains, to the sky, to the horizon, where the Southern Realm lay. The thick canopy of trees created an ocean of green. There was not a thing to be seen except for the healthy tops of the forest.

"It's beautiful," Emira whispered. "All of it."

Tallen did not respond. When Emira turned to face him, his eyes were on her. They stood silently for a moment, gazes locked. Emira's breathing hitched, and the harpy took a step closer, but a swift breeze blew, nearly knocking Emira off of her feet. Tallen reached out quickly, grasping the siren at the elbow as she tried to keep her short robe from blowing upwards.

She laughed loudly, and the harpy loosened his grip.

"Maybe," Emira started, "we should head back soon?"

Tallen paused before answering. "Are you hungry? I could take you into town."

"Really?" Emira exclaimed. She then looked down at her clothes, or lack of.

"Just us," the harpy reminded her.

Emira grinned up at him. "Alright."

THEY FLEW DOWN THE FACE OF THE MOUNTAIN, OVER THE FOREST'S canopy, and into a small opening in the trees. Tallen hovered above the clearing and slowed the beat of his wings, allowing them to lower below the branches and enter the forest.

"Be careful," Tallen said as they landed. He set Emira down on her feet gently and warned, "Watch the roots."

Emira was beaming.

She pushed the disheveled hair from her face and swept it back into a braid.

"I can't believe we're here," she exclaimed as her eyes roamed over her surroundings. The thick underbrush was brilliantly green. Moss, shrubs, weeds, and flowers made up the wild carpet upon which they stood.

Tallen smiled and took her hand in his, leading her forward through the trees.

"There's more," he promised.

Emira allowed the harpy to lead her through the forest. Her stomach turned as he squeezed her hand in his, his grip strong and protective. They finally passed in between two massive trees that opened up onto a clearing. Cradled within the forest, unseeable from above, a town appeared before their eyes.

It was unlike anything Emira had ever seen. Beneath the shadows of the forest canopy, the town was still cloaked in darkness. The trunks of the trees were thick and strong, wide enough that it would easily take up to fifty people to form a circle around each one. And rather than being cut down to make space for new architecture, many of the trees were hollowed out, allowing for shops, restaurants, and homes to be built into them. Candles were placed in small glass jars, which were hung on branches to light the town.

Dirt pathways weaved between the obstacles, but the forest felt otherwise untouched.

"This forest is thousands of years old," Tallen said as he led Emira through the village. "These trees"—he glanced up as he spoke—"have seen more than any can fathom."

They walked hand in hand through the forest village, alight only with the candles that swung from the overhead branches, and the weak beams of sunlight that pushed through the thick canopy. As they passed homes built into the trees, each window remained dark as the inhabitants slumbered within. Emira never would have thought that this was what lay within the Southern Realm's forest.

Tallen stepped up to the window of a nearby restaurant. It was carved into a tree and appeared to also have multiple levels as the glass windows climbed up the trunk. Emira peered up. Many of the surrounding shops were multiple levels, connected to one another with wooden bridges that swung silently from tree to tree.

Tallen tapped on one of the front windows and peered inside.

A moment later, a stout, brunette fae female appeared from within and unlocked the door. Her pointed ears sprouted from beneath her dark, gray streaked hair. She wore a simple brown dress, draped with a dark green, stained apron. Her cheeks were flushed, but her dark eyes lit up kindly when she opened the door.

"Tallen!" she said, happily surprised, wiping her hands on the apron. "You know we don't open for another hour?"

"Bri," he said. "Can I trouble you for an early meal?"

The woman tilted her head curiously, likely not expecting such a request from the harpy. But then her eyes fell on Emira, standing quietly behind the warrior's massive frame. She looked back to Tallen and smiled.

"I think I can figure something out. Come in."

THE INSIDE OF THE TAVERN WAS DIMLY LIT WITH CANDLES IN JARS, ONE on each of the worn, wooden tables. A set of narrow stairs led to where Emira presumed the kitchens to be. The floors, decorated with old tiles, had moss growing over them, yet the hollowed-out tree smelled surprisingly fresh, like pine syrup.

"Thank you," Emira said to Bri shyly as the woman led her and the harpy to a small table at the back of the pub. "I hope we aren't intruding," she added, noting the empty dining room.

Bri smiled as she lifted a pair of golden goblets from the table and filled them from a nearby water pitcher.

"No intrusion at all," she began. Her gaze turned towards the harpy as she continued, "I'm happy to see Tallen outside of a business assignment."

Emira smirked and remarked, "I think, technically, I'm still a business assignment."

Bri chuckled at Emira's comment, keeping her gentle eyes pinned on the harpy.

"She's quite pretty," the barmaid murmured, filling the second goblet and setting it down. Tallen's neck flushed as she did so, yet his expression remained fixed. The pub owner smirked once more before promising a short wait for their meal, walking away and heading up the narrow staircase.

"She's nice." Emira chuckled, lifting the cup to her lips.

Tallen nodded once in agreement.

"Alicus used to come here as a child with Zuri and Xemile. Bri would give them cream ale and pies, even though it was past curfew. She'd send a raven to Valinor and Amarie, letting them know that their crown prince and his betrothed were in her pub with their obnoxious ginger haired friend. That's the story I've been told anyway."

Emira nearly choked on her water as Tallen spoke.

"*Betrothed?*" she repeated, wiping at the corners of her mouth. "Alicus and Zuri were promised as children?"

Tallen nodded. "Zuri comes from a noble family. Her parents were good friends to the late king and queen. Luckily, Alicus and Zuri are likened in personality, and their arrangement has been one of happiness. Not many royal matches end as theirs has."

Emira took another sip, allowing the information to process while the cool water settled on her tongue.

"So, Alicus' parents," she began. "They are dead?"

Tallen nodded solemnly.

"They were crowned after the genocide," he began, "like the other rulers of the realms, but they became ill soon after. Alicus was crowned as king within the same hour of their death."

"Gods," Emira muttered under her breath. "That's awful."

"He is the youngest king in the Fae Realm," Tallen added.

"Is that why he was referred to as child?" she asked, remembering Vyrion's words the first night she met Tallen and Xemile. The harpy only nodded.

That was when she suddenly realized the burden that had been placed on Alicus. He was betrothed young and thrust onto the throne, previously ruled by a beloved king and queen. Such a young fae was likely seen as incapable of ruling such a vast realm. And this all occurred while he mourned the death of both of his parents.

Their silence was interrupted when Bri came back down the staircase rapidly, holding a plate in each hand. Each one was stacked high with fluffy, golden pancakes, slathered in sticky, sweet smelling syrup. She set them down on the small table, earning a quiet, '*Thank you,*' from Tallen.

"Miss Emira," he started as Bri left them alone once more.

"Just Emira," she cut in as she speared the pancakes with her fork. "Please."

The harpy shifted in his seat, seemingly uncomfortably at the request.

"Emira…" he continued. But as he looked at her, Tallen's expression softened. Gone was the stone-faced warrior. His jaw slackened, and his lips parted slightly. His eyebrows relaxed, making the hard lines in his face soften as well. His wings were eased at his sides, no longer held tightly against his body.

"Tallen?" Emira said curiously, raising an eyebrow at the harpy as she took a bite of the hot, buttery breakfast.

"I want to tell you about me," he started, his body tightening, and his face growing expressionless again. "And where I come from."

Emira's spine straightened, surprised by Tallen's statement. She looked at him thoughtfully and replied, "Okay…"

"I left Harpy Rock as an adolescent," he started.

"To be with your father," she added, recalling her conversation with Tallen on one of her earlier nights in the Southern Realm. He had spoken of his mother and his upbringing in the cliffside territory where the harpies called home.

"Yes. I had nowhere else to go, as an undesirable halfblooded member of the harpies. But, my father is…" His voice trailed off, and he looked away, jaw ticking at the vulnerability that Emira presumed gnawed in his chest.

"Is he cruel?" she attempted.

Tallen huffed nervously and faced her again.

"My father," he continued, "is King Ellis of the Northern Realm."

Emira's breath caught, and her lips parted. She stared back at Tallen's blue eyes as the silence stretched between them. Tallen was born of royal blood. He was a northern royal who held allegiance with the south. And as the son of a king, that meant that he was also…

"You're a prince?" Emira choked out.

"A bastard," he corrected quickly. "My father took me in when I left the flock. But not as an heir. I was to be a tool. A weapon. His soldiers and spies trained me for quite a time before I left and came to the Southern Realm."

"A weapon?" Emira repeated. "What do you mean?"

"Harpy males can affect the weather. My father made it clear to me *and* his court that I was to be an asset to his military. Just imagine, a soldier controlling the weather in battle. It would be a devastating feat to behold. I trained as an assassin and a spy and a soldier, and I've—" the harpy's rambling came to an abrupt halt, allowing him to heave a breath before he continued, "I've murdered men and women as I was ordered to, without question, because I had nowhere else to go."

"*Murdered.*" The word echoed from Emira's lips as a whisper.

"I hated every moment," he continued desperately, leaning forward, his muscular arms propped upon the wooden table. "Emira, you must know that. I *hated* it. I left and came to the Southern Realm, where Alicus and Zuri have offered meaningful and just employment. But every scream, every plea for mercy that I ever caused someone has echoed in my head every single day since…"

His voice trailed off.

Emira recalled when Zuri had told her that Tallen was finding peace, but from what she had not said. She had not imagined it to be from such a tormented existence—being used as a weapon of fear and destruction. The blood on Tallen's hands was immense, more than Emira had ever considered.

"Why are you telling me this?" she asked.

"I want you to know," he began, "that I know what it's like to feel forlorn, and to be distrustful. You aren't alone. Being in the Southern Realm has given me a meaningful and happy life, and it can for you too, if you allow it… if you let it in."

Emira reached across the table and took ahold of Tallen's hands, gripping them tightly in her own.

"I'm so sorry," she uttered truthfully.

"There's one more thing you must know…" he started, voice so low that Emira had to lean forward to hear. "Em—"

"Hey, we're opening the doors in five," came Bri's voice from halfway up the winding staircase. Emira drew back her hands from Tallen quickly. She huffed a nervous laugh and tucked a loose piece of hair behind her pointed ear.

"We should go," she said, gesturing to her robe and short nightgown. "I'm not really dressed for public eyes."

Tallen quickly nodded his head and rose from his chair, his face hardening again, morphing into the trained soldier that he was, ignoring the plate of untouched breakfast before him.

"Of course," he said dryly. "Of course, I'll bring you back."

CHAPTER

FIFTEEN

Xemile's sword sliced through the air, making its way to land upon Tallen, but the harpy quickly blocked it with a crisscrossing of his daggers. Xemile smirked, his reddened, sweat drenched face only inches from Tallen's own. The harpy pushed the fae warrior back, sending the impressive sword with him.

It was peculiarly warm for the season, and the midday rays beat down on their bodies as they sparred in the stone arena. Emira remained inside, claiming that the heat was unfavorable. Tallen had agreed and suggested she join Queen Zuri and Vyla for lunch.

Emira did not ask Tallen any further questions about their previous conversation once they arrived home earlier that morning. Why Tallen felt compelled to tell her anything personal about himself was bewildering. The harpy prided himself on maintaining his privacy as it made for a good soldier, and an even better spy. But he ignored his confusion, choosing to indulge his curiosity instead, for when it came to Emira, he felt a significant compulsion to divulge his histories.

"Are you getting enough sleep?" Xemile asked, referring to Tallen's night guard duties, which had remained in place.

"Are you?" Tallen teased, sheathing his dagger, and choosing a sword from the available stock of training weapons. "I can smell at least three separate females on you."

Xemile ran a hand along the back of his neck sheepishly and chuckled.

"Sorry about that," he said with a grin.

"No, you're not," Tallen responded sarcastically.

He lifted the sword and charged toward the smirking general. Their blades crashed against each other, clanging through the arena and reverberating through the warm air. If the two males had been mortals, their ears would bleed from the vibration of the rattle, eardrums shattered by the frequencies.

They continued to spar, dodging each other's blades and attempted jabs. Tallen used his impressive wings to gain the upper hand on Xemile, who needed time to procure his own, and ended the spar with a blade to the fae's throat.

"I'm sleeping enough," he finally answered, lowering his sword.

Xemile wiped the sweat from his brow and turned to pick up his canteen from the edge of the arena floor.

"And Emira?" he questioned, taking a swig of water. "Have her night terrors stopped?"

Tallen sighed, and Xemile held the canteen out to him. The harpy accepted the water and drank deeply.

"They're better," he answered, wiping his lips with the back of his sweat speckled hand. "But her sleep has not improved. She wakes very early."

"Think it'll last much longer?" Xemile asked, reaching an arm behind his head and stretching his tight muscles.

Tallen considered. "I don't know. Perhaps with time. She's terrified of Vyrion—"

"I don't blame her," Xemile cut in, lowering his arm and shaking it into a relaxed position. "He's a sick sonofabitch."

"She's always on high alert," the harpy continued, lifting the canteen to his lips and drinking the last of the water, "as if Vyrion will turn a sudden corner and steal her away at any moment."

"Has she told you anything else about the Eastern Realm?"

The harpy shook his head. He didn't know much about Emira's life before they had found her in the woods. And although she had released such raw emotion the previous night, he refused to push her into disclosing anything further about her *presumed* enslavement. Not until she was ready.

Xemile finished stretching his other arm and turned to the harpy.

"Soon enough perhaps," he continued with a grin. "Fists?"

Tallen chucked the empty canteen aside and smiled.

"Fists."

CHAPTER
SIXTEEN

Emira glided through the corridors confidently. The dried leaves cascaded along the stone floor with every curiously warm breeze that blew through the castle. The route was familiar now, and she made her way to the dining hall with ease.

As she pushed open the double doors, she found Vyla sitting alone at the ashy, round table.

"Hello," the shifter said, looking up from her familiar notebook.

Her hair was pulled back into a low bun and decorated with shimmering clips. Her silver eyes were lined heavily with kohl and her dark skin glimmered with speckles of golden paint along her sharp cheekbones.

"Good afternoon," Emira responded, walking towards the table and taking a seat. "Is Queen Zuri running late?"

"She is unable to attend lunch with us today," Vyla responded, closing her notebook and moving it aside. "Queenly matters."

"Oh," Emira said, suddenly feeling intrusive. She began to rise from the chair. "Should I—"

"No," Vyla interrupted. "You are welcome to stay."

Emira sat back down awkwardly and looked anywhere but in the shifter's direction, whose fierce eyes remained pinned on her.

"I regret that we have not spoken much since your arrival," Vyla began, gaining Emira's attention. "I have a separate residence within the realm but beyond the castle grounds. It allows me more privacy. But unfortunately it also means that I am not as easily accessible for such conversations to occur."

"It's alright," Emira replied quickly. "I didn't think—"

"That I was intentionally avoiding you?" Vyla finished.

Emira huffed nervously. "Yeah," she answered with a chuckle.

She had not been upset that the shifter made herself scarce, as she was as unnerving as any alien creature could be. Her intense gaze alone was one to tremble beneath, let alone the sharpness of her tongue and the seriousness of her nature. Emira tucked a loose strand of her hair behind her ear. Vyla's gaze flicked to the point it bore and she stared for a moment, without trying to hide her apparent curiosity.

The double doors opened and in came four castle servants carrying trays of meat, fruit, potatoes, bread and tea. As they set the platters upon the table, Vyla continued to stare, as if she had not noticed the arrival of lunch at all.

It wasn't until the servants left, and the doors snicked closed that she finally spoke.

"It is interesting that you, being only half fae, possess so many physical qualities of the fae."

Emira's hand touched the point of her ears that seemed to capture the shifter's curiosity and answered, "I suppose. I truly haven't ever thought about it before."

Vyla took a bite of the smoky ham on her plate before continuing.

"And what other fae qualities do you possess?" she asked.

"Well," Emira started, "the rapid healing is new. I've never done it before."

Vyla nodded once. "Due to your poor health. Continue."

Emira considered before she did so. "I don't know. I've never procured wings like the fae can."

"Have you attempted to do so? And have you considered your siren heritage?" Vyla asked, bringing her tea cup to her full, ruby painted lips.

"No," Emira replied honestly. She had never considered either part of her lineage, or what it meant to be half siren and half fae.

Vyla only raised her eyebrows in response.

"What type of shifter are you?" Emira asked, desperate to take the attention off of herself.

"Predatory feline," Vyla answered casually, lowering her cup.

"Like, a lion? Or a leopard?" Emira asked.

"Lion, leopard," the shifter repeated. "They're all the same. When shifted, I possess agility and strength and speed. My eyesight is unmatched and my physical body morphs into that of a predator."

"It sounds... painful?" Emira guessed.

Vyla smirked. "Not at all."

"And you can transform at will?"

"Yes, as can all shifters."

"Are both of your parents feline shifters?"

Vyla's smile vanished, and her gray eyes darkened. "They were."

Emira's face heated at her mistake. "Oh, gods, I'm sorry. I didn't—"

"It's alright," Vyla interrupted softly, raising a heavily jeweled hand. "They were killed in the Shifter Genocide. Both had been emissaries for the Southern Realm, making them targets for assassination. I was only a child when it happened, but the late King Valinor and Queen Amarie made accommodations for my care."

"You were… a child then?" Emira stammered as the numbers raced through her mind. "But I thought the genocide was hundreds and hundreds of years ago."

Vyla's smirk returned.

"A *thousand* years ago, yes. I matured and became emissary for Valinor and Amarie in my parent's stead. Alicus took the throne, and he has continued my employment for the last three hundred and thirty nine years."

Emira's mind reeled at the surplus of information. "I am sorry for the horrors you must have witnessed."

"Likely similar to the ones you have seen yourself," Vyla countered. "Vyrion is, of course, one of the original kings. He was in favor of the genocide and participated fully."

Emira's stomach twisted at the thought. Vyrion may have been the very one to orchestrate the demise of Vyla's parents. The possibility made bile crawl up her throat and burn her esophagus.

"You're uncomfortable," Vyla stated plainly. "Let us speak of this no longer."

"Alright," Emira agreed hastily, lifting her fork and spearing the seasoned potatoes.

"Have you a gown for Mabon?" the shifter questioned.

Emira paused, her fork halfway to her lips. "What?"

"Mabon is in two days' time," Vyla responded matter-of-factly. "Do you have a gown?"

"Um, no," the siren answered truthfully. "What's Mabon?"

"A celebration of the autumnal equinox," Vyla began, no trace of condescension upon her full, red lips. "A festival will take place in two days' time."

"Tallen hasn't said anything about it," Emira answered.

"He wouldn't," Vyla responded. "Tallen does not typically partake in such events, but this year he will act as your escort."

Memories from the hazy morning flooded Emira's mind. She recalled what it had felt like to be lifted into Tallen's arms. She remembered the way his hands felt upon her waist, the thin silk of her robe the only barrier between them. Emira wondered what those hands would feel like gliding along her bare skin.

Emira felt her neck flush. The shifter's silver eyes flashed to the siren's reddening skin, her expression unreadable as she stared.

Emira cleared her throat, shifting in her seat. "You..." she began, searching for something to fill the silence. "You said you have a home elsewhere?"

Vyla nodded as she bit into a ripe strawberry. "Not a far ride on horseback," she said, "and barely a few minutes when shifted."

"How long have you lived there?"

Vyla thought for a moment. "It must be quite a while now. Valinor and Amarie gifted it to me around the time of Alicus' birth. Perhaps six hundred years or so."

"I can't imagine living somewhere for so long," Emira said lightly, now scooping some scrambled eggs with her fork.

Vyla smirked, and she bit another strawberry.

"What is your age?" she asked blatantly.

Emira's gaze flicked downwards. She suddenly felt like a child.

"Twenty-five," she answered sheepishly.

"Ahhh," Vyla purred. "By fae standards you would be fully matured this year."

"Full maturity is deemed at twenty-five years old?" Emira asked, slightly stunned. "Even though the fae are immortal?"

Vyla chuckled. "Yes, the math *is* strange but it is what it is."

"How old is everyone else?" Emira questioned, suddenly realizing that she did not know the answer, and would not know what to even begin guessing.

"Alicus and Zuri are the youngest," Vyla began, "respectively five hundred ninety five and five hundred ninety three years. Xemile would be next at five hundred ninety eight. And Tallen, he is the oldest after me..." Emira held her breath as Vyla continued, "...at seven hundred eighty four."

"I see," Emira chuckled incredulously.

"You were expecting another answer," Vyla probed.

Emira took a bite of the perfectly roasted potatoes and shook her head.

"I'm not sure what I expected," she answered truthfully. "I'm not sure of anything."

Emira avoided eye contact with the shifter and focused on the plate in front of her. She could feel Vyla's never blinking, predatory eyes analyzing, and dissecting. It wasn't surprising that Vyla was more than a thousand years old. She spoke as if she had seen the world and was no longer shocked by the things Emira still found incredible.

But she had not considered the ages of the others, and the knowledge that she was hundreds of years younger, made her feel inadequate and burdensome.

"Do not fret over it," Vyla purred. "Wisdom does not always come with age, but with circumstance. You are wiser than most, as you have endured more than most. At least," she said, a hint of sarcasm entering her tone, "allegedly."

Emira finally smiled and met Vyla's unblinking gaze.

"Thank you," she said, her shoulders relaxing.

The shifter sat across from her, as still as stone, with only a fierce smirk as a response. Emira would have felt on edge if she had not just learned the depth of the shifter's heart.

CHAPTER
SEVENTEEN

The day of the Mabon celebration came quickly, and with it, a chaotic atmosphere of preparations. The corridors of the castle bustled with busy servants, carrying linens and trays of food, stringing lights and arranging centerpieces. The busyness unnerved Emira, and so she remained in her room for most of the day, seeking quiet idleness.

A dress had been made for her to wear for the evening's festivities. When it had been delivered earlier that morning, Emira thought she had never seen a more beautiful gown. It was a smokey blue gray, with a bodice made from glittering lace. The tulle skirts flared at the waist, and cascaded downwards, sparkling as the light caressed the fabric. A slit up the side of the skirt would reveal most of her leg, while a matching, velvet cape would cover her shoulders when the evening began to chill.

An attached note read:

A gown fit for a siren
-Vyla

The sun began to set, and as it did, music and laughter replaced the hurried footsteps of servants outside Emira's door. She understood it as a sign to dress. She twisted her flowing, golden hair into a braid, allowing shorter pieces to frame and curl around her face. Breathless, she admired how the skirts moved around her like smoke. As she slid on a pair of silvery slippers, a knock sounded at her door.

Emira answered to find Tallen standing in the doorway. He was dressed head to toe in his usual black, but his leather was traded for a cotton tunic trimmed with a similar silky gray as her gown. His weapons and whip, however, remained strapped to his body, and his powerful wings were tucked behind his large frame.

"Emira," he breathed, catching her gaze. His ebony curls casted shadows upon his hard face as he straightened and held out an arm, clearing his throat before saying stiffly, "You look beautiful."

"Thank you," Emira responded, taking her place on his arm. "You look less intimidating than usual."

Tallen chuckled, and his shoulders relaxed at her jest.

"Well, that does me no good," the harpy replied with a grin. "I have a reputation to uphold."

"Of emotionless brute?" she joked.

"Something like that."

He led Emira through the castle, where they met Alicus, Zuri, Xemile and Vyla off of one of the many balconies facing the village below.

The king and queen were both dressed in matching emerald robes, gold accents decorating the trim of the exquisite fabric. Their golden crowns were similarly designed, with emeralds and the Southern Realm's signature vine and floral textures. Alicus wore his hair in straight strands, the forest green of it almost blending in with his robe. Zuri's hair was curled, twisted, and tucked into her diadem. But the most impressive sight was that both of their wings were on full display, an aesthetic choice rather than a functional one. Alicus' wings were similar to that of a dragonfly, sheer, with a hint of green, and crossed into the shape of an X, giving the illusion that he had four wings instead of two. Zuri's wings were likened to that of a dove. They were a stark white, beautifully contrasted against her mahogany skin. Unlike the harpy's wings, which were broad and stocky, Zuri's wings were elegantly trim, boasting length over depth.

Xemile wore a tunic akin to the harpy's although his was made of linen in shades of brown and burgundy. He too, wore his weapons on full display, sword at his hip and daggers in each of his brown boots. His auburn hair was pulled back in its signature bun, an anticipatory smirk smeared across his face and the promise of mischief alight in his amber eyes.

Vyla stood out the most. She wore a sleek and mostly sheer gown of midnight. It had long flowing skirts, with slits up either side, and the strapless bodice accentuated her magnificently toned arms. She was bedecked with golden jewelry, hanging about her ears, neck, and wrists. She had painted a shimmering gold over her high cheekbones, making her sharp features even more alluring. Her long black hair was box braided and twisted into a top knot.

"Mabon blessings, friends." Zuri smiled as Tallen and Emira arrived. "Your gown is exquisite, Emira."

Emira glanced down at the dress, admiring it once more. "Thank you so much," she responded with a soft smile.

"Vyla truly has meticulous taste," Alicus added.

Emira faced the shifter. "It's the most precious gift I've ever received."

The only gift I've ever received, she thought to herself.

Vyla only responded with a slight nod.

"We will see you all in the village," Alicus said, taking his queen's hand in his own. With a reverberating *crack,* they vanished, transferring away from the group and down to the celebration.

"I want a rematch for last year," Xemile stated to Vyla sternly as his amber wings sprang from his back. "The wind got me; it was an unfair ruling."

Vyla rolled her eyes in annoyance. As she did, her silver pupils transformed into ghostly slits, cat like and predatory. Her midnight skin mottled with silver markings, shaped like those of a leopard's, along her face, neck and shoulders. Her perfectly manicured nails elongated, becoming lethal talons, nearly six inches in length, and her canine teeth did the same, becoming pointed and morphing into those of a predator's. Vyla had shifted right before Emira's eyes, the process taking only seconds. The shifter straightened her shoulders and rolled out her neck while releasing a low, ill-boding growl.

"If it will shut you up," she purred, now fully shifted, still a humanoid figure, but with deadly accents.

With a swift pump of his wings, Xemile was in the air and headed for the nearest balcony. Vyla was close behind him, an incredible speed building from her stationary position and the train of her gown billowing behind her like the waves of the sea. They leapt from the railing at the same time, Xemile shooting into the air and Vyla bounding below and landing on her feet.

Emira chuckled as she listened to their competitive hollers shrinking as they grew further and further away from the castle.

"And how would our guest of honor like to arrive?" Tallen asked as Emira looked up at him. "Would you like to ride into town on horseback, or would you prefer to fly?"

"I do not have a fond opinion of horses," Emira confessed.

"Flying it is," he said.

Tallen's wings stretched wide behind him and he lifted Emira swiftly, cradling her against his chest and gathering her skirts under his hand to keep them from tousling in the wind.

Emira looped her arms around his neck as he walked to the balcony. The cool air brushed against her skin as Tallen beat his wings, and together, they lifted into the autumn air.

CHAPTER

EIGHTEEN

Tallen and Emira landed in the middle of the equinox celebrations. She held onto Tallen's arm firmly to steady herself, first against the pull of gravity as he placed her on her feet and then at the exquisite sight before them.

The quiet woodland village that she had seen a few mornings previously was lit with hundreds of lanterns and string lights, all hanging from the tops of trees, bridge railings and even on the villagers themselves in the forms of necklaces and headdresses.

Along the narrow, mossy streets were tables covered in a variety of foods from dried meats to fresh fruits, cakes and sweets, and faerie wine. The doors to the pubs and restaurants and shops remained ajar as patrons came and went, purchasing goods and wishing good fortune for the coming cold months.

Children weaved between the trees, catching the fireflies and moths that were attracted to the many lights. Most of them held small lanterns of their own or crafts that they had made earlier in the day.

Music poured from the treetops, and Emira cast her eyes upward to see many of the Southern Realm's people sitting among the branches, playing a variety of wind and string instruments.

And far ahead, there was a clearing in the trees, where a raging bonfire was lit, surrounded by multiple dancing figures.

"Alicus and Zuri will be there," Tallen said, gesturing to the fire and placing a hand on the small of Emira's back to urge her forward.

Emira gaped as they passed through the festival, not only at the elaborate decorations, but at the people who resided within the forest village. They looked as if they were born from the trees themselves. While many had peachy or bronzed skin tones, others possessed skin of dark green or brilliant blue hues. Mushrooms grew from the skin of some of the locals, adorning their shoulders and faces with brown morels and red amanitas. Emira spotted moss growing along the limbs and necks of others, decorating their skin with the soft growth of willow and peat. Animals were represented in the antlers upon some of their heads, the claws proudly sharpened upon some of their hands, and the cleft hooves at the ends of some of their feet.

As they passed through the festival, the locals showed their affection for the harpy. Some bowed their heads or placed their hands over their hearts as he passed. Many children gaped and pointed at his wings, which Tallen would stretch every now and then to their amazement. Emira smiled at each encounter, astounded to see the preponderance of respect the realm had for him.

She also felt curious eyes on her as they walked through the festival. She wondered what the realm knew of her, and her reasons for being alongside the harpy.

They reached the bonfire, where Alicus and Zuri danced wildly in each other's arms, smiles plastered to their faces. Xemile and Vyla stood nearby, the warrior loudly arguing that he had *definitely* been the first to arrive from the castle, while the shifter sipped her red wine smugly.

Emira couldn't help but laugh loudly upon seeing them. Her joy was a feeling that was still foreign, but very welcome. Tallen accepted two glasses of honeysuckle champagne from a nearby tray, and offered one to her. She took a timid sip, but the sweet, bubbly nectar was unlike anything she had ever tried, and she happily downed the contents as she watched those who danced around the fire alongside their king and queen.

The realm was mostly inhabited by fae and creatures of the forest, but Emira also recognized witches and shifters among them. They danced enthusiastically together as the fire crackled and sent embers the size of pebbles into the darkening sky.

Then, an old woman, a witch, approached them. Her skin was tanned and weathered, her hair was a gray cape that fell down her backside, and her small body was hunched forward. But her brown eyes sparkled as she held out a bracelet made from green and amber gems.

"Mabon blessings to the guest of our king and queen!" she exclaimed, taking Emira's hand in hers and clasping the jewelry around her wrist. The witch's warm fingers held Emira's as she continued, "I hope you are enjoying your time in our realm."

"It's wonderful," Emira responded kindly, both about the bracelet and the kingdom.

The witch turned to Tallen and grinned. "I hope *you're* staying out of trouble," she said as she pointed a bony, shaking finger at the harpy.

He huffed a laugh and answered, "As much as I am able, ma'am."

The witch *tsked* thrice and turned her attention back to Emira.

"Keep your eyes on that one," she joked. Emira giggled in response before the witch stepped away to rejoin the festival.

"So, the spy is being spied on," Emira chuckled, finishing the last of her champagne and reaching for another.

"I suppose so," Tallen responded lightly.

"They don't seem afraid of you," she added.

Emira felt Tallen's body stiffen the moment the words sprang from her lips.

The harpy's tone was opposing as he responded, "These are the people I am sworn to protect. They should not fear me."

"No," Emira agreed quickly. "They should not."

The following silence between them was deafening, even more so than the music that played and the people who laughed and hollered excitedly.

"Emira," Tallen started finally, "are you afraid of me?"

Emira inhaled sharply and her gaze snapped to the harpy.

"No!" she responded defensively. "No, I mean… I mean, I *was*. When we first met."

She scrambled to explain, the words spilling from her mouth like sour milk. Tallen's expression fell as she spoke, only causing her to feel more flustered.

"In the woods," she continued, "you used your whip to disarm my master and—"

"He is *not* your master," Tallen interjected, voice hard and icy eyes sharp to match.

"I only mean," Emira continued, slowing down to choose her next words more carefully, "I was already afraid. And I didn't know you. Or Xemile. I was afraid of you both then."

Tallen nodded, eyes going back to the fire. Emira stepped forward and turned to stand in the harpy's line of sight. He tilted his chin down, allowing their eyes to meet once more, and she added, "I am not afraid of you, Tallen."

He placed a hand on her cheek and cupped it gently.

"My intention was never to frighten you, Emira," he responded, running his calloused thumb along her pale, autumn chilled skin. Both her eyes and her heart fluttered at the sensation.

"I know," Emira responded, leaning into his touch. "Your intention is to serve your king and follow the orders he has given you."

Tallen's expression grew cold and he quickly dropped his hand. He cleared his throat and straightened his shoulders, looking past Emira and at the flames beyond where she stood.

"Yes," he agreed. "My orders."

Tallen reached for a goblet of ale as a serving tray passed by. He tipped the cup back and took a swig while Emira turned her attention, once again, to the fire.

A JUBILANT ZURI APPROACHED TALLEN AND EMIRA A FEW MOMENTS later. Emira was grateful for it. Tallen and she had stood silently since her assumption regarding the level of fear the harpy unknowingly struck into others.

Zuri's flushed face wore an expression of pure joy. Her crown was askew, and her hair was unruly from wildly dancing around the fire. Her deep brown eyes shone brightly against the darkness that was slowly taking over the sky.

"Come dance, Emira!" she ordered, holding out a hand.

Emira reluctantly accepted Zuri's offer. As she did, the queen spun her away from the harpy who was joined by an out of breath Alicus.

"I cannot keep up with her!" the king said with a wink as Emira was twirled away.

The heat from the bonfire licked at Emira's skin as she and Zuri spun together. There were no steps or patterns for them to follow, just the beating of drums and the plucking of strings. The flickering light shone upon the queen's face, alighting her already bright eyes and glistening smile. Her emerald robes danced around her ankles and she spun, the gold trim catching the firelight like a shimmering river.

Emira and the queen laughed as they twirled, stumbled, and twirled some more. They were surrounded by men, women, and children of the realm, who did the same. In this moment, there was no hierarchy. In this moment, Zuri was not their queen, but their equal, as if she were a neighbor, even a friend.

A hand grabbed her waist, and before Emira could react, she was spun around and facing Xemile. His bloodshot eyes and foul breath told Emira that he was drunk, but his smile and gentle grip assured her of his harmlessness.

"May I steal a dance?" he asked, mockingly offering a lazy, unbalanced curtsy.

Emira laughed and placed her hands on his broad shoulders, pushing him upright and steadying him once more.

"You may." She chuckled as Zuri found a dance partner in a ruddy-cheeked fae child.

His hands clasped hers, and with a resounding laugh, Xemile and Emira spun chaotically, circling the immense fire and weaving between the other dancers.

"Are you having fun?" Xemile hollered over the roaring of the flames.

"*So* much fun," Emira responded as Xemile twirled her in place, holding her hand above her head like a spinning top. "I've never been to a celebration like this before. It's the most amazing thing I've ever seen!"

"Wait until Yule," Xemile promised, pulling her back into a friendly grip. "Spiced rum, cranberry wine, cinnamon champagne…"

"Is alcohol the only thing you care for?" Emira joked.

Xemile winked as he replied, "And the females."

Emira let out an effervescent laugh as they continued to dance.

In between songs, Emira glanced up where they had left the king and the harpy. Each time she looked, Alicus' lips were rapidly moving, no doubt encouraged by the faerie wine, but the unmoving harpy was not looking at his king.

He was looking at her.

THE CELEBRATION CONTINUED LATE INTO THE NIGHT. AS THE FIRE slowly died down, so did the laughter and dancing. Parents cradled their sleeping children away and disappeared into the forest, to return to their wooded homes. Merchants and restaurant owners tidied their store fronts of debris and spilled goods. Those left over cleaned the dirt pathways as they went, returning the forest to its previously untouched state.

As the embers of the bonfire were doused, and the candlelit treetops dimmed, Emira stepped alongside the harpy, who was readying for flight. Her attention turned to Xemile, who loudly proclaimed that he *absolutely* was sober enough to fly.

"Just go with Vyla," Zuri was saying.

"You are in no state to fly," Alicus added.

Vyla was mid shift as she bound Xemile's wrists and wrapped them over her neck and shoulders. He drunkenly struggled against her but was no match as her body strengthened.

"I'm-perfectly-fine-to-fly-on-my-own," Xemile slurred.

"This is what you get for being a drunken idiot," Vyla said bitterly as she tightened his bonds. "Control your liquor next time, and do *not* throw up on me. Or I'll leave you in the woods to fend for yourself."

"Yeah, that's a real threat," Xemile started sarcastically.

"Your king *orders* that you go with Vyla," Alicus cut in sternly. "Be sure he arrives safely," he added in the shifter's direction. She nodded her head subserviently before darting into the forest at top speed. Xemile's disgruntled voice grew softer and softer as they disappeared into the darkness.

"Ready my king?" Zuri asked Alicus flirtatiously as she leaned into his shoulder and entwined her fingers in his own. He smiled down at her, and they disappeared with the familiar *crack* of transference, without another word.

Tallen and Emira were now alone in the forest, the village finally quiet around them. The only light came from the flickering of candles shining through the windows of homes in the trees, and the moonlight that dimly seeped through the thick canopy above.

"Tallen," Emira attempted awkwardly. "I—"

The harpy lifted Emira from the ground and stretched his wings.

"Ready?" he asked emotionlessly. His tone felt unfamiliar, distant, so Emira only nodded in response. They lifted into the air without another word and returned to the castle silently.

CHAPTER
NINETEEN

As she listened to the sound of the massive tub fill with steaming water, the floral scent of the added lavender oils wrapped around Emira's senses warmly. She sipped on Sarolina's prescribed bedtime tonic, undressed, and examined the reflection of her unclothed body in the wall-length mirror.

Her newly filled out, pear-shaped figure bloomed with healthy pink and red undertones. Her wavy, blonde hair, now undone from its braid, cascaded over her breasts. Her green eyes were alight with hope, no longer dulled by the strife she had once known. Pride swelled in her chest at the lively form she saw reflecting back. She felt healthier, stronger, and more energetic. She also felt a new sense of confidence, building greater and greater every day. She recognized it in her voice, and in her straightened posture, and in the feelings of love she now had for herself.

Emira finished the last drop of the tonic and slid into the water. The warmth enveloped her tired muscles, and she wondered for a moment if she, like Xemile, had overindulged at the Mabon celebration.

Baths were unheard of in the Eastern Realm. Slaves were given wet rags with which to wash themselves. But the luxury of being able to soak in the water every night, in addition to her private conversation with Vyla a few days earlier, had given Emira a reason to consider the siren half of her lineage. It came to mind more frequently, and she was no longer able to ignore the empty gnawing in her chest.

Her mother had been a siren, her father fae. Both had been slaves serving Vyrion, and both had been dead before she could remember either of them. As hard as she tried, she could not procure a memory. And though Emira knew enough about the fae species, and the shifters and witches, she knew nothing of her siren half—not a single detail.

Emira's mind wandered, and her eyelids fluttered with exhaustion. Steam drifted upwards, carrying with it the calming lavender aroma.

The friendships and loyalty that Emira had seen in the Southern Realm exceeded anything she ever hoped existed. She thought about Tallen, his ocean eyes and his deep voice. She remembered the fear that had stricken her when she had seen his silhouette that first night in the forest, and she smiled, knowing now that her feelings about him were far from fearful. In fact, what she felt was admiration.

Adoration.

Affection?

Her chest felt hollow for a moment as she remembered his saddened expression, speckled with firelight, at the Mabon celebration. She had made Tallen feel like a monster. How could she have been so insensitive, especially after he shared with her the trauma of his previous position in the north? She would have to apologize and hope that he didn't hold her crassness against her.

As the faucet continued to fill the tub with steaming water, Emira's thoughts drifted on. Finally, her body succumbed to the fatigue. She fell into a heavy sleep and slid under the surface of the water.

EMIRA HAD WANTED TO BATHE, SO TALLEN HEADED INTO THE EMPTY kitchen and pulled a piece of dark chocolate from the back of the cooler. He opened the golden foil, releasing the sweet aroma. As he broke a piece off and lifted it to his lips, Vyla knocked on the frame of the entryway door from behind him.

"Dark chocolate?" she smirked, her cat-like eyes glinting intently. She was not in her shifted form but back to her base form, not a single strand of her black hair out of place, nor a wrinkle or a speck of dirt to be found on her gown.

Tallen turned to her and huffed a laugh as he lowered the wrapping.

"You caught me."

Vyla sauntered forward, keeping her silvery eyes fixed on the harpy, who held a piece out to share with the shifter.

"Xemile alright?" Tallen started.

Vyla scoffed, accepting the chocolate. "He'll be just fine, the imbecile."

Tallen smirked in response, and Vyla stepped alongside the harpy, popping the treat into her mouth.

"How is your current assignment faring?" she questioned.

"Fine…" Tallen answered suspiciously, biting into the bar and rewrapping the foil over the remaining pieces.

"And the siren?" Vyla continued, as she flicked away some crumbs from the countertop nonchalantly. "How are you managing with her?"

"Well enough," the harpy answered politely. "She is—"

Vyla raised an eyebrow at Tallen, a knowing expression upon her gold-stained face. Tallen rolled his shoulders, understanding her objective to be more than casual. He should have known. The shifter did not participate in small talk, something he appreciated about her. But now, she was investigating.

He tossed the chocolate back into the cooler as he responded, "I'm following orders. That is all."

"You're a fool if you believe that lie," the shifter exclaimed, pushing herself from the counter and standing tall. "I saw how you were this evening. You couldn't look anywhere else."

"I am following orders given by my king to guard her," Tallen replied sternly.

"And why do you become defensive when the possibility is brought up?"

"What possibility?" Tallen growled, taking a threatening step forward. He would make Vyla state exactly what she meant. He felt cornered, and his instinct was to lash out, to protect himself. He did not like being easily read and refused to submit to such an attack.

"The *possibility*," Vyla started, unafraid of the harpy's challenge, "that you may feel something more than soldierly duty." Tallen's eyes bore into the shifter, but she only stared back at him. "You feel something more for her."

The harpy stilled at the truth he was desperately avoiding to be spoken aloud. Never, in his near eight-hundred years, had he felt more vulnerable than he did now. Emira did something to his mind, his body, his heart, and it was now clear that he was not hiding it as well as he had thought. But the engrained warrior in him clawed to the surface, pushing away his assailable emotions and forcing his expression back to that of a trained, lethal assassin.

"Enough," Tallen interjected, wings flaring slightly as her words peeled at him, exposing him layer by layer. "I will not be interrogated." The shifter did not flinch as the harpy walked past her swiftly and made his way for the exit.

"You can try to fool yourself," Vyla said to his back, "but Zuri saw it too."

TALLEN MARCHED DOWN THE CORRIDOR, AWAY FROM THE KITCHEN and away from Vyla. He would not entertain her questions about his intentions with Emira. He was a soldier, a spy, an assassin of the Southern Realm, and he was following orders.

Tallen ran both hands through his black hair and huffed frustratedly as he made his way to his post for the night, but Emira's face flashed in his mind's eye—her cheeks, wind kissed after flight, her naturally mauve-y lips, quirked into a smile. He could smell the lavender and library on her skin and hair. He heard her laugh, remembered the softness of her hands on his when they shared breakfast at Bri's pub. In his mind, he saw her slender neck, the curve of her waist, and the arch of her spine, and the shape of her backside. His hands flexed at his sides as his arousal tightened against the front of his pants.

Tallen shook the images from his head and continued prowling towards Emira's room to his post.

He couldn't care for Emira. His position as her guard would become compromised and his judgment altered. He was trained as a warrior, and would not allow for others to see him weakened in any way. His priority was loyalty to Alicus and Zuri, the south, and the orders that he had been given.

And Emira had made it clear that she had no amorous feelings towards him at the Mabon celebration; she saw him as a predator, someone that others should fear.

The squelch of liquid beneath his boot halted the harpy's thoughts and steps. He stood still and looked down at the warm water that swiftly pooled at his feet. It twirled about on the stone floors, whirling around the base of his boot before trickling past him. His gaze lifted to follow the direction from which the water came, and he furrowed his brow as he witnessed the trail of liquid flow through the corridor. With another squelch beneath his step, Tallen continued prowling forward. He followed the water until it led him to Emira's bedroom, where it trickled from beneath her door.

Tallen entered without a knock. His eyes ran along the trail that continued across the floor, past the fireplace, to where it originated from beneath the closed bathroom door. The sound of the flowing faucet and trickling water penetrated his eardrums, but he did not hear Emira.

The harpy strode across the room and reached for the handle, but it was locked.

"Emira?" he shouted over the rushing water.

She did not respond.

Tallen pounded his clenched fist on the door and called out, "Emira!"

No answer.

No sound.

As if she was not in the bathroom at all. Or if she was...

The thought drove the harpy into a frenzy, and he threw his shoulder into the door, immediately cracking the frame and breaking the lock. The white tile floor glistened with flooded water, the faucet spewing into the overflowing tub.

The harpy's whip slithered anxiously at his side as Tallen stalked to the tub's edge where Emira lay at the bottom, unmoving, hair floating about her face. Her eyes were closed, and her mouth was agape, her limbs relaxed at her sides.

Tallen leaped into the scalding water, ignoring the burn against his skin, and heaved Emira to the surface. Her eyes shot open, and she made to push Tallen away as she gasped for air. He clenched her upper arms tightly, refusing to release her.

"Let me go!" Emira screamed, thrashing against him. She kicked up the blistering water, soaking the walls and windows as she did so.

"Emira, are you alright? What happened?" Tallen demanded, shaking her wet frame.

Emira snapped out of her haze and stopped fighting against him. Her eyes darted around the room, gazing at the water on the floor and the overflowing tub. She looked down at her naked body then back to Tallen, who was knee deep in the water with her. His blue eyes searched her face.

"I'm okay," Emira started, voice beginning to shake. "I-I was sleeping."

"What do you mean?" Tallen asked, concern and suspicion lacing his voice.

"I mean… I mean I fell asleep."

Brows furrowed and expression twisted with confusion, Tallen uncurled his grip and stood, reaching for the still flowing faucet. Emira looked up at the harpy as he turned the handle. Water dripped from his black tunic and speckled the skin on his face. She covered her exposed breasts with trembling hands and pulled her knees closer to her body.

I fell asleep, Emira thought to herself as she recounted the evening.

She remembered sliding into the tub and feeling exhausted from the Mabon celebration. The empty cup from the night tonic sat on the tub's edge where she had placed it. But that was all.

I must have, she thought again.

Tallen reached for a towel and held it in Emira's direction, keeping his gaze politely averted. She stood awkwardly and accepted, wrapping the plush fabric around herself quickly.

With her towel in place, he whipped around to face her once more and exclaimed, "Gods spare me, Em! Are you sure you're alright?" The harpy clutched her around the waist and lifted her over the tub wall effortlessly.

"I'm sorry," was all Emira could think to say. She had no explanation to give and not much memory to recall.

Tallen opened the drain and followed her over the tub's edge.

"Come with me," he said, pulling back the splintered wood that had once been her bathroom door. "There's too much water. I'll take you to another room."

CHAPTER

TWENTY

Emira followed Tallen out of her sodden bedroom and through the hall, allowing him to guide her around the water that had trailed along the corridor's stone floors. He led her down a series of halls before coming to an arched door, one that was wider than most doors in the castle. As Tallen turned the handle and pushed the door ajar, Emira understood why it was so. The harpy walked through, his wings fitting comfortably through the frame, rather than brushing the sides of the walls like they usually did. He held the door ajar, motioning for her to follow him inside.

The room was dark and cool. The air smelled like the familiar cedar and dark chocolate scent of the harpy..

"Is this *your* room?" she asked incredulously.

He marched around her to a dark wooden dresser, where he pulled a black shirt from one of the drawers. His shoulders were tense, and he curled his wings tightly against his body as he turned back around and came towards her again.

"I'll need to prepare another room for you to stay, but you can wait here for a moment," he responded stiffly, holding the shirt out in Emiras' direction. "But yes, this is my room."

Emira accepted the clothing and looked around again. Sheer, black curtains draped over the canopied bed. Black and gray blankets made up the comforter, and the mattress was wide enough to accommodate his wings fully out-stretched. A white, brick fireplace took up most of one wall. It was surrounded by two black, velvet chairs, with a small table in between. Various weapons and clothes were slung over the backs of each chair. To the side, light blocking curtains framed the French doors that opened to an oversized balcony with a view of the forest beyond.

"I'll be back in a moment," Tallen said.

He left swiftly. Emira towel-dried her hair and threw on the oversized shirt, the hem of which lightly brushed against her knees. She made her way to the chairs, the plush carpet soft beneath her bare feet. She looked down at the velvet seating area, askew with materials. It didn't appear that the harpy often had company. Awkwardly, she shuffled to the bed and sat, sinking into the pillowy mattress. The blankets were lined with fur that gently brushed her exposed thighs as she picked at her cuticles nervously.

It felt wrong to be here, as if she were intruding upon the harpy's privacy. But she couldn't deny to herself that there was also a strange excitement that came from being in such an intimate space—in *his* space. Her stomach knotted, and her heart lifted into her throat as she waited for what felt like an eternity.

Tallen knocked lightly on the door before re-entering. He stopped for a moment, frozen in the doorway. Their eyes locked and they only stared. As the seconds passed, her stomach became tighter and tighter with anticipation. Emira felt her lips part, and she inhaled a sharp breath as she waited for the harpy to speak. He cleared his throat deeply before rolling his shoulders and finally stepping forward, closing the door behind him.

Emira's heart thundered.

He's angry, she thought to herself.

"There is another room that has been prepared for a guest," he started. "I can take you there for the night, so the water can be cleaned."

"Tallen, I'm so sorry," Emira started as the harpy stepped closer. "I don't know what happened—"

As if he read her mind, he said, "I'm not angry, Emira. I'm… I was—"

Tallen made his way to the bedside and knelt in front of the siren, searching her face again with his piercing blue eyes.

"I saw you under that water, Em, and I thought…"

He turned away, unable to finish the sentence aloud. A muscle in his jaw ticked, and his lips pursed together.

Emira placed her hands on either side of his chiseled face and pulled his gaze back to her own. Desperation lined her voice.

"I don't know what happened, Tallen, but I'm okay. See?" She took his calloused hand and brought it to her cheek. "I'm fine."

Tallen only stared at Emira, his lips pressed together tightly, his hand unmoving from her cool skin. Emira's chest heaved as she continued.

"Tallen, about what I said…" She bit her lip nervously, keeping her gaze fixed on his. "I didn't mean it how it sounded. I'm sorry. I've been very fortunate to have you near me." The harpy only nodded. He ran a thumb along her bottom lip as he stood, sending a chill down her spine.

"Come on," he started, noting her shiver. "You're getting cold."

She stood then, their bodies mere inches from each other. Emira gazed up into his eyes and whispered, "I'm not cold, Tallen."

The harpy came undone. He pulled Emira close and plunged his hands into her wet hair. He pressed his lips to hers, devouring her, tasting her, and she wrapped her arms around his neck, moaning into his mouth and kissing him back with eager ferocity.

With one hand still in her hair, Tallen grabbed one of Emira's exposed thighs and lifted her up against him. She wrapped her legs around his waist, and he groaned as her slick, bare core pressed against the front of his pants. The heat of his arousal teased her bare skin, making her breathing hitch as she ground her pelvis closer to his.

With his wings splayed out wide for balance, Tallen leaned down, lowering the both of them onto the bed, never breaking away from their kiss.

"Em," he growled through his teeth, hovering over her trembling body.

She tightened her thighs around his waist at the sound of her name, and his wings stretched even wider behind them, creating a powerful, feathered canopy.

"Em," Tallen repeated, "you have no idea what you do to me."

Emira smirked through their kiss at his confession and whispered, "Then tell me."

Her words vibrated against their mouths and the harpy huffed an eager breath against her lips. Emira's hands plunged into Tallen's dark curls, and he began to trail his lips down the sensitive skin of her neck.

She arched her face away, opening up to his touch and repeated, "Tell me, Tallen."

The harpy lifted his gaze to hers and answered, voice low, "You could end me with a single word. There is not a single thing in the Fae Realms that I would not do for you."

He lowered his head once more, lips lightly grazing the fabric between her breasts. He inhaled deeply as he did, and Emira gasped at the sensation, moving her hands from his hair down to her sides to clutch the blankets of the massive bed in her trembling fists.

Tallen released a throaty chuckle, dragging his smiling lips down, down, down.

"You are divinity," he murmured.

The kiss of his warm breath through the fabric of the shirt knotted Emira's stomach as heat pooled between her legs. Tallen disappeared lower and lower until she finally felt his soft lips and the stubble of his cheeks on the sensitive inner flesh of her bare thigh.

Her breathing hitched at the sensation and her hands moved to his dark curls once again, gripping his hair at the root as she spoke.

"Please," she begged, voice barely more than a whimper. "Gods, Tallen, please."

The harpy huffed a laugh against her skin, sending shivers up her body. She arched her back against the bed, pushing her hips closer to him. His teeth grazed the hem of her—his—shirt and slowly began to lift it up.

"Tallen," Emira breathed, bucking her hips.

He teasingly lingered for a moment, allowing the building pressure between her legs to become near insufferable before gently inching his mouth along her thigh, teeth trailing along her sensitive flesh, and closer to her heated center. Emira whimpered and begged that he take her, that he bring his lips down to her core and lick away the throbbing arousal that devastated her.

A knock at the door ripped through their haze, and duty bound, Tallen stood faster than Emira was able to blink. He'd turned his back to her, splaying out his wings, shielding her near-naked body from the potential viewer.

Xemile's voice came from the other side of the door.

"You in there, Tallen? Where in the name of the gods did all of this water come from?"

CHAPTER

TWENTY-ONE

Emira had waited in Tallen's room while the harpy explained the water seeping through the halls to Xemile. She had then awkwardly shuffled to the available guest room, still draped in Tallen's black shirt, and hid under the covers, praying to any god who would listen that Xemile wouldn't sense the passion that had ignited between her and the harpy. What consequences would come if Alicus and Zuri were informed that their second in command had been intimate with her? Would Tallen be punished? Would she?

That night, Tallen guarded her room as usual, but Emira refused to look in his direction, mortified that they had nearly been seen. The harpy made no attempt to converse, and Emira could not decide if she was grateful or disappointed for it.

The following morning, King Alicus and Queen Zuriel called everyone to the library, where Emira now sat nervously among the Southern Realm's most trusted consorts. They received report from an expressionless Tallen regarding the chaotic events of the previous evening; the water overflowing and that Emira had seemingly fallen asleep under the surface, entirely unharmed. Thankfully, if anyone also knew of her and the harpy's dalliance, it was not discussed.

"How is it possible that you fell asleep under water?" Zuri asked, incredulously.

Emira opened her mouth to respond, but she had no answer. She looked around the group, hoping someone else may have a theory.

Vyla spoke, "It's the siren in you."

The shifter glanced at her freshly manicured nails casually while the others held their breath waiting for more. It did not come without prompting.

"It's never happened before," Emira confessed.

"You've been enslaved and lingering near death for your entire life," Vyla said, with little sympathy in her voice; only fact. Zuri winced at the shifter's directness while Tallen released a discontented sigh and rolled his shoulders before painting his face again expressionless. "Any power you may possess will have been diminished by your poor health."

"And the ability to sleep underwater," Emira started, "is something that sirens can do?"

Vyla's eyes flicked in Emira's direction.

"Sirens need sleep somehow," she answered matter-of-factly.

Alicus spoke next. "What other sorts of power do sirens possess?"

"They're a private people," Vyla answered, turning to her king. "Most remain under water, avoiding the land races at all costs. The scope of abilities they may have is unknown."

"And when did you become a siren expert?" Xemile teased. His amber eyes cut to Emira, and he winked, causing her to relax her shoulders. Emira was glad to see him back to himself after the Mabon celebration.

Vyla's eyes flashed in the general's direction menacingly. Xemile did not flinch, but returned the act with his own dominant gaze, smirk never faltering.

"I began my research the night she arrived, when I scented siren within our walls. Although, progress has been slow. As I said, they are a private people and therefore minimal information exists."

"Keep looking," Zuri insisted. "We must learn what we can."

"Yes, my queen," Vyla purred.

"Are there not others?" Alicus asked. "Other sirens with whom we can speak? Learn from?"

"No," Vyla answered. "At least, if there are, their location is unknown. Unrecorded."

The air left Emira's lungs as Vyla spoke. If there were other sirens, they didn't want to be found. And although they were a part of her, she would likely never know another. But the possibility of their existence was enough to tug at Emira's heart.

Were there others like her somewhere in the Fae Realms? In the sea?

Zuri spoke to Emira next, cutting her train of thought short. "You should learn to make use of any power that emerges. Learn to control it."

Emira nodded. "I'll try," she promised. "Although, I'm not sure how."

Xemile grinned mischievously. "I can help with that. I wonder what an ass kicking from a siren is like."

Tallen looked down at his crossed arms as a smirk stretched across his face at his comrade's words.

"We'll start tomorrow," Xemile beamed. "Bright and early."

Alicus nodded his agreement, setting Emira's fate in stone.

AFTER THE MEETING, EMIRA SAT ON THE COUNTER IN THE KITCHEN, enjoying a solitary breakfast of fresh, mixed fruits, roasted potatoes spiced with rosemary and paprika, and scrambled eggs topped with cheese. While popping grapes into her mouth, she considered what abilities the siren people may have and what power may begin to emerge in her.

Besides, of course, taking naps underwater.

She chuckled at the absurdity of it, and of what her life had become since her rescue from King Vyrion.

Tallen entered through the arched doorway, icy eyes pinned on her. They had still not spoken much since the night before, but heat pooled low in Emira's stomach at the magnificent sight of him. He smirked, as if reading the indecent thoughts coursing through her mind.

"Come for some of your chocolate stash?" Emira teased.

Tallen's brows knitted together. "How did you find it?"

She laughed and felt her cheeks flush warmly.

"For an infamous warrior spy of the Southern Realm," she began sarcastically, "I would've thought you'd hide your snacks somewhere less obvious than in the kitchen."

He smirked. "I see."

He watched her pop another grape into her mouth and his eyes caught on her parted lips. He was drawn forward, leaning his powerful arms upon the counter, one on each side of Emira's full thighs.

Only a few inches separated the harpy and the siren now, causing her heart to pump adrenaline faster and faster through her veins. He was intoxicating—his scent, his presence. They stared at each other intensely for a moment before Tallen finally spoke.

"I have an assignment that will take me away for a few days."

Emira's heart sank at the news.

He continued, "Xemile can post guard at your door while I'm gone—"

"It's alright," Emira cut in coldly, slipping past the harpy to hop off of the counter and creating distance between them once more. "Sarolina's tonic has me sleeping well enough."

Tallen's eyes narrowed suspiciously.

"What's the assignment?" she asked, quickly changing the subject.

Emira wasn't lying about Sarolina's tonic. She had not dreamed about the Eastern Realm, or Vyrion, since the witch made the brew. But the thought of being away from Tallen, especially after the passion that had erupted between them the evening before, somehow made her feel vulnerable and insecure.

"Border patrol," the harpy responded. "Xemile's soldiers have been covering, but my shift is long overdue." Tallen prowled closer to Emira, closing the distance between them once more.

"I leave in an hour," he informed, so close now that his breath tickled her senses.

"So soon?" she breathed, chest heaving as Tallen continued to stalk closer and closer. The harpy pinned Emira against the counter, one of his massive arms on either side of her, trapping her there.

He leaned in closer, his lips grazing Emira's pointed ear. Agonizing pressure built between her legs, and she squeezed her thighs together. Her lips parted, sucking in a breath as the moisture from his words kissed her skin.

"Regrettably soon," he purred.

The harpy pressed his body against hers, pinning her even more tightly, his hard length nudging firmly against her abdomen. Emira's eyes trailed up the leather he wore across his broad chest, past the thick cords of muscle along his neck, and into his fierce, blue eyes.

"Tallen," she whispered. "I—We—" The siren stammered, distracted by his looming presence. "Is this *allowed?*"

The image of Rocas' mangled body flashed in her mind, a sickening reminder of the last time she became close with another. She believed that Tallen would not meet the same gruesome fate as the quiet stablehand from the east. Alicus and Zuri were kind rulers, and respected love and life. But doubt seeped its way through her rational thought, and she recoiled at the possibility of being punished; at *Tallen* being punished.

The harpy smiled softly as he answered. "Em, the only reason this would not be allowed is if you did not want it. Gods know I've tried to ignore my feelings, but all it has done is squander the time I may have had with you."

Emira felt her shoulders relax at his words, his reassurance.

"I *do* want this," she replied softly. "Please, Tallen."

His name on her lips was the harpy's undoing.

His mouth crashed against hers, and Emira brought her hands up to his dark curls, gripping them at the root and moaning against his mouth. Tallen's growl rumbled against her kiss, his arousal pressing even harder into her.

"Tallen," Emira repeated as the harpy's hands left the counter's edges and found their way to her hips. "Are you going to finish what you started?" The boldness of her words had her heart pounding so violently that she wondered if the harpy could hear it.

"Yes," he responded gruffly, mouth still pressed firmly to hers. His grip on her tightened, and he seated her upon the counter before settling himself between her legs. Tallen kissed Emira even more deeply, their tongues and teeth clashing as a desperate whimper slipped from Emira's lips once more. She wrapped her legs around his trim waist, attempting to pull him impossibly closer. Her hands ran down through his hair, past his stubbled cheeks, and onto his broad shoulders. She felt the cords of his muscles working beneath her touch, as his hands roamed to her backside, where he gripped her possessively. She arched into his touch, a breathy sigh escaping her lips and caught by his own.

Suddenly, the harpy pulled his lips away. He did so swiftly, stopping before he was too possessed by passion. He looked at Emira, who wore an expression of confusion behind her flushed cheeks.

"But not today," he finished hesitantly.

Emira swallowed her disappointment, wiping at her swollen lips and turning away. Tallen's hand came to her chin, and he gently brought her face back to his own.

He rested his forehead against hers and said, "I have an assignment that requires me to leave the realm only moments from now." His gaze hardened as he promised, "I will not be rushed with you. When I taste you, I intend to take my time and savor you."

Emira's breathing hitched as the harpy wrapped his arms around her and lowered her so that her feet were once again on the ground. He pressed a final kiss to her forehead before turning and walking from the room, leaving her out of breath and craving more.

CHAPTER
TWENTY-TWO

Emira waited on the balcony arena the next morning. She had dressed in black leggings, tucked into a pair of gray hiking boots. Her shirt was linen, and hit just past her wide hips. The light material flowed in the autumn air, a cool breeze for which Emira was thankful. She had slept well enough to feel determined about beginning her training with Xemile, but it had been odd knowing that Tallen was not sitting nearby as usual. There had been an empty gnawing in her chest as she drank her tonic and drifted to sleep the night before.

Xemile arrived dressed head to toe in his brown leathers. His auburn hair was tied back in a bun, and a sword was strapped to his back. His expression was both mischievous and determined. Emira had not seen Xemile look so intimidating since the first night they had met, and doubt seeped into her mind. Perhaps she had misjudged herself.

"How'd you sleep, mermaid?" Xemile said, unbuckling the sword's sheath and setting it on the ground.

Emira scoffed. "I'm not a mermaid."

"Alright, half mermaid," he joked.

She rolled her eyes and met him in the center of the arena, where Xemile was pulling a dagger from his boot and examining the blade.

"Yep," he started, running his finger along the sharp edge then offering the handle of the knife to her. "We'll start with this."

Emira accepted the weapon slowly. It was heavier than she had anticipated, simple but beautiful with gold encrusted along the hilt.

"I don't understand," she said while admiring the blade. "I thought we were doing, I don't know, siren stuff?"

"I can't teach you what I don't know," Xemile answered, taking a few steps backward. "But what I do know is weapons. I also know that you're holding that dagger in the perfect position for a broken wrist."

Emira looked down at the dagger incredulously.

"How can you tell?" she asked.

Xemile huffed a laugh and gestured to himself. "*Head of Military Command for the Southern Realm*, remember?" he replied, sarcasm lacing his tone and a boastful smile upon his face.

She scoffed again, looking back to the dagger in her hand.

"More like Head of Smartass Command," she muttered.

Xemile smirked. "That's the fire I want, mermaid. We have a lot of work to do, but if I push you hard enough, maybe those dormant siren powers will want to come out and kick my ass all the way to the Mortal Realm."

XEMILE AND EMIRA SPENT MOST OF THE MORNING FOCUSING ON HER form, holding her body in the most effective position during combat.

"Keep your wrist straight, and your stance wide," Xemile started. "Let your opponent use their energy charging you, and then you attack, not the other way around."

She made a mental note; *let them come to me.*

"Always be aware of your surroundings," he continued, demonstrating how to check his blind spots. "You have fae eyes and ears—use them."

Emira nodded, absorbing everything the commander told her.

They practiced various ways to hold the dagger, and Emira learned what felt the most comfortable in her grip. Her left hand was dominant, unlike Xemile's, so she had to alter her stance, mirroring him rather than doing exactly as he did.

Xemile explained where to find weak spots in most armor - the neck and under the arm.

"If you're down and can't wound your opponent in either spot," he said, "go for the back of the ankle or behind the knee. Sever that tendon, and they'll come down like a sack of bricks. That's when you can make your killing strike."

When the sun was at its highest, Xemile showed Emira a series of movements to disarm an opponent. They broke briefly to eat and were back in the training arena in the afternoon, working into the evening.

"Have you heard anything from Tallen?" she asked, checking her stance and readying herself.

"No, but that isn't unusual," Xemile answered. "Ready?"

Emira nodded, and Xemile charged. She ducked, avoiding the blade of his sword, and simulated slicing the back of his knee.

"Good," he said zealously, stepping backwards once more.

Emira heaved a breath and wiped sweat from her brow. "He doesn't send word while he's gone?"

Xemile traded his sword for a knife before answering. "No news is good news. Tallen won't report until he returns."

Emira's chest deflated.

This time, Xemile didn't give a warning before rushing towards her, blade raised. Her thoughts raced; what had he taught her to do?

Block. Block the blow.

She did. Barely.

"Good," he said again. "Disarm me this time."

Emira nodded, blowing a piece of stray hair away from her sweat slicked face. She widened her stance and adjusted the grip on her dagger.

"Ready, mermaid?" Xemile questioned.

Emira nodded.

He did not hold back. The commander charged at full speed, knife poised. Emira had to think quickly. She spun outwards, avoiding the fae warrior. As she did, she kicked out her leg, colliding it with the front of Xemile's ankles. His balance was thrown off and Emira seized the opportunity. She stepped back two paces before using all of her strength to kick Xemile in the back, attempting to get him prone on the ground. If he dropped his weapon, that was even better.

But her strength was not enough. Xemile righted himself, and Emira did nothing but leave a dusty footprint on his leathers.

"Try again," he said as he turned to face her. She retreated a step with every one he took forward. "You can't out muscle me. What can you do instead?"

Emira continued stepping backwards, creating an even greater distance between her and Xemile. Exhaustion from their rigorous training was beginning to make her feel slow, physically and mentally.

Xemile barreled towards her. She ducked, dodging his blade and threw a punch to his gut before sliding away, creating more distance. He grunted with the blow but did not fall. It only gave Emira a few seconds of time to formulate a plan. As he came for her again, Emira swooped under his raised arm, grabbing a hold of his bicep as she did, and yanking it down and backwards. Xemile released his weapon as Emira continued pulling, swiftly bringing his arm behind his back. With her other arm, dagger in hand, she simulated cutting his throat.

"Good!" Xemile praised when Emira released him. The fae male looked towards the setting sun and sighed.

"You kicked ass today, mermaid," he said, giving Emira a friendly jab in the shoulder. "Come on. Vyla's probably waiting in the kitchen. We've earned a whiskey."

THE ALCOHOL BURNED DOWN EMIRA'S THROAT AND SEEPED INTO HER aching muscles. Vyla had not found any new information in the library, but she, Xemile, and Emira indulged in drink after drink until the sun disappeared behind the horizon and the sky lit up with stars. Her head spun as she laughed, listening to the stories her friends told.

Xemile recounted when Alicus, Zuri and he were younger and the trouble in which they would find themselves when they would sneak out past curfew. Vyla sent Emira into a fit of giggles while doing a vulgar impression of Xemile before commenting that Alicus and Zuri would be envious over missing the entertainment that the whiskey was providing them.

"I cannot fathom how they manage to go to bed before ten o'clock," Vyla mused.

Xemile smirked, the opportunity to poke fun at the shifter too great. "That's because you're *nocturnal*, aren't you kitty?"

The glare from her silver eyes seemed to glow with agitation, and Emira nearly burst with laughter.

After her third whiskey, Emira could barely see straight. She bade goodnight to her friends and began to stumble towards her room.

When she arrived, too drunk and too tired to do much at all, she peeled off her training clothes and slipped on a gauzy, linen nightgown before sliding under the cool covers. Her bones groaned as she relaxed into the mattress, and her eyes began to flutter.

She thought of Tallen as she drifted. She imagined his piercing eyes and remembered the feeling of his coarse, wavy hair in her desperate grip. She recalled the weight of him on top of her in his bedroom and then pressed against her in the kitchen. Her cheeks warmed as she replayed their dalliances in her mind, and she prayed to the gods that, wherever he was, he was safe and would return unharmed.

Her body succumbed to the exhaustion that she had earned from training with Xemile. Her eyes closed, and she fell asleep, while on the nearby table, Sarolina's nighttime tonic sat cold and untouched.

CHAPTER
TWENTY-THREE

E mira sat upright, aroused by the cold, damp, mildewy air. She adjusted her eyes and searched the darkness.

This was her room.

Not the light, clean, comfortable room in the Southern Realm.

No, this was the Eastern Realm.

Her chest heaved as she started to hyperventilate. She went to grasp her soft, clean blankets, only to be met with the rotten padding that she had been forced to sleep upon. She glanced around the darkness frantically. The familiar stone cellar surrounded her. Empty beds lay on the ground beside her own. The intrusive sound of dripping water sliced at her ear drums, but the cell was otherwise silent.

Until…

"I told you I would make you pay," Vyrion's voice hissed.

Her master emerged from the shadowy corner, his sharp, emerald eyes glinting. Emira gasped and pushed herself away, her back thumping against the damp, stone wall.

Vyrion took a step forward and unsheathed his curved dagger.

"Did you think you could hide forever?" he growled.

"H-how?" she managed to say. "How am I here?"

"You're not," he responded coolly. "Not really."

In a flash, Vyrion charged and held his clenched hand around her throat. Emira screamed, arching away from the pain in her back as the stone wall dug into her spine. His fae grip was strong, and she could not take in enough air. The twisted king cackled and held his cold blade up to her cheek.

Close enough that his hot breath suffocated her senses, he promised, "But I will ensure that you feel every last bit of torture I inflict upon you."

With that, Vyrion pushed the blade's edge onto the skin of Emira's cheek and dragged it slowly down her face. She shrieked and uselessly kicked her legs against him as the blade sliced into her skin, leaving behind an unbearable burning sensation.

Her warm blood trickled over the hand he still held to her throat and down his powerful arm. His eyes glinted in delight as he watched the blade slide down her soft flesh. When it reached her chin, he shifted and began to slice the other side.

Emira's screams echoed off of the stone walls. Vyrion took a step back and scanned her face, sadistically, as if admiring his work.

"Everyone will know who you truly belong to now."

Salty tears stung the fresh wounds, and Emira's body began to tremor. She was sure she would vomit from the pain, the surging adrenaline. Vyrion swiftly kicked her side, and her rib snapped like a twig before she landed face down on the rotting mattress.

She tried but was unable to inhale a breath without crushing pain. She was drowning, slowly being pulled under an invisible surface from which she couldn't free herself.

"Why?" Emira choked, clutching her side. "Why me? I've told them nothing about the east. Just let me go! Let me go or kill me, please!"

She coughed, the sick tang of blood filling her mouth.

"I won't be killing you yet," Vyrion said casually, admiring the crimson that dripped from his dagger's blade. "You may still be of use to me." His attention shifted back to Emira. "Fingernails first. Then I plan to whip your backside to a nearly unrecognizable state."

Emira wailed, burying her face into the mattress as her master recited his agenda. She released another calamitous scream before he pulled her up from the floor by her hair and began.

XEMILE AND VYLA WERE FINISHING THE LAST OF THE WHISKEY WHEN Emira's ear-shattering wail echoed through the corridors of the castle. The predator within the shifter roiled with adrenaline as Xemile and she dashed from the kitchen, heading towards the siren's chambers.

Emira's screaming rattled their eardrums, the high pitch crawling its way through their ear canals and into their brains. Xemile and Vyla rushed into Emira's room, where she was fast asleep—yet thrashing and twisting on the bed.

Vyla darted to the bedside and clenched at Emira's flailing arms, holding them down and calling out the siren's name, beckoning her to wake. But her eyes remained shut, squeezed tightly together like the petals of a flower before bloom.

"Find Alicus and Zuri," Vyla ordered the general urgently. Xemile left the room immediately, pushing past a gathering of servants who had also been stirred by the commotion, from the opposite end of the castle.

In her nightmarish haze, Emira clawed at Vyla's cheek, but even as the trickle of blood warmed the emissary's skin, she held the siren firmly.

"Emira! Wake up!" she commanded. "It is a nightmare! Wake up!"

The bed was drenched with sweat, and the blankets were tousled haphazardly. Spotting the untouched tonic at Emira's bedside, Vyla cursed and used the weight of her body to hold the siren down and keep them both from hurling from the bed.

Xemile arrived moments later, with Alicus and Zuri trailing closely behind him. The glimpse Vyla saw of their faces read that they were stricken by the sight. The blood on her face had smeared in their struggle, and now coated one side of her cheek.

"The brew," Vyla stated, nodding to the full cup.

"Tallen said she was waking on her own before," Xemile hollered to his rulers over Emira's screams of terror. He came to the shifter's side and assumed the task of holding the siren in place. "She can't seem to wake now."

Alicus grabbed the cold elixir and stalked to the edge of the bed.

"Open her mouth," he ordered the commander.

With one muscular arm secured across her torso, Xemile held Emira's jaw with his free hand and firmly squeezed, keeping her lips separated between screams.

She choked on the liquid as Alicus slowly poured the draught between her lips. His gaze was dark and focused.

"Be careful," Zuri muttered from beside the king.

As the tonic seeped its way down her throat, Emira's thrashing slowed. Her screaming morphed into whimpering and eventual silence.

Alicus placed the empty cup on the bedside table and Xemile cautiously released her now still body. Vyla wiped away the blood dripping from her cheek as Zuri and she watched and waited.

The siren gasped deeply and shot upright. She looked around the room, focusing on each detail with bloodshot eyes.

"Emira?" Alicus started, voice barely above a whisper. He took a cautious step forward. "Are you—"

But he was interrupted as Emira began violently vomiting.

Xemile grabbed a nearby plant and tore it from its decorative pot. He held the empty container to her face and caught what bile he could.

"Vyla, water," he said softly. The shifter turned to find the water station, shooing at the servants who lingered at the door, looking on with pale faces. Zuri came to the bedside and wiped the sweat drenched hair from Emira's face as she heaved into the pot. The siren emptied her stomach, laid back on the pillow and began to sob immeasurably.

"Away," Alicus commanded the gaggle of servants that remained in the doorway. They obeyed their king, whispering amongst themselves as they made their way back to their chambers.

Vyla poured a glass of water. Xemile and Alicus stood nearby, their faces grave and contorted with worry. Zuri sat alongside Emira, brushing stray hair away from her scorching, clammy face as she cried into the blankets. The shifter set the water down and joined the group.

They remained quietly nearby while the siren wept through the night.

CHAPTER
TWENTY-FOUR

The wounds that Emira sustained in her nightmare began to appear on her sickly, white skin as she woke, growing more prominent as the morning went on. And while she was fast to begin healing, she suffered multiple marks as a result of the torture Vyrion had inflicted. It was an unknown magic to be able to access another's physical body through their dreams. King Alicus sent Vyla to the library to research such things while Queen Zuriel remained by Emira's side, assisting Sarolina as needed.

Alicus and Xemile watched the pink sunrise from a balcony facing the Eastern Realm. The king sat silently, gray eyes dark and face hardened in anger. Xemile leaned against the stone of the castle, sipping from a glass of whiskey.

"What could this be, Alicus?" the general questioned. "I've never known a fae able to access someone through dreams this way."

He did not turn his head, or acknowledge Xemile's words, but only stared out across his realm, forest green brows furrowing at every implication of the previous night. The Southern Realm was warded, and the shield's magic remained in place overnight. Xemile personally flew to the borders before the sun rose to ensure it. And Tallen was on border patrol tonight; the harpy would have eviscerated any threat before it came too close.

But Vyrion somehow breached them, accessing a guest of the king, within his own palace walls. It was an act of war.

Xemile pinched the bridge of his nose and rubbed at his bloodshot, tired eyes. Emira's screams rang in his mind, the deafening noise one that he would not likely forget. She had quickly become a part of the Southern Realm's family, and an unofficial member of their court. They had all come to care for the siren, despite her initial wariness.

Suddenly, the crash of thunder and a strong gust of wind blew across the balcony, whipping through the vines that crawled up the sides of the castle walls, and sweeping away the leafy debris on the ground. Already on edge, Xemile instinctively reached for one of his blades as Tallen rained down through the gray clouds, appearing momentarily only as a silhouette before landing on the balcony edge.

"Shit, Tallen," Xemile grumbled, taking his hand off the hilt of his knife.

"Report," Alicus started, standing eagerly. "How are the borders? The villages?"

Tallen prowled forward, leaping from the railing and landing seamlessly on the ground.

"Where is she?" he demanded, voice as hard as stone. Alicus and Xemile gaped at him for a moment, processing the anger on his face.

"Where. Is. Emira," the harpy repeated.

"We need to discuss her too," Alicus began, disregarding his soldier's question.

Tallen turned away from his king without a word and marched for the siren's room, eyes as sharp as knives.

"Tallen!" Alicus called after him, but the harpy did not stop.

Xemile followed, prepared to reprimand him for his insubordination, but before he could catch up, Tallen reached Emira's room. Without knocking, he flung the bedroom door open, causing Zuri to startle. Emira, however, did not react. Xemile craned his neck to look between the harpy's shoulder and wing as Zuri's wide eyes met Tallen's.

"Gods spare me, Tallen!" Zuri exclaimed, hand over her thumping heart. But Tallen was frozen, unable to breathe as he looked upon Emira.

Her fingernails were gone, ripped off one by one and replaced with dried blood that had been fresh hours earlier. Bloodied whip-like marks numerously lined her backside while cuts and bruises scattered her skin from various beatings.

And worse than anything else, her beautiful face had been carved. It was blood crusted and swollen. Tallen gritted his teeth in anger as the horrifying sight sunk in.

V Y R was sliced into one cheek while I O N marred the other.

Tallen had never felt anger as he did now. Heat warmed his entire body, and he felt his face turn a murderous shade of red. His fists balled at his sides and the beating beneath his chest increased, adrenaline rushing through him.

"A broken rib as well," Zuri added, as she resumed running her fingers in Emira's hair. Tallen's eyes shifted to Emira's side, and one of her blackened hands that she used to clutch at the bone as her fae magic slowly mended it.

Tallen's jaw tightened as he turned back the way he came. Xemile followed, still attempting to speak with the harpy. Alicus remained standing on the balcony, eyeing him intensely. The harpy made his way again to the railing, stepped onto the ledge, and opened his wings.

"Where are you going?" Xemile questioned.

"I'm going to kill that son-of-a-bitch," Tallen growled as he leapt from the castle, disappearing into the storm clouds.

"Shit," Xemile mumbled.

Alicus turned to his general once more. "Intercept him."

TALLEN BEAT HIS FEATHERED WINGS HARDER AND HARDER AS HE edged his way closer to the borders of the Southern Realm. Clouds rolled around him, gray and black, raining down torrential storms that threatened to flood kingdoms.

"Tallen!" Xemile called. His batlike wings weren't as large or as strong as Tallen's, and he was far behind the vengeful harpy. If he had heard, Tallen ignored Xemile's beckoning, eyes focused, his anger forcing him to see in tunnel vision in the direction of the Eastern Realm.

"Tallen!" the fae called again, slowly catching up to the wrathful warrior as rain pelted his face and body. "What the hell is going on? Talk to me!"

Tallen turned his head slightly but continued en route for Vyrion.

"I'm going to make him wish he had never been born," the harpy promised. "I'm going to bleed him over and over again until he's begging for his mother. And then I'm going to snap his fucking neck."

"What happened?" Xemile inquired as he finally made his way alongside his friend. "What do you know?"

"Everything," the harpy replied, too calmly.

"Gods spare me, Tallen!"

Xemile finally caught up with Tallen and gripped his shoulder, halting him. They beat their wings against gravity, floating midair and looking at each other. When Xemile finally caught his breath, he brushed the rain from his eyes and asked again, "What is going on?"

"No more waiting," Tallen began. "We don't need to wait for her confession to act. This ends now."

He turned to continue on, but Xemile stopped him again. "You've been given an order to wait, to stand down."

Tallen's blue eyes pierced through Xemile's amber ones as he responded, "That's an order I will not follow."

Xemile's face blanched, and his auburn brows furrowed together. "Alicus is our king, Tallen," he stated.

The harpy said nothing, rage still marring his face.

"Tallen!" the general yelled, his voice shaking with disbelief at the insubordination. "Alicus is your *king!*"

"I felt everything!" Tallen roared over the thunder that rattled the sky around them. "The entire night, Xem!"

"What do you mean?"

The harpy's head dropped forward, and he ran both hands through his rain-soaked hair.

"I knew something was wrong," he started. "I can't describe it. Deep in my gut, I felt every ounce of fear and every sickening turn of her stomach."

"Shit," Xemile muttered as realization seeped through his bones. "You… you felt it?"

"I couldn't leave my post, leave the borders unguarded," Tallen continued as the rain began to cease. "I knew that. I made sure to rip apart every single creature that crossed me. It was all I could do to drown out the fact that…."

His voice trailed off, and silence waned between them, aside from the sound of the wind ripping through the sky.

"Tallen," Xemile began.

But the harpy continued, "I saw her, and there are *marks,*" he seethed. "The bastard carved his fucking name on her."

"We don't know how he did it," the fae cut in, "but you have to go back and be there for her." He grasped the harpy's shoulders again. "You can't kill Vyrion on your own—"

"I can—"

"But you *can* help Emira. She needs you. She asked for you the moment she woke."

She needed him, *wanted* him there.

Tallen inhaled deeply. The swirling storm that had enveloped them began to calm as he blew out the tension and rolled his shoulders, nodding at his general's words.

Xemile finished calmly, "Be there for your Bonded Soul."

CHAPTER
TWENTY-FIVE

Tallen entered the throne room with his chin high and his wings tucked tightly. He was prepared to accept the reprimand of his rulers with dignity and presented himself so.

Aside from the stone beams that held the ceiling high, and the ashy wooden thrones at the head of the room, it was otherwise empty, causing the harpy's heavy footsteps to echo along the stone walls.

Alicus and Zuri stood in the center of the room, rather than sitting in the thrones that were made for them. This purposeful gesture eased Tallen's tense muscles. This was to be an informal conversation, one he held with friends. As he entered, their heads snapped up in his direction, their expressions unreadable.

Tallen halted his footfalls when he reached their circle. He lowered his head and bent down to one knee subserviently.

"My king," the harpy started without lifting his gaze. "My queen."

Alicus cut him off with a raised hand.

"Rise, friend," he commanded.

Tallen obeyed.

"My sincerest apologies," the harpy began, eyes still lowered to the ground, "for the disregard I've shown for your authority. My loyalty is to the Southern Realm, and I accept the punishment that you have declared fit for my insubordination."

Zuri placed her hand on Tallen's forearm, signaling him to lift his gaze.

"There is no punishment to be dealt, Tallen," the queen stated kindly.

"Your actions are forgiven," Alicus added.

And just like that, it was as if there were never a misstep between them.

"Have you seen Emira yet?" the queen questioned.

"No," Tallen responded solemnly. "I came straight here. I will see her when you dismiss me."

Silence stretched between them. Alicus and Zuri kept their gazes on Tallen as he stood, straight-backed and awaiting orders.

"We know everything, Tallen," Alicus said carefully.

The harpy's dark brows pulled together suspiciously.

Zuri smiled. "Your soul is bound to Emira's."

Tallen's chest heaved at the statement, spoken aloud, no longer a secret to be kept.

"Yes," he answered, blowing out a breath of relief. "It is."

At his confession, Alicus' eyes brightened and the corners of his mouth lifted in a grin as he took a step forward and placed a hand on Tallen's shoulder.

"Congratulations! What wonderful news for the two of you! If only you had not kept it a secret for so long."

Tallen did not return his king's celebration. His face remained solemn, and he let his wings sag behind him slightly.

"Dear gods, Tallen," Zuri started, her brown eyes wide with realization. "Does she not know?"

"Emira does not know?" Alicus repeated. His hand flew from the harpy's shoulder to his own forehead in disbelief. "How could she not? How could you not tell her?"

"You *must* tell her!" Zuri added insistently.

"I cannot," Tallen replied quickly. "Not now, not like this."

There was a pause between them as Alicus and Zuri waited for Tallen's explanation. His jaw ticked, and he inhaled deeply before he spoke.

"Imagine after *everything* she's been through, and now feeling so close to freedom, and healing like she has, only to have it all ripped away. You know how the bond works. She will feel as if I'm taking her captive all over again. I can't do that to her."

Zuri's gaze softened, and her full, red lips turned downwards slightly.

"If you have been keeping this to yourself, for fear that she will reject you," the queen began, "then you are a fool. And she would be a fool to do so."

"A kingdom full of fools," Alicus interjected lightheartedly.

"I mean it," Zuri continued, eyeing her husband agitatedly. Alicus and Tallen exchanged smirks as she continued. "You have more to offer than you realize, and it has nothing to do with your blood or your titles."

"It's true," came Xemile's voice from the entrance of the throne room. He swaggered towards the group with his signature grin smeared across his face. "From someone who has had a taste or two of many varying bloodlines—"

"Alright," Alicus cut in with a grin. "That is more information than requested…"

However, Xemile continued, "You're a catch, brother."

Tallen's wings shuddered as he huffed a laugh.

"The bond *can* feel intrusive," Xemile offered, "but they say it can also provide a sense of security and belonging. And Emira needs that." The red headed warrior's eyes trailed downwards to the glassy floor, and his tone shifted as he whispered, "She's awake."

Tallen looked at his rulers, eagerly awaiting their dismissal.

Alicus straightened his shoulders as he spoke, his voice that of a king once more. "Emira is your Soul Bond, a very rare thing indeed, and so she is family. Even if she does not yet realize it. And Vyrion's acts against her are now considered personal."

CHAPTER
TWENTY-SIX

Emira lay on her side in bed, squeezing her eyes shut and gritting her teeth against the pain that coursed its way over her body. Sarolina stood at the bedside, hastily mixing medicines in a large bowl as Emira groaned and clenched her muscles tightly, trying to fight against the agony of the leftover wounds. She held her arms over her chest, her wrists curved outwards and her fingers bent awry. Her fingernails were gone, lifted with the point of Vyrion's dagger and ripped clean off. The tips of her fingers were now swollen and caked with dried blood, tingling and stinging as the surrounding air licked at the wounds. The cuts that caressed either side of her face burned as tears spilled from her eyes, and the whip marks down her back stung and prodded at her spine with every uneven inhale of breath she took. Her broken rib, as it was an internal injury, Sarolina was able to mend immediately with a concoction of quartz and amethyst.

"Almost done," Sarolina offered tenderly as she mixed the contents of her bowl. "We'll soak your fingers in this. It will help."

She didn't offer more. Emira could only focus on was the pain that was untouched by the failed attempts of easement by the witch.

The siren caught a glimpse through her squinted eyes as Tallen entered the bedroom. He did so hurriedly, without knocking. His expression was, for the first time, truly decipherable. Tallen was shaken; concerned for Emira and her safety, and perhaps disturbed to face the severity of the wounds she bore. Her gaze on him didn't last long. She couldn't help but keep her eyes squeezed shut and grit against the agony.

"Gods," he murmured as he approached. "Em—"

"Tallen," Sarolina interrupted sternly, "hold this."

Emira heard them shuffling beside her hurriedly.

"Emira," the witch started, "I'm going to soak your hands in this salve. It will speed up your rapid healing and help to grow your nails again." Her voice turned severe as she finished, "It is going to be very painful, but it is necessary."

Emira nodded her understanding and held her trembling hands out, offering them for treatment.

Sarolina placed the bowl next to Emira on the mattress as Tallen guided her wrists down into the cold mixture. The bones in her fingers screamed as they were submerged, and she cried out in agony as the emollient fulfilled its purpose.

She tried to pull away, but Sarolina ordered the harpy, "Hold her firmly!"

Tallen held her wrists in place as Sarolina added healing balms to the marks down her back and face. The bruising, the witch had said, fae blood would heal on its own.

Emira tried to pull her arms away from the salve, but Tallen's strong grip remained, holding her hands under the surface of the liquid. The tips of her fingers burned as her nails slowly emerged, covering the bare, fleshy patches on her fingertips.

"It's almost done," Tallen whispered to Emira. "Hold on. It's almost finished."

As the minutes passed, Sarolina finished treating the rest of Emira's wounds, and the pain in her fingers slowly eased. The witch monitored her patient's hands, signaling when the harpy was finally able to release them. Emira pulled her hands from the bowl with a gasp and looked at her newly grown nails. The smeared blood remained, but the pain was gone. She breathed a sigh of relief as Sarolina removed the bowl.

"Thank you," Emira croaked, throat raw from her screams.

"I'll come back in an hour to reassess," she murmured. The vials and jars in her wicker basket clinked together as she lifted it from the table and headed for the door. "I've already given you the nighttime tonic. You should try to sleep." She eyed the harpy in warning, and he nodded gently in understanding.

When the witch closed the door behind her, and they were left alone, the harpy's pretense dissolved. He lay beside Emira and gently wrapped his arms around her sore body, holding her close and burying his face in the crook of her neck. Emira released a sob as she slowly reached her arms up around him.

"I should have been here," he said, his lips touched the sensitive skin above her shoulder.

"No," Emira responded, voice cracking as her pained vocal chords worked the sound from her throat.

The harpy pulled himself away and lay Emira back down on the bed. He then shuffled himself to lay beside her, draped one wing over the both of them, creating a dark, warm cocoon.

"I thought I was going to die," Emira confessed as her eyes fluttered closed. Tallen squeezed her tighter and pressed his lips to her forehead.

"That isn't going to happen," he responded sternly.

Emira shifted her gaze up to his, forcing her heavy lids to remain open.

"I've accepted that my end will come at the hands of Vyrion." Tallen's lips parted to speak, but she placed a raw hand to his chest to silence him. "He *will* kill me," she continued. "No matter what I do, he will. I have to tell Alicus and Zuri about the Eastern Realm before that happens."

"Later," Tallen said. "Now, you rest. I will not leave unless you order me away."

A smile tugged at Emira's lips. "You've said that before."

"And I will say it again," he swore. Emira nestled into his chest, breathing in his dark chocolate and cedar scent. He gently kissed the top of her head as her eyes fluttered closed again.

"Sleep," he whispered.

And she did.

CHAPTER
TWENTY-SEVEN

Days later, Emira found herself sitting in the familiar library alcove with the Southern Realm's court.

"Emira," Zuri started, "thank you for choosing to help us."

Her voice remained low, as if speaking to a wounded animal, and Emira felt like she was one. She kept her shoulders pulled tightly together and her back hunched. She had taken all of her meals in bed the past week and rested well as she healed, but her face said otherwise. Although the green hued bruises and crimson scars had healed entirely, and Vyrion's wretched name no longer marred her face, her eyes remained puffy with exhaustion. Tallen had remained by her side throughout the week, coaxing her into calm idleness when she stirred, and suggesting she walk the corridors to exercise her sore muscles.

Emira turned towards Alicus and Zuri and asked solemnly, "What do you want to know?"

Vyla opened her notebook and began scribbling when Alicus asked, "Are we correct in our belief that Vyrion has somehow broken the treaty? Is Vyrion keeping slaves in the east?"

"Yes," Emira answered surely. She would not falter.

"Explain," Vyla demanded softly.

Emira paused, keeping her eyes fixed on the emissary. Although she heard Vyrion's whispered threats in her mind, she refused to back down.

"Everyone serves him. We work from sunrise until the moon is the only light we have left. Most of us are mercilessly beaten, and many are killed, my parents among them." Emira took in a shuddering breath as the words spilled from her lips. Blinking back the tears that she refused to shed over Vyrion, she continued, "He kidnaps travelers and enslaves them. He knows no limits when he kills—men, women, and children are all under his power."

Tallen rolled his shoulders at the saturation of her confession, and Emira felt a pit in her stomach. Xemile's signature smirk was unseen, replaced with a hard frown, and Vyla was scribbling every spoken word into her notebook.

"How many slaves?" asked Alicus.

"Countless. Hundreds. There is no one in the realm that is not a slave besides our mas—besides Vyrion."

"How does one fae control so many under such tyranny?" Alicus continued. "Surely he has a court? A council? An army? Why do they continue to serve him?"

"Fear," Emira replied. "All who serve him in such a way do so for their own well-being. Some believe they will earn a place higher than those of mere slaves. Others are just trying to survive. They will do his bidding, as will his militia, with only their own survival in mind."

Alicus sighed and rubbed the bridge of his nose.

"What does this mean, Alicus?" Zuri asked, placing a delicate hand on her husband's arm.

He brought his fingers away from his face and closed them around his wife's fingers.

"It means, my love, that Vyrion has indeed found a loophole in the contract. He has found a way to breach the treaty without the consequence of death."

"What are our orders?" Tallen asked his rulers eagerly.

"The law of our land dictates a meeting of kings," Alicus answered. Zuri nodded. "The other realms must be informed of this treason before we take further action."

Emira sat silently, trying to force the echoing voice of Vyrion from her mind. She had accepted at a young age that her death would be at his hands, and she knew her time in the Southern Realm would not change that. Vyrion *would* find her, and he *would* kill her for speaking against him. But before he could succeed, Emira understood that this may be her only chance to save a few others first.

"Send the ravens immediately," Alicus ordered Vyla. "Keep Vyrion in the dark."

The shifter's gray eyes lowered in acknowledgement. She stood and swept her way out of the room as the king turned his attention back to the siren. "Thank you, Emira."

Emira nodded quickly, gulping back the salivation that had pooled in the back of her throat.

"We grant you all dismissal," Zuri said. Xemile stood, followed soon by Tallen and Emira. The three of them bowed slightly to the still seated rulers before turning to leave.

After breakfast, Emira walked wearily through the halls alongside Tallen. Her body had healed, but her mind remained tormented. Servants passed, eyeing the harpy and the siren as they whispered to each other about what they had witnessed from her doorway days prior.

Tallen stopped suddenly, and Emira followed suit.

"What?" she asked.

He released a breath and responded, "Let me fly you across the realm. Let's go somewhere *quiet*." His icy eyes shifted towards the group of servants that had most recently passed by.

Emira narrowed her eyes and looked back down the hall.

"Are we not needed here?" she questioned.

"Alicus and Zuri can handle a day on their own," Tallen replied. "Come on."

His hands trembled as he held them both out for Emira to accept, and his eyes remained unblinking, pleading.

Emira bit her lip and smirked. With one swift movement, Tallen grasped her hands and lifted her into the air, flinging her over his broad shoulder playfully. Emira shrieked happily, and the harpy chuckled deeply beneath her. He stepped to the nearest balcony and leapt into the sky.

Tallen's powerful wings beat against the cool air, and they were lifted higher and higher, gliding over the rocky mountains, the green forest, and the villages below. The sky was clear, and Emira felt as if the air was cleansing her mind.

Tallen flew until they were surrounded by nothing but clouds. Continuing to rap his wings powerfully, the harpy slowed to a hover. Emira, now cradled in his embrace, tilted her head back and splayed her arms wide, breathing deeply as she did so. The chill wind froze her lungs as she inhaled. An invisible weight lifted as she exhaled, like all of the hurt in her world had melted away.

Tallen remained silent, hovering amid the plush clouds and looking down at Emira's exposed neck. She needed this; this moment of peace. Her chest heaved with every deep breath she took, her blonde hair billowed in the crisp breeze, which also carried with it her intoxicating lavender and library scent.

"I never thought," Emira started, bringing her gaze back up to Tallen's, "that I could feel so alive."

Hands occupied with supporting her, the harpy studied her windswept face.

"From this moment forward, I expect you to *live*," he demanded gently. Her green eyes were wide, listening to and observing him. He placed his forehead against her own and continued, "No more fear, Em. No more tears spilled over him. You belong to the Southern Realm. You belong to me."

CHAPTER
TWENTY-EIGHT

The harpy flew them farther and farther from the castle walls until Emira spotted a calm, glassy river that cut between the trees, and the rocky border of the Caseli Mountains, where just over them lay the Western Realm.

Tallen held Emira tightly as he slowly descended onto the shore of the glistening river. Emira huffed a breath as Tallen set her on her feet, and she brushed the wild hair from her face.

"I don't think I'll ever grow bored with flying," Emira beamed.

Tallen's chest swelled with pride.

"You won't," he promised.

"Where are we?" she asked, eyes moving to the river.

The glassy water was as clear as crystal, the pebble covered floor visible through the calm surface.

"The Valeldran River," Tallen answered. "It leads north and cuts through my father's territory. It's the widest there; that's why the north is a port town. And southwest, it leads to the ocean. But we are far enough that this water is fresh to drink. It's always cold and quiet."

"I wonder," Emira started, kicking off her slipper-like shoes and stepping to the edge of the water. She dipped her feet carefully, and inhaled when the water touched her skin.

"It's only a little chilled," she continued, reaching for the harpy. "Come on."

Tallen grinned, unbuckled his knife's sheath and let it fall to the gravelly shore. He took Emira's outstretched hand, and together, they walked into the Valeldran.

The cool water enveloped the both of them, seeping into their clothes and chilling their skin underneath. As it grew deeper, Tallen took a hold of Emira's waist and held her pressed against his chest. He used his powerful legs to propel them further from land. Emira dipped her head back, soaked her hair and pushed it away from her face. Tallen watched, like a predator watching prey.

The harpy was treading water when Emira's eyes fell back on his face. She wrapped her legs around his waist and curled her fingers into his hair, resting her forehead against his.

"Tallen," she breathed, eyes fluttering closed. The feeling of his name on her lips felt safe, and comfortable. It felt like home.

Water droplets tickled her skin as they dripped down her face. Her gauzy dress clung to each curve of her body as she tilted her lips closer to his. His anticipatory breath tickled her skin. Emira's thighs tightened around his waist, and she felt his hard length pressed against her.

"Em," he growled, taking one hand from her side and running it up the length of her arched back. His fingers entwined in her golden hair, and she tipped her head back in response, exposing her neck. He pressed a light kiss to her throat, and she trembled in his grip.

"Say you want this," he commanded against her skin. "Say you want me."

Emira's breath caught at his words, and excitement pulsed through her body. The harpy had confirmed that there would be no consequences to their interest in one another, and the conflict that she had felt was now completely gone. She could enjoy this, savor this, *want* this. Without lifting her head, she answered, voice quivering, "I want you, Tallen."

With the hand he still held tangled in her hair, he swiftly lifted Emira's head back up and pinned his lips to hers. Their tongues clashed and she released a moan into Tallen's mouth. He slid his other hand from her waist and gripped her thigh, squeezing and pulling her as close to his body as he could.

"Tallen," Emira breathed, throwing her arms around his neck.

She traced his bottom lip with her tongue, and he groaned, his arousal intensifying. She chuckled, tongue still on his lips, delighted in his building desire.

"You have no idea how consumed I am by you, Emira," he murmured.

Emira slid her mauve-tinted lips from his and trailed to his ear, where her breath warmed the harpy against the cool river. She clutched his coarse hair in her hands and whispered, "And you will never know how much you have saved me."

Tallen tipped his head back slightly, releasing his grip on her hair and savored her words. Her warm breath trickled down from his ear to his jaw and onto his neck, where she planted kiss after kiss, whimpering lightly against his skin, and pushing her hips into him beneath the water.

"Tallen," Emira whispered. He lifted his head and met her gaze, his blue eyes alight with eagerness and pleasure. "Make me yours."

The harpy came undone.

With a swift beat of his raven-like wings against the surface of the water, Tallen easily lifted their soaked bodies from the Valeldran River and into the sky. He clutched Emira to his chest possessively as he ravenously kissed and nipped at her skin.

After only a few seconds in the air, they landed where they were surrounded by rocky cliff sides and a scattering of scanty, young trees. The Southern Realm below was now nothing but a speckling of green cradled in a rocky embrace. Sunlight peeked through the few overhead immature branches, and despite the shade, a soft patch of grass grew wildly beneath their feet.

"Say it again," Tallen demanded, pressing his lips back onto the siren's.

His hands roamed from her waist, up over her breasts and into her hair. Her wet dress clung closely to her trembling body with the fresh pull of gravity. Tallen began to lower the shoulders of her gown. "Say it again, Em."

"Make me yours, Tallen," she pleaded.

With trembling hands, he slid the wet fabric down past her arms, completely exposing her torso. His predatory gaze dropped to her naked breasts and her nipples that were peaking against the cool air. Emira's heart pounded beneath her chest as the harpy gazed, his eyes predatory and hungry.

With one swift movement, Tallen had Emira gently pressed up against one of the thin trees, his mouth upon her skin, kissing and sucking down her neck and over her collarbones. The contrast of his soft lips and rough stubble sent a chill up the siren's spine. She arched into him, pressing her thighs together in an attempt to relieve the torturous pressure that was building between her legs.

Tallen's lips continued planting kisses over her shoulders and down her chest. When he reached her bare breasts, the harpy knelt so that he was eye level with them. One of his large hands went to her waist, while the other grabbed her breast, holding it tightly in place as he placed his mouth upon her nipple.

Emira gasped, the sensation of his tongue flicking her sensitive flesh agonizingly tantalizing. She brought both hands to his hair, running her fingers through his wet curls and leaned her head back against the tree. The rays of the autumn sun warmed her skin as Tallen began working her other nipple, gently biting and tasting her flesh.

The harpy dragged his lips up the valley between her breasts as he stood, and Emira let out a shaky moan. His wings shuddered, and he kissed her once more, devouring her, moving his hands to either side of her face in an attempt to bring her even closer than was possible.

"I need you, Tallen," Emira begged, squeezing her thighs even tighter together.

Tallen smirked through their kiss and murmured, "I said I would not be rushed with you. I intend to keep my word."

The front of his pants protruded as his cock drove it's way forward. The harpy lifted Emira off of the ground, wrapping her legs around his waist and pressing his mouth to her breasts again. Emira writhed in his grip, the feeling of his unyielding erection hard against her. The soaked skirts of her dress, which still hung in heaps around her body, made it difficult to move freely, but she ground her hips against him, attempting to relieve the throbbing pressure between her legs.

Tallen moaned as she moved, the feeling of her core grinding against him causing his arousal to intensify. His erection pressed so firmly against the waist of his pants that the urge to remove them became too great.

He pulled away from Emira and gently lowered her onto the soft patch of grass beneath their feet. Tallen stood over her, the broad frame of his body casting a shadow over her face. With his fierce eyes fixed on her, the harpy removed his boots and swiftly pulled his shirt around his wings and over his head. He smirked as he knelt down, grasping the fabric that had gathered around Emira's hips. He slid it off effortlessly, leaving her completely bare.

A rush of adrenaline swept through Emira's veins as Tallen looked down upon her. Still on his knees, he gazed between her legs, hungry eyes fixed on the slick wetness between them. He grabbed her thighs, spreading them wider than they already were and dipped his head downwards. The sensation of his tongue gently flicking her clit had Emira grasping his black curls and gasping in with pleasure.

The harpy huffed a laugh at her reaction, his warm breath making the building pressure nearly unbearable. He swiped his tongue up the length of her, and Emira released a raw moan of pleasure. She fisted her breasts as he continued, swirling his tongue on her clit, flicking the sensitive bud until Emira's vision blurred. The orgasm ripped through her, quickly, like a crashing wave. She cried out as the peak came and went.

The harpy licked her clean, running his hands along her thighs, up her abdomen and onto her breasts as he did so.

Tallen slid his body upwards, kissing along Emira's supple, blushing skin as he did, until they were face to face. With one hand holding his body up, black and gold feathered wings tucked in tightly, Tallen kissed Emira deeply. With his free hand, he cupped the back of her neck, lifting her slightly to meet his lips.

The siren continued to grind her hips into the harpy, his durable training leathers a frustrating barrier between them. Emira reached down and hooked her thumbs into the waist of his pants, pushing and wrenching. She could not free him, and she moaned defeatedly into Tallen's kiss.

He pushed himself upright, hovering over Emira on his knees, wings splayed out for balance. His torso was covered in hard, muscular lines. Cords in his arms and neck moved as he did while his abs looked as if they could cut diamonds. A speckling of dark hair covered his pecs, as well as below his navel, trailing down beneath the waist of his infuriating pants.

Emira continued to writhe beneath his looming presence, eager for him to return to her. With a few swift movements, Tallen removed the last of his clothes, allowing his erection to spring free.

The siren gaped. Her squirming stilled for a moment, as her eyes raked over his naked body. He was glorious in every way, from the icy blue of his eyes, to his cut-from-stone figure, to the thick cock he presented to her.

Emira sat upright. The harpy, kneeling before her, was still much taller than she was sitting. She palmed his erection, relishing how smooth and warm his skin felt in her grasp. Tallen hooked his fingers through her hair, holding it firmly at the root. Then Emira placed her swollen, slightly parted lips to the head of his cock, and the harpy released a deep, throaty moan.

She worked him, using her hands and her mouth, swirling her tongue around the tip before taking all of him. The salty taste of his building pleasure clung to the back of her throat, and she moaned around his cock, causing the harpy to shudder. A bolt of lightning cracked across the clear sky, shaking the ground and trees around them. Emira pressed her lips even more firmly around his erection. The sensation of him filling her, thrusting his hips to amplify his pleasure, made the throbbing between her legs nearly insufferable.

Tallen pulled away from her, his expression raw with pleasure. His brows were furrowed and his lips were slightly parted as he released his grip on her hair.

The harpy bent forward, tucking in his wings and pressing his lips to Emira's. They lowered themselves once more, Emira's back on the grass and Tallen leaning over her.

"I'm going to make you come again, Emira," the harpy growled against her lips. She squirmed at his promise, hips bucking eagerly.

"Please," she begged, sending the harpy nearly into a frenzy. "Tallen, please, please, please…"

He swept his mouth over hers once more before palming his arousal and positioning himself at her entrance.

"Ready?" he said, his voice a low growl, husky with pleasure.

Emira nodded.

Tallen slowly pressed his body into hers. He filled her, and hissed as her core squeezed down on his cock. Emira arched, the first pinch of pain a rapid shock before pleasure took over. He stretched her, filled her to the hilt. For a moment, he remained still, buried inside her cunt. The harpy leaned forward, planting kisses along Emira's neck and collarbones. He grasped at her blonde hair, her soft hands and her full thighs before thrusting his hips and picking up speed. Lightning flashed across the sky again, and the ground beneath them skittered with energy.

Emira fisted her breasts as Tallen plunged in and out of her. She wrapped her ankles around the backs of his powerful thighs and allowed her head to roll backwards. The pleasure swam through her, running through her veins just as her blood did.

Emira cried out Tallen's name, over and over until he was moments away from coming entirely undone.

"Em," he groaned. "Gods, Em, you're going to make me come."

She clawed at his forearms as Tallen thrusted, faster and harder.

"Make me yours, Tallen," she moaned. "Make me yours."

Their pleasure peaked at the same moment. Tallen withdrew, spilling himself upon the ground as Emira's core clenched and unclenched with her orgasm. A final flash of lightning, this one silent, speared across the sky as they rode their high together, a brilliant, hazy fog encompassing their senses.

Breathing heavily, Tallen slowly planted a kiss on Emira's forehead.

"Mine," he stated against her skin.

She smiled up at him, hair tangled in the blades of grass, and wrapped her arms around his massive chest. He settled next to her, and they lay upon the earth together, bodies entangled as the sun dried their discarded clothes.

CHAPTER
TWENTY-NINE

Xemile instructed Emira to meet him near the river's edge
the next morning for training. The sky was purple with the
coming sunrise and the air was a frigid chill. The Valeldran waters rushed with the rapid breeze of mid-autumn, creating
a serenity that, even against her chattering teeth, Emira could not
deny was alluring. She adjusted her cloak, pulling it tighter around
her shoulders as Tallen walked by her side. The harpy had insisted
on escorting her, curious as to what the commander had planned
that involved the use of the river.

Xemile was waiting when they arrived, already knee deep in
the rushing current. His powerful legs, dressed in his usual dark
brown leathers, held him steady against the strong waters. The
early morning rays bounced off of his auburn hair, creating the illusion of flames dancing around his face. The warrior's expression
was smug as he unsheathed a knife, delicately pressing his thumb
to the sharp edge to test its lethality.

Emira stepped into the water, the cold biting at her ankles, while Tallen remained on shore, settling himself comfort-

ably against one of the many large boulders that bordered the wide river.

"What's the plan?" the siren asked, standing a hundred yards away from her fae trainer. "Why are we meeting here?"

But her questioning was cut short when Xemile hurled his dagger in her direction. It whipped through the air, spinning like a frantic, silver bird. Emira ducked, dodging the sharp edge, as the dagger spun overhead and landed in the water, the pointed end stuck in the rocky substrate. Xemile immediately hurled another. Emira dodged again, this time crashing into the shallow, bitter-cold water.

Tallen, still on shore, stood tall. His feathered wings flared behind him instinctively as his eyes darted between his comrade and Emira.

"What the hell, Xem?" Emira sputtered, pulling herself from the under current and eyeing the second blade that had landed only inches from where she stood. Her soaked body shivered against the frigid air, and her wet hair clung to her scalp, freezing her face before the water could drip down her cheeks.

"I have a theory," he answered.

There was no malice in his voice, as if casually throwing weapons at someone wasn't abnormal. He trudged closer, kicking up water as he went. His usual smirk was smeared across his face as he reached down and pulled a rock the size of his fist from the river.

"Xem, no!" Tallen shouted, leaping from where he stood.

Emira glared at Xemile murderously as he lifted the rock over his head and flung it in her direction. Fury pooled in her gut at his nonsensical method.

"Enough!" she screamed angrily, diving again.

Her body hit the surface of the water with a powerful *crack!*

The sound echoed through the surrounding valley, reverberating off of the mountainsides and bouncing off of the vibrating river face.

As her body fell beneath the water, a wave, four times as tall as she, rose up from the Valeldran. The mighty crest flowed rapidly towards her attacker. It crashed into Xemile, knocking him violently backwards and pushing him below the surface. Tallen sprinted into the Valeldran, making his way to pull them both from the swift currents. As the wave took Xemile under, it settled back into the river, becoming still once again.

The harpy reached Emira's side as she pulled herself from the water. He helped to steady her feet as she frantically wiped the water from her eyes. She looked in Xemile's direction anxiously, watching as he pushed himself into an upright seated position in the water. The commander's brow was bloodied, cut open from the force of the wave slamming him against the stoney riverbed. She scanned him quickly for other injuries that she may have inflicted.

Their eyes met and after a brief pause, Xemile began laughing maniacally.

"I knew it!" Xemile boasted, slapping the water's surface and pumping his fist into the air. Tallen and Emira blanched at each other, neither understanding their friend's celebration.

Xemile finally stood, shaking the excess water from his now unkempt hair like a deranged animal.

"Come on, mermaid," he dared, his amber eyes glinting against the sunrays. "Let's see what else you can do."

Emira remained standing ankle deep in the water, gaping at Xemile; his grin spreading wildly at his discovery.

"Xem, what-what the hell happened?" she stammered. Her eyes shifted between the commander, the blood on his brow that he didn't seem to notice, and the rushing water at her feet.

Tallen stepped closer to the siren and placed a heavy hand on the small of her back, icy eyes searching her face for injuries. When he was satisfied, he looked towards the fae warrior and stated incredulously, "You threw a rock."

"I ran out of daggers," Xemile mocked.

"Tell me what the hell just happened!" Emira demanded.

Xemile stepped forward and began searching the shallow water for the knives he had thrown.

"Vyla found some new information in the library," he started. "Not much, but enough to start forming a theory or two."

He reached down, pushing his disheveled, red hair from his eyes and lifted a glistening blade from under the surface.

"She was right," he continued, sheathing the weapon. "Sirens are a private people, but their known history is violent, willing to sink entire fleets when threatened. And that's where your power will come from. *Danger.*" He reached down again, plucking the second blade from the water.

"That can't be right," Emira countered, watching him. She refused to let her guard down, now that he had both daggers on his person. "I was threatened daily in the Eastern Realm, and nothing like this ever came from that."

Tallen's eyes snapped in her direction as the answer dawned on him.

"You weren't healthy," he stated as the thoughts processed. "Like Sarolina said, you're quicker to heal now that you aren't on the brink of death, and your siren abilities are emerging. Vyrion kept you weak so you couldn't fight back."

She considered his logic for a moment but couldn't find a reason to suspect that he was wrong. Xemile kicked up water as he made his way back to his original post. He had another rock, tossing it up and down in the air like a ball.

"Only one way to find out," he said with a smirk.

Before Emira could dispute his proposition, the warrior hurled the rock. The heavy stone whipped through the air with incredible precision, spinning like a throwing star, curving slightly and making aim for the harpy.

"No!" Emira shouted, instinctively reaching for the jagged stone.

As she did, a powerful stream of water shot from her hand. The water collided with the rock and sent it careening onto the shore. As it hit the ground, her power ceased, and her hands trembled from the forceful vibration it had created.

Tallen's wide gaze darted to Emira's, and he gave a disbelieving laugh. Emira's mouth was agape as she stared at her palm, but eventually, she too laughed at the absurdity. The harpy placed his hands on the sides of her wet face and ran them up through her hair.

"You," he growled, "are spectacular."

Tallen didn't give Emira time to respond when he pressed his lips to hers, the water from her still drenched hair dripping it's way slowly down his arms.

"I'm getting a bigger rock!" Xemile shouted from somewhere along the shoreline.

Emira broke her kiss from the harpy and responded abrasively, "Alright, you wanted an ass kicking from a mermaid? Let's go."

Tallen smiled and slowly began stepping backwards onto land.

"Give him hell, Em."

EMIRA STOOD IN THE SHOWER, RELISHING IN THE FEELING OF THE warm water flowing over her aching muscles. Her bones groaned, sore from the earlier training, but her mind ran wild. She had manipulated water; she had created it from nothing. Emira tilted her head upwards and let the stream run down her face. Squeezing her eyes closed, she pictured what she wanted the water to become. The steady flow slowed before stopping to nothing when she opened her eyes.

Droplets floated around her like frozen, shattering glass. It was as if she was encased in diamonds, hovering around her naked body like bewitched jewelry.

With a swift pushing motion of her arms, the droplets shot outwards in all directions, and the water began to flow again. Emira laughed, covering her face with her hands. Her magic came so easily now. All she had to do was visualize what she wanted to happen, to will it into existence. Something that once may have felt so complex, even arduous, came so naturally. It was as easy as breathing.

A swift knock at the door pulled Emira's mind to the surface. Tallen was prowling toward her from the doorway. With only a thin, glass door between them, there was no hiding her naked body from his view.

Not that she wanted to.

"Can I help you?" Emira grinned.

She peered through the water speckled glass at his broad figure, which was now leaning against the wall, arms crossed over his massive chest, a smirk spreading across his face.

"Perhaps," he teased, stretching his wings flirtatiously.

Emira rolled her eyes. She swept a hand once along the glass, wiping away the steam that had accumulated.

"Are you just going to stare?"

"Why not?" Tallen countered. "You're beautiful."

Emira huffed a laugh, eyeing the harpy through the foggy glass.

"I don't think that's why you came in here," she started.

He shrugged, but did not move from where he stood.

"Well, if you're just going to stand there..."—her voice turned sultry and Tallen's face heated—"I'll just have to take care of things myself."

Emira lowered a hand between her legs, keeping her eyes fixed on the harpy through the steam. She slid a single finger between the lips of her cunt, caressing her clit as she did so. A shockwave of pleasure rippled through her body, and Emira sighed heavily. Leaning her head against the shower wall, she stroked herself a second, third, fourth time.

Tallen shifted, the scent of her arousal wrapping around his body. The steam from the shower caressed his skin, filling the bathroom in its hazy embrace. Tallen remained leaning against the wall, arms crossed and eyes on the siren.

Between the fluttering of her eyelids, Emira watched him back, the adrenaline coursing through her body tightening its grip on her lungs.

Tallen's jaw tightened as she gasped, her climax intensely rushing over her body. His gaze remained on Emira, taking in the curve of her parted lips, the arch of her back, the sound of her moan. And as her body relaxed, he moved forward.

He swiftly disrobed and pulled the glass door back, allowing the steam from the hot water to further penetrate his skin. Tallen stepped over the shower's threshold and pinned his lips to Emira's, while grasping her hips and pulling her naked body closer to his own.

He growled into her mouth when her wet skin pressed against his arousal. Tallen wrapped his large wings around them and began to slowly trailing kisses down her neck, her breasts, her hips. He knelt before her, and she raked her fingers through his coarse, wet hair. His lips trailed even farther down, kissing the insides of her thighs.

Emira gasped as his tongue teased her clit and lapped at the product of her previous orgasm. She arched her back and pressed her hips into him. Tallen's wings wrapped around her, pulling their bodies closer and deepening her pleasure.

He grasped at her thigh and lifted it over his muscled shoulder, opening her body up to him. The pleasure intensified, and Emira's body tensed in anticipation. Tallen huffed a laugh against her core, and she nearly came apart.

"Tallen," she breathed, fisting his black hair.

His grip on her tightened again at the sound of his name on her lips. His tongue firmly circled her clit, and she exhaled a moan, pleasure caressing her from the inside out as she came.

The harpy relished the taste, drinking up every last drop of her orgasm.

"You taste like divinity," he growled, slowly rising back up to his feet. He clutched her relaxed body as her eyes fluttered and her heart raced. Tallen cupped the back of Emira's head, angling her to face him. With his lips a breadth away from her own, the harpy whispered, "Taste it."

He moved his mouth over hers, sweeping his tongue between her lips and over her teeth. The sweet tang of arousal attacked Emira's senses, and she arched closer to the harpy. His hands slid from her head, down her neck, and over her breasts. Emira gripped at his waist, pulling him flat against her, before raking her hands down the sculpted muscles of his backside.

Tallen, never breaking away from their kiss, reached for both of Emira's thighs. With one swift motion, he lifted her, and positioned her legs around himself. Emira felt the cool shower wall at her back as the harpy pinned her, and angled himself at her entrance.

The harpy hissed against Emira's mouth when her slick arousal touched the head of his cock. He finally pulled away from their kiss, and allowed his eyes to sweep over her face. The siren's cheeks were pink with pleasure, and her swollen lips were slightly parted. Tallen nudged her cunt, forcing a whimpering plea to escape her tightly squeezed lungs.

"I'm going to watch," the harpy said, keeping his hips painfully still. "I'm going to watch as I fuck you. I want to see your face when I make you come."

Emira bit her bottom lip as he spoke, excitement and adrenaline rushing through her. The pressure that had built between her legs was nearly unbearable, and she desperately grated her hips in an attempt to relieve some of the ache.

"Eyes on me," Tallen demanded.

He slid one hand to her cheek, firmly holding her face in place as he pressed into her.

Emira's eyes rolled as he filled her to the hilt. Her legs pulled him closer, and her hands flew to his shoulders, nails digging into his tanned skin as her cunt tightened around his cock.

"Open your eyes," he growled, taking himself away from her completely. Emira whimpered, rotating her hips beseechingly.

"Please, Tallen," she begged frustratedly.

"I'm going to watch you come, Emira," the harpy repeated, gripping her face tighter and squeezing her cheeks together. "I'm going to watch the pleasure dance behind your gaze when I make you scream. Open. Your. Eyes."

Emira blinked and refocused her gaze. As soon as her eyes met Tallen's, he pounded into her, his icy expression never breaking away from her own.

With each thrust, the harpy brushed against Emira's clit. She desperately held his gaze, not wanting him to stop.

Tallen moved faster and faster, his hands gripping her thighs, and his wings tucked tightly behind him. Water dripped from his black hair, and down his hardened face. Emira kissed him, licking away the droplets that sat on his lips.

The siren's core tightened and she moaned, nestling the back of her head against the shower wall.

"You're going to come for me, Emira," Tallen said. His eyes remained fixed on Emira's face, her parted lips, her red cheeks. "Show me how you come for me." The harpy continued thrusting, each pump sending a wave of pleasure through the siren.

"Tallen," Emira gasped, focusing on the harpy. "Tallen, I can't—" She started to close her eyes, but Tallen's hand tightened further on her face.

"Open your eyes *now*," he demanded.

Emira obeyed.

"Come, Em. Come all over my cock."

Tallen continued filling her, his hips grinding rhythmically as he did. He felt as Emira's core squeezed down on him, relaxing only as she came. Her mouth agape as she cried out, the siren dug her nails into Tallen's shoulders as her pleasure clouded her mind and rattled her body.

Settling Emira on the floor once more, the harpy swiftly pulled out and spilled himself on the shower floor, the rushing water sweeping it away.

The harpy pressed a gentle kiss to Emira's forehead as he reached for the faucet and turned the water off.

"Good girl," he said, lips still pressed to her wet skin.

He carefully led Emira over the lip of the shower and wrapped a clean, white towel against her spent, goosebump-covered body.

Emira looked up at Tallen with a small smile. "You've made us late for dinner."

CHAPTER

THIRTY

Dinner that night was light hearted, for which Emira was thankful. Alicus and Zuri sat closely, their loving feelings towards each other on full display in the form of whispers and trailing fingers. Xemile and Vyla were back to bickering, likely over something competitive but unimportant. Tallen spotted Emira smiling at them, and confidently contributing to conversations, unafraid of consequences or judgment. It warmed him to see her so joyful.

Emira excused herself to the restroom when dessert was announced to be on the way. The harpy watched the sway of her full hips and the flip of her wavy, blonde hair as she walked from the dining hall. When he turned back to the table, all eyes were pinned on him, and the conversation had ceased.

Tallen straightened defensively. "What?"

"You know damn well what," Xemile teased.

"I don't," the harpy responded.

"When are you going to tell her?" Vyla hissed.

"What are you talking about?" Tallen demanded, heat rising in his throat.

"Cut the shit," Xemile offered with a smirk.

"Xem," Zuri warned with a forward tilt of her head.

"Everyone here is aware that Emira is your Bonded Soul," Alicus started calmly, "except Emira herself."

"You have to tell her," Vyla said.

"I cannot," Tallen stated, gripping the arms of his chair. He was unfamiliar with this sensation. He was not a coward, but when it came to Emira, he did not know himself.

"You can," Zuri replied softly. "You must. It's not fair to keep this secret from her."

Tallen dropped his head, his jaw ticking.

"She's already been through so much," he started. "If I tell her now…" His voice trailed off as the thought ran through his head. If he told her now, she could reject the bond. She could reject him.

Alicus' voice came next. "War with the Eastern Realm is coming. She deserves to know before it's too late."

Tallen's gaze snapped to his king. He had not, could not, consider the alternative; that a time may come when it was too late to tell Emira the truth.

The harpy released his grip on the chair, and rolled his shoulders.

"I can't lose her," he admitted, voice low. His eyes swept over the faces of his friends. "If I smother her with this information, she is sure to pull away."

Zuri's soft brown eyes begged Tallen to reconsider.

"A time may soon come," she started, "when you are no longer able to tell her. War *will* come."

Silence stretched through the dining hall. Tallen, in his five decades of employment in the south, had never shown weakness until this moment.

Vyla's sharp voice sliced through the silence. "You must tell her."

The harpy swallowed and nodded stiffly.

"Okay," he rasped.

"Make your king a promise," Alicus said. "You will tell her tonight."

Tallen nodded stiffly again, and quickly responded when Emira's returning footsteps echoed through the corridor.

"I swear it. I'll tell her. Tonight."

CHAPTER
THIRTY-ONE

Tallen made no effort to hide the romantic relationship that had blossomed between him and Emira. The harpy had invited her to begin sleeping in his room instead of her own, to which she enthusiastically accepted. It was darker and cooler than her own quarters were, and the scent of dark chocolate and cedar filled her lungs each time she entered. Tallen would also be able to return to a normal sleep schedule, spending his nights in bed with Emira, and his days awake and, mostly, by her side.

They entered their room at the end of the evening. Tallen closed the door behind them and kicked off his boots. He shuffled over to the dresser and began removing his weapons from his person. One at a time, they thumped onto the wooden surface until he removed his whip last. It slithered at his touch and seemed to fall asleep when released.

"Are you alright?" Emira asked, stepping towards his turned back.

The harpy didn't answer.

"You were quiet at dinner," she added.

He finally turned to face Emira, his expression stoic.

"We need to discuss something of great importance," he responded solemnly.

Tallen took her hand and led her to the edge of the bed, where he gestured for Emira to sit down. She desperately searched his face, looking for an answer to the many questions crossing her mind.

"Did I offend you? Earlier?"

Tallen's brow furrowed.

Emira lowered her voice sheepishly, "In the shower?"

Tallen smirked, and Emira laughed in response, playfully striking his arm.

"No," he finally responded. "You didn't offend me. Being with you, like that, it's everything. You are everything to me, Em."

Emira felt her cheeks turn a shade pinker at his words. She reached out and placed a hand in his, and it was swallowed up by the considerable size difference of his to her own.

"What is it then?" Emira asked curiously.

Tallen sighed deeply, his gaze avoiding hers.

"Hey," she continued, placing her free hand on his stubbled cheek. "Talk to me." Emira's eyes remained unblinking and wide with concern at his hesitation. "Are you leaving for an assignment?"

"No."

"Then what could possibly have you so worn?"

"Em," he began, "Have you heard the term *Soul Bond*? Do you know what it means?"

Emira was quiet for a moment while she considered her answer. She was still ignorant to so many things, as she had spent her time as a slave focused on staying alive.

"I have heard it," she admitted, "but I do not know the meaning. I suppose I've never really thought about it."

"It's a sort of connection," Tallen said. "An intimate link between souls. It's rare, and it's special. Very, very special."

"Okay…" She thought for a moment. "Do you choose your Soul Bond?"

"No," Tallen replied. "Some say it's the will of the gods; others say it has to do with being created from the same stardust at the beginning of time. Whatever the truth, it's rare. And real."

Silence filled the room as Emira tried to understand where the harpy was leading.

"Em," Tallen began, clutching both of her soft hands and shifting closer. "Nothing changes. You owe me nothing."

"I don't understand, Tallen. What are you trying to tell me?"

He gripped her hands tightly and heaved a sigh as he spoke. "You need to know. You *deserve* to know—"

"Are you bonded to someone?" Emira interrupted, trying to pull her hands from his, but Tallen only gripped her more tightly as he continued.

"You deserve to know that *we* are bonded, Em. *You* are my Soul Bond."

Emira froze, her mind refusing to bring forward words.

"Em," Tallen continued, his eyes pleading with her to listen. "I expect nothing. Do you understand? You owe me *nothing*."

"Why…" she breathed, as his words continued to process. "Why are you telling me this?"

"You deserve to know," he replied, squeezing her hands tighter still. "You deserve the truth and to know what this bond truly means."

"Do you own me?" Emira asked eagerly, fearfully, brazenly.

Tallen's lips parted, and his chest heaved.

"No, Em! Not like how you think. You own me, and I own you—we are one in the same."

Tears began welling in Emira's eyes, and she tried to turn her face away but was rooted in place at the idea of becoming a prisoner once again.

Tallen continued, desperately. "That nightmare you had, when Vyrion hurt you, I felt it." Emira's gaze snapped back to the harpy suspiciously, and she watched his lips as he spoke. "I felt your pain and your fear. I felt your hopelessness. It broke me, Em."

"You... *felt* it?" she whispered.

Tallen nodded slowly, "In a way. It's an intuition. I felt your panic, your horror."

"How long have you known?" Emira asked, her voice returning to a normal level.

Tallen sighed.

A while then, she thought.

"There was that first day in the kitchen," the harpy recalled, "you came looking for something to eat and the moment you placed your hand on that apple—"

Emira's mind trailed back to her second day in the Southern Realm. She had been proud to find the kitchen and startled to see Tallen there. She had picked up an apple...

"As soon as you touched it," he continued, "you thought about Vyrion, and everything that had happened to you. I know you did."

Emira lifted a trembling hand to her mouth. "How?"

Tallen nodded, a smile spreading across his dark face at her realization.

"You felt it?"

"I felt your shift in mood. You became fearful, and I could only imagine what caused your heart to race like that, what would cause you such panic."

Emira's eyes roamed over the harpy; his wings, his face, his hands that were still holding on to her own.

"I wanted to tell you that morning at Bri's," he said. "And every day since, I knew you needed to know. But being Bonded Souls... it can feel intrusive. And you've been through so gods-damned much."

Emira cut him off by swiftly pressing her lips to his. She hooked her arms around him and raked her fingers over his shoulders.

"Tallen," she said against his mouth. Pulling her closer, he lifted her up onto his lap. Emira straddled him, slipped her tongue between his lips, and kissed him deeply.

"I want to be near you. More than anyone else, I want to be near you," she confessed between kisses. "Is this the bond that I've been feeling?"

He draped an arm around her waist and ran his free hand up the length of her spine and into her golden hair.

"Yes," he whispered into her locks.

"I want this," Emira admitted. "If you are mine, then I am yours."

"I am yours, and only yours," Tallen vowed, "until the end of time."

The siren smiled and kissed along his neck, nipping playfully at his ear. She fisted his thick hair and whispered against his skin, "Then make me yours, Tallen."

With a throaty, possessive growl, the harpy tightened his grip on Emira's waist, and flipped her onto the bed. Her blonde hair sprawled over her face, and she chuckled as she brushed it away. Tallen wrenched his shirt over his head, flaring his wings as he freed them from the fabric, and tossed the clothing to the floor. His thick, muscular shoulders rounded into his broad torso. Emira drank in the sight of his sculpted warrior's body, from his chiseled abs and strong arms, to the faint scars and healed craters that peppered his tanned skin. Each muscle, each mark, was the result of nearly eight hundred years of battle and training. Thick cords under his skin flexed as he leaned over her, his Soul Bond, planting kisses along her cheeks, down her neck and along her collarbone.

Pinned beneath him, Emira began to shimmy out of her dress, returning kisses along his full shoulders, arms, and chest. Tallen reached down and freed her from the excessive fabric, wrenching the gown away and tossing it to the floor beside his shirt.

Emira gasped at the chill that crept along her skin as the harpy removed himself from above her. His icy eyes bore down, scanning her pebbling flesh. The siren felt her cheeks flush as he gazed, admiration flooding his features.

She sat upright with her knees parted, and Tallen nestled between them. His hands came to either side of her neck, and he titled her face up to his. The harpy wore an expression of true awe, his jaw slackened and his gaze soft.

"You are the most beautiful creature I have ever beheld," he confessed. As he leaned closer, he whispered, "My Soul Bond," before his lips met hers once more. For a wild moment, they were a passionate clashing of teeth and tongues. Tallen nipped at Emira's lower lip as her tongue swept across his upper one. He tasted like wine and dark chocolate, a delicious combination of bitterness and sweetness.

Emira hooked her fingers into the waist of the harpy's pants, eager to feel the entirety of his weight upon her again. As she slid the clothing down, his massive cock sprang free, thick and swollen with need. The siren clutched him close, starting with his muscle covered ribs, then sliding her grip down to his sculpted backside, and eventually landing on his robust, powerful thighs. The harpy moaned as her hands roamed over his skin, sweeping his tongue between her lips and allowing his hands to move freely as well.

The callouses that speckled Tallen's grip scraped lightly along Emira's flesh, sending shivers along her limbs. He started at the nape of her neck, moving slowly along the curve of her spine and over her full hips. As they landed, his grip tightened, clutching at the supple flesh that made up her curvaceous figure.

"You are everything." He smiled against her lips, leaning in even closer. His cock grazed the slickness between her legs, and twitched eagerly. Emira, too, shuddered at the teasing sensation, before gripping Tallen around the neck and pulling him atop her, the both of them supine on the mattress once more.

"Tallen, please," Emira begged against his lips.

He nudged himself against her slick entrance and she whimpered, bucking her hips closer to him. Slowly, the harpy settled, pressing into her, and slowly filling her to the hilt. She gasped at the pleasure, and squeezed her hands tighter around his shoulders, arching her back into him.

"Holy *gods*," Emira cried.

Tallen pumped his length in and out of her, rolling his hips as he did so, hitting the sensitive spot within Emira that made her muscles clench with pleasure. He swam in the sounds of her moans, reveling in the feeling of her core squeezing down on his cock.

As an orgasm swept over her, Emira felt the harpy's muscles tense. She looked up from her ardent haze to see Tallen's jaw clenched. His grip tightened on her wide spread thighs as his wing spread out behind him. The harpy began pumping his length in and out of her rapidly, his pleasure building faster and faster. His black, feathered wings came down around him and Emira both, cocooning them in downy darkness.

"Fuck," he gritted out.

And then he came with a thundering clamor, spilling himself inside his Soul Bond, before finally slowing himself to a stop.

Without a word, Emira settled beneath Tallen's arm and trailed light kisses along his muscled ribs as he positioned himself beside her, wings still embracing her tightly. He ran his fingers through her golden hair, and their bodies settled into an entanglement of bonded ecstasy.

Emira's heart swelled as she nestled closer to the harpy. Her Soul Bond. A bond that meant forever.

Against his tanned skin, she confessed, "I love you, Tallen."

"Emira," he breathed, turning on his side to face her. He took her face in one of his hands and replied, "I love you. More than you could ever fathom, I love you."

CHAPTER
THIRTY-TWO

Responses to Vyla's summons from the rulers of the other realms had come quickly, and without hesitation. And now, only seven days later, they were expected to arrive at any moment. King Alicus had arranged for his guests to lodge in the castle, in an effort to show hospitality and peace. It was an uncommon event to host so many rulers at once, and the air was thick with the tension and excitement among the servants who bustled about, preparing the fortress for such an occasion.

And while visits to Bri's, and the Valeldran River, became regular occurrences for Tallen and Emira, the curious eyes and gossiping tongues of those who inhabited the forest were anxiety inducing, so Emira chose to stay within the castle walls as often as she could. Tallen tried to assure her that the people remained unaware of the reason for the meeting of kings, but that only made their theories of her past and of her intentions even more outlandish. Emira was sure that rumors would reach to the east, and Vyrion would arrive as an unwelcome guest.

But now the anticipated day had come, and the servants paid little mind to anything besides their chores as they scurried about, cleaning rooms, prepping wash basins, folding linens, and cooking for the feast that was to take place that night.

Back in the bedroom that she now shared with Tallen, Emira gazed at her reflection in the full length mirror. Zuri had left her a gown to wear, one that she called 'perfectly appropriate for such an event.' The dress was the same blue as the Valeldran River, deep and with hints of purple. The neckline plunged between her breasts, and the back was almost entirely open, exposing her shoulder blades and the curve of her spine. The long, flowing sleeves ran down the tops of her hands and looped around her middle finger. As she walked, the skirts flowed like midnight ocean waves. Vyla had also loaned her a stunning sapphire necklace that glistened against her pale skin and complimented the gown.

Emira leaned more closely to the mirror as she added some pins into her hair, which was styled into a loose braid that draped over her shoulder and ran down the length of her torso. She hummed absentmindedly, curling a stray piece of hair around her finger.

Beyond the castle, a trumpet blared, jolting Emira from her nervous trance. She dashed to the balcony, her violet skirts trailing behind her like a waterfall of fine silk. The autumn air licked at her skin as she peered over the edge of the balustrade, pebbling her exposed flesh and sending a chill down her spine.

Lights flickered in the forest beyond, so many that Emira knew it to be the rulers and their parties. The trumpet blared again as the trailing of lights grew brighter, moving their way through the trees and toward the castle. She remained on the balcony for as long as she could bear the chill, hoping for a glimpse of the visitors.

As the first party emerged from the forest, Emira's breath was taken away. Each member of the party, however far away they were, had hair as white as snow. With the distance, Emira could not make out their faces, but their clothing and demeanor proved the leaders of the group to be soldiers. They all wore matching coats of white, while holding long spears at their sides. They marched in perfect rows, their footsteps like a drum beat on the path leading to the castle.

When they continued forward, Emira audibly gasped at the sight emerging from the trees. Following closely behind the army was what appeared to be a colossal bull. With a massive head easily seven feet from the ground, horns nearly three feet long protruding from each side, and hoof beats louder than the cracking of a whip, the beast was a fearsome sight. It's long, shaggy, brown fur swayed slightly with the breeze and with each stride it took. The bull was fitted with a large saddle, and atop it sat a male who Emira presumed to be king. She strained her eyes for a better look, but she was too high to see any clearer.

Emira made her way back inside and readied to descend to the throne room. She passed the mirror, catching a glimpse of the stray curl she had tried to tame. Continuing to hum, calming her nerves and filling the silence of her bedroom, she adjusted the loose curl once more and let her hands fall to her sides.

We're going to stop Vyrion, she thought to herself, exhaling deeply.

Suddenly, the violent crashing caused by the bedroom door being haphazardly flung open shook the ornamental mirror before her. Emira jolted, focusing her vision on the reflection of an unfamiliar fae male staring back at her from the doorway. She whirled to face him, her oceanic gown twirling around her legs with the motion. He was plain in appearance, with olive skin, and caramel hair. His clothing suggested that while he was no king, he was no servant either. His white tunic was trimmed with fine silk, and the rings on his fingers glistened in the evening rays that spilled into the room.

But his eyes were glazed over with a cloudy film. His expressionless gaze scanned the room, finally landing on Emira. They stared each other down as still as stone. Her magic rumbled beneath her skin, ready to burst from her body in defense.

"Leave," Emira commanded, attempting to sound brave. The male took a single step toward her, no expression changing his face.

"I said *leave*," she repeated as he took another step forward. "Stop!" A whirling ball of water pooled in her hand.

As he advanced again, Emira lifted her arm, preparing to strike.

Without warning, a strong gust of wind blew through the bedroom from the open balcony. Emira's gown flowed about wildly, her braid lifting from her shoulder. A small stack of books flew off of the nearby dresser, and the thick, dark curtains whipped about the room. The trees beyond the balcony began to shake as the wind picked up and thunder rumbled in the sky. A massive, dark flash flew across the room, taking down the intruding male.

Tallen.

He barreled into the intruder, their bodies clashing with a thunderous *crack*. They tumbled across the room, smashing into the wooden armoire. The fine furniture exploded underneath the weight of their struggle, and various sizes of splintered wood shot in all directions. Emira raised her arms and turned her head away instinctively, avoiding the debris flying toward her like rogue arrows.

Her gaze snapped back to the brawling males. She squinted against the blasts of air created by Tallen's massive, thrashing wings, propelling his body with every blow he delivered to the intruder's face, now a bloody, unrecognizable pulp. As her eyes focused, she saw Tallen's whip held tightly around his opponent's neck, the male's weak fingers gripping at the leather that held his windpipe closed.

The glinting of Tallen's blade flashed as Alicus' voice suddenly cut through the chaos.

"*Enough!*" the king roared.

Emira turned her head sharply in the direction of his voice. Alicus was standing in the doorway, dressed in finery. His forest green hair laid in straight strands around his pale face while a golden headdress stretched across his forehead, ends tucked behind his protruding, pointed ears.

The command in his voice echoed through the now destroyed space. The room quieted immediately. Tallen froze, holding his dagger in a raised position above the intruder, whose eyes were no longer clouded over, but a glistening hazel consumed with terror. A light sheen of sweat speckled the fae's face as he looked up at the harpy, whose expression commanded fear. His thick brows were furrowed over his hardened gaze, his lips pressed together in a tight line.

"Release him," Alicus ordered.

Tallen stood, a low growl resounding in his throat as he withdrew his whip and sheathed his knife.

The bloodied male turned onto his side, coughing up blood and clutching his purpled neck.

"What happened?" Alicus demanded of his assassin.

"He was coming for Emira," Tallen growled, his blue eyes blazing into the bloodied pulp on the floor in front of him.

"N-no," the male rasped, hand still against his throat. "I don't kn-know her. I don't… r-remember anything."

Tallen's jaw ticked and his icy gaze swirled savagely.

"His eyes," Emira said to Alicus quickly. "They were clouded. He wasn't himself."

"You will do no more damage," Alicus commanded the harpy, who nodded his understanding reluctantly. "Coburn is Ambassador to the Western Realm. He will answer to his king."

Tallen's fierce gaze remained on Coburn as he pointed a finger in the direction of the door.

"Out," he growled.

The ambassador scrambled to a stand, and quickly limped into the corridor, followed closely by a seething harpy.

Alicus held an arm out to Emira, his gentle expression and soft voice returning.

"Come," he said, "I shall escort you to meet the others."

Emira balked at Alicus, eyes moving back and forth between his face and his outstretched arm.

"What—" she stammered. Her gaze moved over the room, to the shattered furniture and the blood coated floor. "I don't understand."

"Neither do I," Alicus said with a smile. "But we must go, lest we be late. I'm sure King Hallend will have a thing or two to say about his ambassador being bloodied by one of my own."

The humor never left Alicus' tone, as if he were amused that Tallen had committed an act of violence.

Emira sighed heavily, turning her attention back to the southern king.

"Alright," she started.

"You look lovely," Alicus added quickly, his voice smeared with humor.

Emira huffed. "Thanks."

Heart still pounding, she accepted his outstretched arm with the silent plea that the rest of the evening occurred with less bloodshed.

CHAPTER
THIRTY-THREE

Emira gripped Alicus' arm fiercely as the double doors to the throne room opened. The fine, typically empty room was fitted with a large, round table of ashen wood. Surrounding it, were the familiar faces of Queen Zuri, Tallen, Xemile, and Vyla. Additionally, the bloodied ambassador stood shakily while being aggressively questioned by a lean fae male Emira did not recognize. His waist length hair of silver glistened at his backside as he motioned angrily between Coburn and Tallen. The tunic he donned was also silver, similar to his hair, and the sapphire-encrusted crown atop his head indicated his realm's wealth.

This had been the male she saw atop the bull earlier that evening.

His amethyst eyes darted to Alicus and Emira as they entered, and his pointed features screwed up in anger. As the target of his animosity, Emira felt intimidated, but when she looked up to King Alicus, his expression remained unbothered.

"A siren?!" the silver-haired fae blanched at Alicus as they walked closer to the center of the room.

The ambassador at his side kept his head lowered to the ground. His once white tunic was stained with the gushing of blood that had come from his nose and mouth. Beneath his eyes, his olive skin had turned purple with bruising. Tallen had beaten his face into a nearly unrecognizable state before attempting to slit his throat.

The angry fae male continued, "Why the fuck do you have one of those water dwelling demons here?"

"King Hallend," Alicus greeted politely, "an honor to see you again."

"What is the meaning of this?" Hallend seethed. "I send my ambassador ahead to inform of our arrival, and he is returned to me bloodied and beaten?"

"I will withhold my explanation of these events," Alicus responded, "until the arrival of the remaining rulers. So as to save myself from explaining twice."

As he spoke, Sarolina shuffled in hurriedly. She beckoned for Coburn to follow her, glancing up and down at his wounds, and tsking. With his king's swift permission, Coburn followed the witch briskly from the throne room.

As the remaining members of the party were seated, Hallend's purple eyes shifted from Alicus to Emira, and his lips curled in revulsion. Tallen took a hold of Emira's hand, their entwined fingers resting upon the table.

"How does the west fare, Hallend?" Zuri asked quickly.

She was dressed head to toe in emerald green and silver, the official colors of the Southern Realm. Her black hair was styled immaculately, braided up and away from her delicate face, with jewels tied into each intricate knot. Alicus, Emira noted, was dressed in matching colors, a show of unity between them.

"It is well," Hallend responded stiffly, eyes moving to the southern queen. He reluctantly took a seat near her. "Better than ever, in fact."

"How wonderful to hear," Zuri responded. Her radiating white smile and bright eyes seemed to slightly ease the tension that hung in the air.

"The mountains," the silver haired king continued, "have been producing an abundance of gems, and ice is never in short supply."

"I have to admit," came a booming, unfamiliar voice from the entryway, "trade with Hallend has been magnificent. With those gems, I can buy anything I want from the Mortal Realm." All eyes turned on the newcomer. There was no hiding who he was.

King Ellis of the Northern Realm.

Tallen's father.

Aside from the thick, red scar that crossed through the king's left eye, Tallen was the spitting image of him. Ellis was tall and broad, with dark hair and icy blue eyes. His frame was muscular, and his sharp jawline looked as if it could cut through steel. Ellis swaggered into the throne room, his black velvet cloak whipping behind him like a flag in the wind. His heavy boots fell in loud footfalls as he approached the table, plopping onto the seat beside Alicus. Emira caught the shimmer of a dagger at his side as his eyes landed on her.

"Your messages failed to mention a siren, emissary," Ellis stated. Emira and Ellis' eyes remained locked as Vyla answered.

"That was of no importance."

"Like hell it wasn't!" Hallend retorted, fist landing heavily upon the table.

"Please, Hallend," Alicus began, "contain your outrage. I have promised you answers, have I not?"

Hallend huffed, glancing again at Emira distrustfully.

"Thank you for coming, King Ellis," Zuri said diplomatically.

"We are appreciative of your long journey," Alicus added. "You are, of course, the furthest from the south. I'm sure the journey was tiring."

"You doubt my stamina." Ellis laughed. "Am I looking that old?"

"How long did you travel?" Xemile asked.

Ellis sat next to the general as he responded. "Five days on the road. We stopped to rest for six hours each night, but the gods were forgiving. No rain or sleet to slow us down."

Emira leaned in closer to Tallen, whispering in his ear, "Why didn't he just use transference?"

Tallen shifted in his chair in order to lean into Emira. "Transference only works within each realm. No one can transfer between the fae realms. The wards make it impossible."

Ellis' eyes landed on the whispering couple, his gaze shifting between them and their entwined hands.

"I'm glad to hear you had no trouble," Zuri finalized. "I hope your accommodations will be satisfactory."

Polite conversation followed. Emira did not speak but watched and listened to the two new kings. They were vastly different in personality, Hallend being more reserved and speaking quietly with a smiling Zuri while Ellis' voice boomed, filling the room with his words and energetic disposition. His gaze rotated between Xemile, who spoke enthusiastically of war strategies with the northern king, and Emira's entwined fingers with the harpy.

After a few minutes, the doors opened once more to reveal a fae couple. A king with brown skin and dark eyes entered with his queen, who was also blessed with the same russet features. The king was dressed in golden robes and his long, dreadlocked hair was held back with golden twine. His queen wore her hair in a wildly curled afro, tamed with a silken ribbon of gold to match her dress, and her husband.

"Melazir!" Alicus beamed. "Luiza! We are grateful to the gods for your arrival."

The newcomers wore expressions of gratitude as they entered, finding empty chairs alongside Ellis.

"We are appreciative of your hospitality," King Melazir said. "The south is sure to be of comfort after the precarious boat ride from the islands."

"The waters were rough?" Xemile asked.

"Autumn seas are like a cat," Queen Luiza answered humorously. "One day, they are lazy, and barely acknowledge your presence at all. But the next, they are a fierce predator set to destroy anything they set their eyes on."

Xemile glanced deliberately at Vyla and muttered, "Don't I know it?"

His snarky remark was met with a hateful glare from the shifter, which only instigated his mischievous smirk.

"Although I hear Coburn has had a more dangerous journey than ourselves," Melazir commented, looking to Alicus for clarification about the rumor he had no doubt heard upon his arrival.

"Yes, but before we begin," Alicus started, "I hope you all will enjoy an extravagant feast. Let us fill our bellies with food and wine before we discuss political matters."

At the promise of wine, Ellis hooted his acceptance while Xemile banged his fist on the table thrice to show his appreciation. Even Hallend's face seemed to relax upon the promise of food and alcohol.

Alicus threw a wink in Emira's direction, easing the tension in her shoulders as servants began shuffling in while carrying silver trays and goblets of faerie wine. The worst was over. It had to be.

DINNER WAS, AS ALICUS PROMISED, DELECTABLE. ASIDE FROM THE Mabon celebration, it was the most food Emira had ever seen in one place. Each tray, once emptied, was swiftly replaced with another by the servants of the Southern Realm. They swooped in like hawks, with new appetizers and desserts that rivaled any she had ever seen or heard of before.

They were blessed with various meats ranging from thick steaks of venison to large filets of fish from the Valeldran River. Candied carrots, mashed potatoes, freshly sauteed green beans and roasted parsnips sat alongside the meats, adding color to the table. Chocolate mousse and strawberry cheesecakes were accessible on either end of the table, and even Tallen, face like stone throughout the meal, was unable to resist their sweet, beckoning scents. Many bottles of faerie wine were opened and finished, opened and finished, as the rulers around the room ate, drank, and spoke as if there had not been a disorderly beginning to the meeting at all.

King Ellis was the liveliest, speaking the most and the loudest, animatedly with his hands and facial expressions. The vermilion scar that ran through his eye danced along his face with every booming laugh or smile the king flashed, only adding to the various countenances he presented. But as social as he was, he did not look in the direction of his son, Tallen, except to occasionally glance at the harpy's hand clutching Emira's.

King Hallend spoke the least. His expression remained sour, his pale lips pressed into a thin line, and his body language stoic. He barely moved, except to aggressively spear a piece of red meat onto his fork. His answers about the west came with few words at a time, only softening his expression slightly when Queen Zuri spoke to him. His amethyst eyes glanced at Emira occasionally. They were full of hatred and distrust, but his gaze would quickly flick away when Tallen leaned slightly forward in warning. Alicus noted the motion but allowed it.

However, Melazir and Luiza were kind to everyone, equally involving themselves in conversation around the table, asking questions about the Southern Realm and the recent Mabon celebration.

"We wish we could have attended," Luiza started. "I would have loved to see the auburn foliage."

"You see, Emira," Melazir began, placing his elbow on the table and leaning in her direction with a smile, "the Island Realm is in a constant state of summer. Our leaves are greener than those of any other realm, and they stay that way year round."

"Is it unbearably warm?" Emira asked curiously.

"Perfectly comfortable," Luiza answered with a smile. Her bright, white teeth contrasted against her rich, mahogany skin, and her eyes narrowed slightly with the upturn of her mouth. "Part of our island is covered in rainforest, so we have a warm, rainy season for some time, followed by the warm, sunny season. It is perfectly balanced, as the gods intended."

"You didn't mention the humidity," Xemile added, his tone beyond snarky. He turned his attention to Emira as he added, "Those few weeks between rain and sun are as wet as the water surrounding the islands themselves."

Melazir and Luiza threw back their heads in laughter at the warrior's complaint, without denying its validity.

The double doors reopened, revealing an entirely healed Coburn. His eyes were bright, as if he had not been entranced only hours ago. His skin looked refreshed as well, no signs of lacerations or bruising to be seen. He bowed his head respectfully before entering the room, and finding a seat next to his king. The room was quiet as he did so, all eyes upon him, searching for the answers to their unspoken queries. Emira found, however, that she could not look directly into his eyes. Shame and fear overwhelmed her, so she kept her eyes cast downwards as he finally sat.

"You're looking well," Queen Zuri stated, holding a plate of fresh food in his direction politely.

"Sarolina is a wonder, Your Highness," the ambassador answered, accepting the meal.

"That she is," Alicus agreed. "I suppose now is as good a time as any to discuss the purpose of our gathering," Alicus tested.

His statement was met with nods and murmurs of agreement. As the rulers around the table placed the goblets and cutlery down, servants rushed forward to clear the surface. Emira followed as Tallen did, allowing her plate and napkins to be whisked away. Cups were refilled with wine, a pot of tea placed before the southern queen, and within minutes, the table was refreshed with not a crumb left behind.

Alicus sighed and stood. Zuri did the same, taking his hand in her own. "I have invited you here today," Alicus began, "to discuss a most pressing issue. Vyrion is keeping slaves in the Eastern Realm, and in doing so, has committed a breach of contract."

The group went silent for a moment, the rulers looking between each other.

"That's not possible," Ellis finally stated. "He is death bound by treaty."

Alicus and Zuriel took turns explaining to the events of the previous weeks, starting with finding Emira in the woods, the night terrors she had endured, the injuries sustained in sleep, her testimony about the eastern king, and ending with her most recent evolution of abilities while training.

"And you believe your siren had something to do with Coburn's unfortunate entrance?" Ellis started.

"*Emira.*"

Tallen growled the first word he spoke aloud to the group. All eyes fell upon the harpy, whose own gaze speared viciously in the direction of his father. "You will address her as Emira. Or Miss Emira if you had any shred of respect."

Ellis' expression darkened as he stared at the harpy from across the table. Emira sucked in a sharp breath, squeezing Tallen's hand in warning.

"I see you have not changed," Ellis responded scornfully. "Still as contemptuous as ever. Tell me, Tallen…" The king of the Northern Realm spoke directly to his estranged son now as the others looked on, an invisible audience to their conversation. Ellis' eyes flicked once more to Tallen and Emira's entwined hands before asking, "Is it the cunt of a siren that has you forgetting your manners?"

Emira's hand jerked as Tallen ripped his own free. He stood swiftly, his wings spreading widely behind him. The whip at his side slithered excitedly as the harpy seethed in the direction of his father. Xemile stood in unison with the harpy, only he extended an arm in Tallen's direction, a silent command to stand down. Ellis did not react, except for smirking in the direction of his bastard son. The two males kept their icy eyes fixed on each other, time standing still around them as old tension filled the space.

"What is it you plan to do?" Ellis taunted from his seat. "Are you going to kill me, Tallen? Will you use the weapon *I* gifted you to squeeze my throat and end my life?"

"Ellis, please," Alicus began.

"Sit *down*, Tallen," Xemile ordered.

Tallen's jaw ticked as the commander spoke. He glanced briefly at Xemile, whose amber eyes were wide, his arm still outstretched in warning. With a quick shift of his wings, Tallen sat once more, gaze never leaving that of his father's. Xemile followed, letting out a relieved breath as he did.

"Emira," Tallen started, voice low and menacing, "is my Soul Bond."

The smugness on King Ellis' face disintegrated and was replaced with disbelief. His eyes shot to Emira, his lips slightly parted, as he allowed the information to sink in.

"Your Soul Bond," Ellis repeated.

Suddenly, King Hallend burst out into laughter. All eyes landed on him as shock filled the room by his response.

"How about that!" he laughed. "The bastard son of the north, bonded to a *siren*, of all the options! You'd best be happy he left your service—" Ellis' face hardened further, his ears turning red.

It was apparent to Emira that Tallen leaving the north was an infuriating topic for the king. "He and that bloodthirsty water beast would have taken down your entire realm!"

"I've heard enough," Ellis boomed. Hallend continued to laugh.

"We are severely off track," Vyla interjected. The sound of her authoritative voice halted the western king's laughter, and quieted the northern king's rage. "Act as the kings you are and cease this meaningless squabbling. Have you all traveled this far to play 'whose dick is bigger'?"

Silence followed the shifter's harrowing command. Xemile's amber eyes trailed slowly to Vyla, and when their gazes met, he winked impishly.

The king of the north turned his attention to Emira. His eyes roamed over her twice before he spoke.

"So, *Emiraaa*," he drew out the length of her name mockingly, "how did you do it? How were you able to overtake Coburn's mind so easily?"

Emira hesitated, unable to answer. Had she been the one to make Coburn lose himself?

"We were unaware of the hypnosis ability shown today," Vyla added quickly. "Emira included."

"Hypnosis?" blanched Zuri.

"Ahh, yes," Melazir cut in. "Maidens that can simply sing to ensnare their prey. Our realm has stories of the waterfolk."

Emira turned her attention to the island rulers.

"It does?" she asked eagerly. "What do they say? What are the stories?"

"I will not sit here and listen to the tall tales of the island fae," Hallend began, standing. Coburn stood as well, eyes remaining lowered. "And I refuse to remain with water demons and those who harbor them."

"You should listen to what we have to say," Xemile began, "for your realm's sake."

"You dare order a king?" Hallend questioned, his crystal-like eyes glinting with anger.

"Vyrion must be held accountable for breaking this treaty," Alicus cut in.

"You are young, Alicus," Hallend began mockingly. "One female's word against a king is little to go to war over, especially not for the sake of a *siren*," Hallend sneered in Emira's direction. He stood tall, glancing at Coburn once before stating, "I tire of this conversation. I will take my leave and retire to my rooms." The king turned and left, Coburn following closely behind while Tallen glared at their backs.

The double doors slammed closed when the males left, leaving the remaining members of the party in the echoing silence.

"He's always been a joy," Xemile stated aloud.

Alicus inhaled deeply before turning his attention to Melazir and Luiza.

"I would like to hear your tales, Melazir," Alicus began. "Unfortunately, my library is lacking in waterfolk references. Perhaps you can shed some light about Emira's kin."

"As an island realm," Luiza began, "we have many stories of the sea that you may not."

Ellis straightened his back as he interjected, "The north is a port realm, my men are at sea all the time. We have no such tales of sirens or waterfolk."

Luiza's golden eyes flashed in the northern king's direction. "Sirens would avoid your realm at all costs, Ellis. Too many land dwellers, all using the sea to their own advantage."

Ellis gave her a mockingly incredulous look. "I've always believed the island fae to be illusory, but you speak of an underwater race that has not been seen or heard from in the gods know how long, if ever. I will not go to war over a children's tale."

"Far from children's tales," King Melazir replied. "The sirens of our stories are fierce and territorial. You should be grateful they do not destroy your ports and take their waters back."

Ellis' expression hardened, and he turned to face Emira.

"Do you wish to tear down my ports, girl?" he questioned.

"I *wish*," Emira began, straightening her spine, "to tear down Vyrion's rule. There are fae and shifters and mortals there at this very moment, who are suffering gravely, because Vyrion has somehow broken the treaty."

"And why," came Ellis' voice, "should we sacrifice lives and resources over something as insignificant as a broken promise?" Tallen shifted in his seat, and his wings rustled behind him. Ellis stood and continued, "I never liked Vyrion, but even if he is keeping slaves, he has only broken a promise, not a law, and I will not waste resources bringing down his court. The realms have only been at peace for a thousand years. Much of the trauma from the Shifter Genocide is still fresh to those who lived through it."

Alicus' chest heaved as Ellis, throwing one last angry look in Tallen's direction, turned, and left the throne room.

Melazir sighed regrettably. He looked at Luiza and took her hand in his.

"I wish we could help," the king said to Alicus and Zuriel. His gaze turned to Emira's. "I'm sympathetic to your trauma. Truly." The king and queen of the Island Realm stood in unison.

"Please reconsider," Zuri begged.

"You must understand," Melazir started, "that Coburn is a fairly powerful male, and your siren took hold of his mind without even being in the same room."

Emira's breath caught at his words. Perhaps if she had not felt compelled to hum away her nerves, the realms would be more willing to help.

"We can offer gold and weapons to aid your mission," Queen Luiza started, "but we cannot ask our people to fight for something, or someone, they do not understand. The others have seen their fair share of bloodshed. They will be guarded against more if it can be avoided."

Silence.

Emira's stomach dropped. Vyrion would continue his treachery. The other realms were going to allow it. The very ones that fought against the past kings in the Shifter Genocide were going to ignore the keeping and brutalization of slaves in the east.

And she was powerless.

"Perhaps," came Alicus' voice, "you will think on it while in the south." The king stood, followed by Zuri, who stepped around her chair to his side.

"We can offer that in exchange for your hospitality." Luiza smiled.

The rulers ended the meeting diplomatically, but Emira couldn't hear their words over the buzzing in her mind. Tallen gripped her hand and led her from the throne room, back to their chambers, where she raged into the night.

CHAPTER
THIRTY-FOUR

Emira found herself in the training arena with Xemile after lunch. Her anger over the failed meeting had bled into the following day, with no end in sight. How could the other realms have made their decisions so quickly? How could they, after fighting so hard to end the shifter genocide, allow Vyrion to keep slaves?

Emira channeled her anger, using the force of vexation within her, to bloody Xemile's lip, blacken his eye and pin him beneath her boot.

"Damn, Emira," Xemile said from beneath her shoe, "you're a beast today."

Emira did not smile but removed her foot and held her hand out to the general. He accepted, gripping firmly, and stood. Xemile clapped his free hand upon her shoulder.

"It doesn't have anything to do with yesterday, does it?" he jested.

"I don't want to talk about it," Emira snapped, ripping her hand free from his and lunging backwards into position.

"Alright," Xemile answered, a curved smile spreading across his bruised face. "I suppose you can just keep beating me into oblivion."

Emira pulled a dagger from her boot and spun it skillfully in her hand, testing its weight and adjusting her grip.

"Whoa, whoa!" Xemile started, hands raised defensively. "No weapons, not while you're this fired up."

"I'm *fine,*" Emira said through gritted teeth.

"If you come at me with that right now, I'm bound to lose an eye," Xemile retorted.

"Scared of a *female*, Xemile?" came a voice from the top of the arena stairs. Xemile's eyes moved past Emira, and she spun. King Ellis was strolling down the stone steps, his black cape trailing behind him.

Emira turned back to the general with her jaw clenched and her chest heaving. She'd decided that she hated the northern king. She hated him for the role he played in Tallen's youth as well as for his words the day before. He was a venomous snake, an arrogant slug that did not deserve her attention.

"You turn your back on a king?" Ellis' voice was closer now, his footsteps growing louder and louder until Emira felt his presence right behind her.

"I have nothing to say to you," she responded, sliding the dagger back into her boot. Xemile raised a brow at her insubordinate response, but Ellis only released a booming laugh.

Emira spun, fuming at the northern ruler's conceit.

"How *dare* you?" she started, stomping towards the fae male.

"Emira, don't!" Xemile shouted upon deaf ears.

"You insult me," she continued, marching ever closer to Ellis. "You insult Tallen. You *refuse* to help a realm in need. And now you approach me demanding the respect of a king?"

"Emira!" Xemile gripped her arm, but she pulled away and stood chest to chest with Ellis.

He was so tall that she had to crane her neck to see his face. His blue eyes looked down on her and glistened with curiosity, the red scar across his eye crinkling as he smirked.

"You are no king that I respect," Emira stated.

"But Tallen has your respect? A half-blood harpy with no allegiance to his own realm?" Ellis dared.

Xemile stepped beside them, torn between honoring royal hierarchy and defending a member of his realm's court.

"Emira, step back," the general commanded. Emira did not listen.

"Tallen may be half harpy," she started, "but he has more honor in one wing than you do in your entire *full-blooded fae* body."

Xemile released a puff of breath, defeated.

Ellis leaned back and looked Emira up and down. With a smirk, he muttered, "Soul Bond indeed."

There was a beat of silence between the three of them before Ellis spoke again.

"Has Xemile been your combat coach thus far?" He stepped away from Emira and headed for the various weapons that were kept off to the side of the arena.

"Yes," Emira answered warily.

Ellis picked up a large dagger, longer than his hand, and curved in the blade.

"Want to show me what you've learned, siren?" the northern ruler taunted.

"It would be an unfair fight, and you know it," Emira responded.

"I'll go easy on you," Ellis answered. "Show me what the southern general has taught you thus far."

"I have no intention of sparring with you, nor do I want to continue this conversation."

Emira turned on her heel and made her way towards the ascending steps.

A whirring of silver flashed past her eye, and Emira turned to see that Ellis had hurled the dagger in her direction. The king's smile had grown, and before Xemile could intervene, Emira lunged.

Ripping the dagger free from her boot, Emira raised the blade against Ellis. He countered with a blade he had hidden at his side, and both weapons came down upon each other with an ear shattering *clang.* Emira spun out and away from her massive opponent, throwing an elbow into his ribs as she did so. Ellis buckled, grasping at his side and the injury he did not expect the siren to inflict. With a grunt, he undid the clasp of his cape, allowing it to flutter to the stone ground. He pulled another dagger from his belt and flipped both blades skillfully in his hands.

"Clever girl," Ellis teased.

"Emira," Xemile interjected, "cease this immediately. He is a *king.*"

"He is not *my* king," Emira responded, her eyes burning into the northern ruler.

"Come then," Ellis challenged, stepping towards her. "Can you only block a blow and escape?"

"To what end would you like to see my skill?" Emira challenged, venom dripping from her words.

"Until my satisfaction," the fae ruler responded. He stepped towards her again, and Emira responded in kind, marching towards him with a flip of her weapon. She was sick of his arrogance and his entitlement. She was going to end this.

Now.

She blocked his blow as he aimed for her abdomen, using her knife's blade against his. With a firm rotation of her wrist, she pushed his weapon away and lifted her own. In return, he grabbed her arm and held it in place above her head. She pushed her knee hard into his gut, and as he bent forward with the intensity of the strike, she threw her forehead into his nose with crack.

Ellis staggered back, touching the bloodied flesh with a jarred expression. His eyes roamed from the blood on his hand to Emira.

"Satisfied?" Emira taunted.

Ellis stormed forward, his icy blue eyes swirling viciously. For a moment, Emira faltered. With a swift kick to Emira's hand, Ellis relieved her of her weapon, sending waves of pain through her arm. He used sheer muscle and force to grab her by the front of her training leathers and held her a few inches from the ground. They were now face to face, Emira weaponless, feet dangling—and Ellis' bloodied, pride hurt.

"An unfair fight you say," he repeated, turning to the side and spitting blood.

Still in his grip, Emira swallowed and lifted her gaze to his.

"For you," she responded.

Before Ellis was able to understand her meaning, Emira drove her knee between the northern ruler's legs. He dropped to the ground, releasing her as he did so. Emira stumbled as the king crumpled before her. She found her balance and took a few steps backwards to pick up the knife he had kicked away.

"Do not underestimate me again," she said, voice strong and sure. "And do not speak of my *cunt* again, or next time I will ensure to cut off your balls so that you may have one of your very own."

Xemile gaped, entirely too shocked to react. Emira turned on her heel and headed for the stone steps. Her gaze shifted to the top, where Tallen stood, arms crossed over his chest, wings splayed, and a smile upon his face.

CHAPTER
THIRTY-FIVE

"I apologize if I've made things more difficult for you," Emira said to Tallen as he escorted her back to their shared bedroom. She needed to remove her sweat and blood stained training leathers. And shower. And eat.

"You've done no such thing," the harpy responded, holding open the door as they entered. As soon as she heard the lock click, Emira peeled off the sullied clothing, her bare, sweat slicked body on full display. As she made her way to the bathing chamber, Tallen admired the way she moved, the way her hair fell against her back in golden waves as she untied it from its braid. His waistband tightened slightly, and he pulled his gaze away with a smirk.

"The only thing you've done," he continued, "is make my father respect you."

The rushing water of the tub echoed as Emira answered, voice raised over the sound, "How do you mean?"

Tallen strolled to the doorway and leaned against the frame as Emira dipped her body slowly into the steaming water.

"Ellis was a highly trained war general before he was ever a king," the harpy reminded her. "He values strength and skill over titles. Beating him in the arena is one of the only ways to gain that respect."

"It was a dishonorable win," Emira argued, dipping her hair back into the water. "I would have lost if I had not let my anger get in the way of my integrity."

"That's a credit to your character, Em, to believe that." Tallen's eyes followed as Emira sat upright and lathered her hair with soap. "But integrity does not exist on the battlefield as it does in the training arena. You were challenged, and you met that challenge."

Emira smiled softly at the harpy before rinsing her hair and squeezing out the excess water. "Do you think Alicus and Zuri will be upset with me? Xemile didn't seem pleased."

Tallen huffed a laugh. "Ellis will not speak of this to anyone. His pride has been hurt, and he won't be seeking to admit defeat, especially not to another ruler."

Emira felt her shoulders relax at Tallen's words. She believed him. Ellis was boastful, and she knew nothing ill would come from their sparring. She reached for the still running faucet, and turned the water off.

"If only it was so easy to gain the favor of Hallend," Emira mumbled.

Tallen, still leaning against the doorframe, responded, "Ellis respects strength, and the ability to wield a blade. But Hallend has a strategic and intellectual mind. And he's stubborn as hell. It's what made him a triumphant war leader."

Emira considered his words. If she were to gain Hallend's favor, she could try again to rally him to her cause. But it was clear that sparring would not earn her the same respect with Hallend as it did with Ellis. She would have to manipulate the western ruler's values as she did in the arena with the northern ruler.

She formed a plan as she finished washing. She lifted the drain plug and stepped out of the tub basin. Tallen handed her a towel, and as she cocooned herself in the warm, plush fabric, the harpy snuggled her close in one swift pull of his arms. With his thumb and forefinger, he gently lifted her chin, their eyes locking instantly.

"You are everything," the harpy purred, his voice low.

"You say that all the time," Emira smirked. "What does it even mean?"

Tallen placed a gentle kiss on her forehead, the tip of her nose, and each of her cheeks before finally grazing her lips with his own. "It means you are my everything, Em. You are my light. You are my stars. You are the very air I breathe. Everything I do, every-thing I am, it is with you on the forefront of my mind."

Emira's heart lurched at his words, at the sincerity of them. She looped her arms around his neck, allowing her towel to fall to the floor, and pressed a kiss to his lips. As she pressed her naked body against the fabric of his clothing, she felt his body tighten, and the waist of his pants protruding.

The siren parted her lips, allowing his tongue to sweep in over her own. She sucked on his lower lip in return, which earned a groan from deep within Tallen's throat.

"Bed?" Emira asked, as she began trailing kisses along the harpy's neck.

Tallen gripped her waist, his hands roaming along the smooth skin of her hips. "I'm perfectly capable of taking you right here," he responded.

With that, the harpy lifted Emira and held her tightly against him. She pressed her lips to his, as Tallen took a few steps forward, pinning Emira against the wall. Adjusting his grip to hold under-neath her thighs, Tallen lowered himself to one knee, and ran his mouth down between her breasts, along her abdomen and below her navel.

"Tallen," Emira breathed as her body tensed, hips rolling in his tight grip. Her core tightened as his face disappeared beneath her.

The first stroke of his tongue sent fire rushing through her body. He licked her cunt slowly, lazily, and it drove Emira mad. With no blanket or pillow to grip, Emira clenched her fists in Tallen's black curls.

The second stroke of his tongue remained slow but penetrated her more deeply. Her body quivered, still only being held up by Tallen's sheer strength.

The third stroke of his tongue quickened and ended with him gently sucking on her clit. A rush of heat traveled through Emira as her pleasure built. She gripped his hair harder, searching for some semblance of grounding as the harpy shifted his hands, placing them on her bottom and lifting her up even higher against the wall. He stood, and Emira felt as if she were floating.

The siren placed her legs over each of the harpy's shoulders, stabilizing herself as she felt her climax approaching. Tallen continued sucking on her clit, lazily lapping at the wetness between her legs. As she came, Emira cried out the harpy's name, and in return, he held her tightly, keeping her back pressed against the wall while never breaking contact between his mouth and her core.

Emira's body relaxed as she swam in the remnants of her orgasm. Tallen slowly lowered her back down, not releasing his grip until her feet touched the floor. His hands went to either side of her face, and he claimed her with a deep kiss.

"I'm not done with you," he growled into her mouth.

With a swift flip, the harpy turned Emira, her back now pressed up against his chest. He reached around her curvaceous frame, one hand gripping her breast, as the other working between her legs.

Emira felt her body go limp in his grasp. Her knees buckled as his fingers stroked her core, pumping in and out until she could no longer stand it.

"The tub," Tallen said, passionate desperation lining his voice. "Hold the edge of the tub."

Emira did as she was told, leaning down and placing both hands on the edge of the porcelain rim. The shuffling of Tallen undoing his belt sounded behind her, and she bit her lip in anticipation.

One of Tallen's strong hands gripped Emira's hip while he used the other to guide himself to her entrance. Emira arched her back, waiting for the release that Tallen was about to provide. With one gentle push, he filled her, and Emira cried out in relief. She gripped the edge of the tub harder as he began thrusting. His cock filled her, stretched her, and she panted as he found a rhythm.

"Fuuuck, Em," Tallen growled as his hands roamed over her backside, caressing her ass and running up the length of her spine. He touched her hair, still wet from her bath, and gripped it at the root. Emira moaned as he lifted her head up. With his other hand, Tallen reached around the siren and down between her legs. He rubbed her clit in lazy circles as he picked up speed behind her.

Emira's vision went hazy as her orgasm built. The harpy worked her, and the tightness that was low in her belly felt like it would explode at any moment.

"Tallen," she gasped. "I'm so close, gods, Tallen."

"That's it, Em," he responded, his voice gruff. "Come for me."

With a cry, Emira climaxed, her orgasm flowing through her body like electricity. And as she came, Tallen sped up, his thrusting becoming desperate and frenzied. A deep roll of thunder rattled the walls as the harpy finished, his cock pumping come into the siren.

He slowed, breathing heavily. Emira released one last moan as the harpy finally unsheathed himself. She stood, turning to face her Soul Bond. His wings enveloped the both of them, and he planted kisses atop her head.

Emira glanced up, the harpy's blue gaze already on her.

"*You* are everything, Tallen."

CHAPTER
THIRTY-SIX

Emira awoke early the next morning and found herself unable to calm her racing thoughts. She slid from the bed, careful to not wake the harpy, before she dressed and padded through the corridors of the castle.

She made for the library, seeking out the comfort of books and silence as well as the warmth of the early morning rays that shone through the domed window above the athenaeum. When she entered, she strolled leisurely past the shelves of novels and tomes and history books that she had been scouring since her arrival in the south. As she silently read the titles to herself, she was able to quiet her own swift and self-destructive thoughts.

But her peace was soon interrupted. As she turned a corner, she came face to face with King Hallend. They both stopped abruptly, taking in the sight of each other for a moment. The western king was dressed in fine robes of white, his equally snowy hair pulled back and braided away from his face. His sharp features stared down at her, his violet eyes fiercely examining the siren.

She held his stare, refusing to take a step back.

"King Hallend," Emira said icily, bowing her head ever so slightly.

"*Siren*," he sneered in reply.

Emira swallowed the lump of anger rising in her throat. "What brings you here so early?"

The western ruler's gaze flicked to the shelves of books, and he scanned them as he answered, "The sun is insufferable."

"What?"

"The sun," Hallend repeated. "It rises earlier and sets later here than in my kingdom."

"Oh," Emira answered, unsure what else to say. "I…" she began, "I couldn't sleep either."

Hallend only grunted in response before walking around the siren and continuing forward. Emira watched his back as he passed, mind racing once again.

This was her chance. This was possibly her *only* chance to gain Hallend's favor.

"Your kingdom," Emira started, halting the ruler. He did not turn as she continued, "mines ice and gems."

Hallend turned his head slightly so that he could gaze upon her with disdain.

"*Very good*," he responded patronizingly.

Emira snubbed out the rage that built in her chest, choosing instead to walk up alongside the king and continue speaking.

"Is Coburn well?" she asked, swiftly changing the subject.

Hallend stopped mid stride, Emira halting beside him. He looked down at her as he answered, "Why are you speaking to me?"

His voice dripped with derision.

"Is your hatred for me so great?" Emira balked.

Hallend only scoffed in response. Emira searched his hard face for a clue, an answer. But one did not come.

"Your contempt cannot be so strong that you would ignore the enslavement of thousands of others? Did you not fight for the shifter's lives only a thousand years ago?"

"I do not *trust* you," he responded through gritted teeth. "And I do not trust the judgment of so young a king as Alicus."

Hallend turned, his back shrinking away from Emira once more. She stammered, searching for the words that would make him change his mind. It hit her like a punch to the gut, the air leaving her lungs before she could speak.

"Queen Zuriel has placed her trust in me," Emira finally said to the icy king's back. "She will fight."

Hallend pivoted, his expression cold and his violet eyes sharply observing the siren before him. Emira continued, quickly so as to not lose his attention, "*She* would die for those who suffer in the east."

Hallend seemed to grow taller as he inhaled deeply, straightened his shoulders, and turned up his nose. "Queen Zuriel is none of my concern."

"No?" Emira replied incredulously. She took slow, steady steps towards the fae king. "Yesterday was enough to prove otherwise."

Hallend's eyes flashed, the only sign that he may have been shocked by Emira's boldness. His gaze quickly returned to his usual frigid stare as he responded. "Get to the point, *siren*."

"You do not care for the lives of those who suffer in the east. You do not care that Vyrion is using an unknown magic to enter my mind. And I'm sure to believe you do not care for much outside of your own wants and needs." There was a pause as Emira stopped before the king, close enough that, if he wanted to, he could reach out and grab her around the throat. "But you *care* for the southern queen."

Hallend and Emira stared at each other. Seconds ticked by, but neither one of them softened their gaze.

Finally, the fae king's shoulders relaxed slightly. A smile tugged at the corners of his mouth, but his expression remained cold.

"I admire your stubbornness," he finally said. "But Queen Zuriel's choices do not affect my own. I will not come to your aid."

With that, Hallend turned and walked away, a ghostly silhouette against the morning sun.

CHAPTER THIRTY-SEVEN

Emira did not participate in the conversation being held at dinner that evening. She was overwrought with her failure to secure the western king's alliance, and she glanced at him only occasionally from across the large, round table. But his focus remained fixed on the food in front of him or the southern queen when she spoke.

"You promised us stories," the queen began in the direction of the island rulers.

Melazir's face beamed at the opportunity to speak of his home.

"Any sort, or siren related?" he asked, throwing a wink in Emira's direction.

"Perhaps siren related would be the most beneficial to us," Alicus answered humorously.

"Not that we don't enjoy all of your tales, Melazir," Zuri added.

The island king laughed, his dark eyes crinkling at the corners as he did.

"You will only encourage him," Luiza smiled.

"Our land has many tales of the waterfolk," Melazir began theatrically. It was met with an eye roll from his queen and a chuckle from Zuri. "The tale of the siren is probably one of the oldest."

Emira shifted in her seat, eager and anxious at the same time. She reminded herself that a story may not hold any truth, but she was hopeful that something the island king said would lead to further information.

"Sirens present as beautiful females, nothing more than any other land dweller in form," Melazir continued. "But truly, they are ruthless creatures of the deep, luring males to the depths of the seas."

Hallend grunted bitterly. Emira gritted her teeth against her annoyance and continued listening to Melazir.

"That, we know," the island king continued, looking in Emira's direction, "is an exaggeration. Emira seems perfectly content to live amongst land dwellers. No instinct to take any of us away to the wild waters!"

Melazir and Luiza chuckled politely, and Emira smiled.

"No," she responded, "I don't plan on stealing anyone away to... Where was it you said?"

"The wild waters," Luiza answered. "It just means the sea, or the ocean. Not the lakes or rivers with fresh waters, but the salty abyss where sirens dwell."

Emira didn't answer, but looked between her southern friends confusedly.

"Gods, have you not yet been to the ocean, Emira?" Melazir asked incredulously. When she didn't answer, he turned his attention to Alicus. "Well, that's where you'll find your answers! I'll bet the moment Emira is near the sea, her siren instincts will take over and she'll feel more like herself than ever before."

Emira stood suddenly, silencing her dinner mates. She turned swiftly and made for the door, without a word to those behind her.

"Emira?" Xemile began. Tallen stood and rushed to the siren's side, worry contorting his features. He gently gripped Emira's arm and spun her to face him.

"I'm going to the ocean," she stated plainly.

Alicus and Zuri stood now, concerned at the quick shift of intensity in the air.

"There is no access to the sea within the Southern Realm," Alicus informed. "The closest seashore would be in the east. Or the west."

All eyes shifted to Hallend. His violet gaze hardened as he said, "No."

"It *would* be closer than going north," Ellis commented humorously, enjoying the tension that was building in the air.

"I will fly you there," Tallen stated.

"Without my permission, the wards will keep you out," the western king added sternly.

A stale silence hung in the now quiet room. Emira glared at Hallend. She *hated* him, more than she hated Ellis. She had an opportunity to get some answers, to find out what it truly meant to be a siren. And her only barrier remaining was the icy, western king.

Finally, Zuri spoke. "It would help a great deal if you would allow Emira access to your shores. I know that you don't trust her, I understand that you will not fight against Vyrion. But please, Hallend…"

The icy king's gaze softened as the queen said his name.

"We have been friends for many years," she continued. "And Emira is my friend. Please, help her in this small way."

Emira held her breath as Hallend's eyes remained fixed on Zuri's. She did not look away from his emotionless stare, but rather basked in it, keeping her soft brown eyes on his, imploring him to accept.

"You ask this of me?" the western king finally said.

"I do," Zuri replied. "Not the southern realm, not Alicus or Emira. *Me.*"

Hallend's eyes remained on Zuri for a beat longer before shifting to the siren.

"You may enter my realm for access to the sea, but that is all. I will be the one to transfer the both of us there," he stated.

"Deal," Emira answered quickly, relief releasing its treacherous hold on her lungs.

"We will disable the wards for your safe journey between realms," Alicus chimed.

Hallend stood from his chair, rounded the table and made his way to the siren. He stood before her, expression hard and unreadable. He reached out his hand and said stoically, "The harpy will fly."

CHAPTER
THIRTY-EIGHT

The sickening twist in her stomach brought Emira's mind back to her near execution, and the first time she had experienced transference with Vyrion. But as quickly as her gut wrenched, it stopped, and instead of landing in an overgrown, forgotten forest, Hallend had brought her to the coast of the west. She felt her feet slam onto a rocky shore as the biting cold stung her face, and the furious gusts of wind whipped her hair about. As her eyes began to focus, she saw before her the unending sea, salty air smacking her senses with every crashing wave. The setting sun blossomed pink upon the gray, glassy water that stretched out further than she could see.

Overwhelming anger stabbed her chest. The shore had been just beyond Vyrion's castle, but she had never seen it, never been allowed to leave the boundaries of his kingdom. All those years enslaved by Vyrion had kept her away from this beauty and restricted her power. But she could feel it now. Magic tingled beneath her skin, as if it could sense that the ocean was only mere paces away.

The rustle of footsteps on the rocks sounded behind her. Tallen and Xemile had flown to shore, leaving Alicus, Zuri and Vyla behind in the south. They must have flown faster than they ever had before, or perhaps she had been staring out to sea longer than she realized, Hallend remaining quietly on shore.

Emira did not turn to greet them but kept her gaze fixed on the ocean before her. Her blue gown rustled against the frigid breeze, the same one that gave the waves their power to rise up and crash onto shore. A chill ran down her exposed spine. She looked at the pink horizon and thought of the hundreds of slaves who were currently in Vyrion's grasp.

What would happen if she took those next steps and entered the water?

Tallen came up beside her.

"You don't have to," he said gently, looking out to the horizon with her.

As her eyes welled, Emira replied firmly, "I need to know."

Tallen pressed his lips to her temple, inhaling her scent deeply before stepping back slowly to rejoin Xemile and Hallend on shore.

Emira drew in a deep, salty breath and blew out the last of her fear and doubt.

Five steps forward and she was ankle deep in the water. The icy, rushing current threatened to suck her feet under the sandy substrate, but she stood firmly, ignoring the numbing of her skin against the freezing sea. The hem of her gown floated around her, swaying with each pull of the tide.

Agonizingly long moments passed, and nothing happened.

Emira didn't know what she had expected, but disappointment tugged at her throat. She blinked back the tears that threatened to fall and join the salty water and forced herself to remain still for one, two, five more minutes.

Tallen's heavy footsteps finally splashed in the water. Standing behind her, he placed his hand gently on the small of her back.

Emira turned to him and buried her face in his chest, allowing the tears to finally soak her cheeks. She sobbed, and he held her shuddering body as they both stood in the ocean together.

"This emptiness," Emira choked, "it will never be filled. I cannot be whole."

"Em," the harpy began, stroking the frozen skin of her bare back.

Suddenly, the water around their ankles began to ripple violently. They looked down, and Tallen's hand went instinctively for his hissing whip. Toward the horizon, a whirlpool formed. The harpy tried to pull Emira to shore, but she resisted, eyes fixed on the growing swell of water.

From the center, a male emerged, but he was not fae. He was the furthest thing from fae. His skin was a pale blue, almost gray, and his eyes were large, black circles with no pupils or eyelids. His strong chest was bare, the muscles beneath his slate exterior rippling against the force of the whirlpool from which he emerged. His shoulders were bedecked with scaled armor as were his forearms and the sides of his torso, along his ribcage. In his webbed and clawed hand, he held a spear made from whale bone and the tooth of a megalodon.

Upon seeing Emira and Tallen near the shore, his mouth opened in awe, exposing many rows of sharp, serrated teeth, like those of a shark. He slowly swam forward, the whirlpool still spinning around his waist.

"It cannot be," he said in a screeching voice; one that was not meant to be heard out of water. His head tilted animalistically and he repeated, "It *cannot* be."

He glided even closer, now only a few feet from them. Tallen pulled his hissing whip from its binding and made his way to step in front of Emira.

But the male lowered his spear and bowed deeply, crying out, "Princess Emira, it truly is you!"

"WHO THE HELL ARE YOU?" TALLEN SNARLED, GRASPING EMIRA'S arm protectively. The others came closer, ready to defend against the newcomer. The sound of blades unsheathing on shore told Emira that her comrades were heavily armed.

The male lowered his head slightly in introduction, seemingly unbothered by the potential threat before him. "They call me Fjord, deliverer of mer royalty."

Hallend cut him off, his violet gaze eyeing the stranger suspiciously. "Explain your meaning."

"The shore calls to me," the male continued in his screeching, echoing voice, "when royalty enters the water." His attention turned to Emira, and she stared back at his black pits for eyes. "I've come to guide you safely home," he said, "as I do with anyone of divine merblood."

She took a cautious step forward.

"Take me… *home*?"

His invitation intrigued her. His words rang in her ear, like a gnawing, buzzing bee. Fjord held out a blue webbed hand, with claws almost 6 inches long, but Tallen snatched Emira back before she could consider her acceptance of it.

"How do we know you aren't full of shit?" came Xemile's thundering voice from the shoreline, followed by the splashing of his steps entering the water.

Fjord eyed the others waiting alongside Emira, but when the creature turned back to her, head tilting this way and that, he said, "I would recognize a daughter of Queen Leilitha if she was oceans away."

Leilitha.

Emira's legs gave way at the sound of her mother's name. It had not been spoken aloud for years, and to hear it upon the lips of Fjord, the closest she'd ever come to meeting another like her, felt like being pulled under the water by a vicious wave. As her knees buckled, Tallen caught her around the waist, holding her up before she collapsed into the salty, rushing water.

"You" she started, steadying herself against the harpy, "knew my mother?" Emira drew in a shaky breath and whispered, "Leilitha."

The words dripped from her lips like honey, slowly and sweetly.

Fjord gave a gentle smile, hiding the rows of teeth behind his blue lips.

"Very well," he responded, reaching out his hand again. "She was my queen. Allow me to take you home. Your people will rejoice in seeing you alive."

"Emira isn't going anywhere with you," Tallen snarled, the whip in his grasp slithering with anticipation.

Fjord's gaze flicked to the harpy as he snarled back, "You do not speak for her."

Tallen pushed his way in front of Emira and prowled towards the blue creature. He unsheathed his dagger, holding it firmly in his free hand as Fjord adjusted the grip he held on his spear. He glided forward to meet the harpy, cutting through the whirlpool around his waist like a knife to butter.

"No! Stop!" Emira begged.

Fjord immediately stilled, lowering his head in her direction. Tallen stopped seconds later, taken aback by the mer's obedience. Emira turned her head to look at the shore behind her, sucked in a salty breath and looked again at Tallen.

"I'm going."

Xemile stepped further into the sea, now alongside Tallen.

"I can smell tricks on this creature," Hallend sneered.

"He knew my mother," Emira countered. "He knew her name."

"That can't be enough reason to follow him into the godsforsaken sea," Xemile retorted.

"Nothing has been found in the library, and Vyla said herself that the sirens are a private people. If I'm going to get any answers at all, they will be from him."

"There's no way I can let you go," Tallen said, his voice deep and commanding. And desperate.

"I'm going, Tallen," Emira replied. "I've been a prisoner my entire life. I've been afraid and running my entire life."

"You don't have to be that any longer," the harpy pleaded. "You are safe here, but you do not know this"—his eyes slid to Fjord, unease spreading across his features—"this male."

"I asked you once if I was a prisoner to the Southern Realm," Emira responded calmly. "You said that I was not." The harpy's eyes glistened as she spoke. "My life has been nothing but a cell, a place I cannot escape. That ends now."

Tallen gripped her waist and pulled her closer to him. The tide sucked their feet deeper into the sandy bottom of the ocean. His blue eyes bore into Emira's green ones, and his wings shuddered against the freezing wind. He pressed a kiss to her mouth as she put her arms around his neck.

"I know your plight," he said against her, "but I can't lose you, Em."

"It will be alright," she lied.

She didn't truly trust Fjord, but she felt so close to answers. She couldn't turn the opportunity away. Tallen pressed another kiss to her lips, running a calloused hand through her loose braid.

"I will wait here," he swore. "Em, I will dive into the deepest trenches of this ocean for you, if you need me."

"I know," she responded softly.

With trembling hands, Emira removed the sapphire necklace and held it out for Xemile to take. He did so slowly, eyes pinned on the mer a few feet from them.

Tallen took Emira in his grip, one hand firmly placed on either side of her face and kissed her deeply. His tongue swept between her teeth as she coiled her arms around his neck. Their bodies pressed together, and Emira shivered as the warmth from the harpy's wings spread through her. Slowly, she broke their kiss, knowing that Tallen would not be the one to do so.

Emira slowly stepped away from Tallen, and deeper into the water. She was now knee deep, and within Fjord's grasp. She glanced once more towards shore. Tallen stood with his wings sagging behind him. His jaw was clenched and his fists were balled at his sides. Xemile moved closer, ready to heave the harpy back if needed. Hallend stood further back from the water, an expression of distrust smeared across his pale face.

Emira turned to face Fjord, who bowed at the waist upon meeting her gaze.

"You will take me below," she began, command lining her voice. "You will answer my questions, show me what I must see, and then you will bring me back."

He answered, "The people will mourn to see you leave, Your Highness."

Emira repeated sternly and without falter, "You will bring me back, Fjord."

With that, he nodded his agreement and they moved together towards the unending horizon. His head dipped below the surface. Emira watched for a moment as the mer disappeared beneath the glassy sea, and a strange instinct took over her body. Before she could question how she was meant to keep up with him, she dipped beneath the water and followed.

Emira was engulfed by the sea, and she heard Tallen release a guttural scream when she disappeared into the depths of the ocean.

CHAPTER

THIRTY-NINE

The water beneath the surface was as clear as glass. Above, the rays of the sun shone through, slicing through the water like daggers. The light illuminated the sea floor, which dipped lower and lower, metamorphosing from the rocky shore, into the rippled, sandy seabed. Emira's eyes remained open as she easily gazed at her new surroundings. The salt water did not burn like she had expected it to upon descending with Fjord. She saw clearly, as if she was made for this.

'I *am* made for this,' she reminded herself.

Fjord swam alongside Emira. From the waist down, he had the body of a shark. His muscular tail, trimmed with pointed fins of blue and black, cut through the water both powerfully and gracefully. Surprisingly, Emira's own body was able to keep pace with the mer, despite being finless, and she swam against the current with ease.

"How far are we going?" she asked.

Under the water, her voice sounded melodic, as if she had sung the question. She managed to hide her shock as the mer looked over.

Fjord answered in a similar, musical tone, no longer screeching like he had on shore. Emira understood now that his voice was made to be heard under the water. It was strong, and deep, and caused the water around them to vibrate slightly.

"It was once very far," he started, "hidden in the deepest pocket of the sea. In recent years, your kingdom has been moved to be closer to the Fae Realms."

"My kingdom?"

"Telaria," he answered, his pointed teeth glimmering as he smiled, "the Realm of the Sirens."

"It doesn't belong to me," Emira retorted, tearing her eyes away from the mer and looking ahead at the vast, unending blue before them.

"Oh, but it does, Your Highness," Fjord continued. "You are our crown princess."

Right, she thought to herself. *Queen Leilitha...*

"Tell me of my mother," Emira ordered gently. "You knew her?"

Fjord sighed, forcing water to rush from the gills along his neck that Emira had not seen before.

"I was one of her personal guards," he started. "Queen Leilitha was kind, and beautiful, and just. She created a safe haven for marine species during the genocide of the shifters. Our people adored her more than any monarch Telaria has ever seen."

The mer's voice trailed as he reminisced, sadness clouding his black eyes. Emira continued swimming alongside him, patiently waiting for more.

"But," he finally said, his melodic voice now laced with anger, "she was taken from us, before your birth, obsessed over by a fae male." Fjord paused for a moment to look at Emira. "Your father."

She gaped as his words sunk in. Her legs slowed their kicking, and Fjord's fins followed, leaving them to tread water.

"My father?" she repeated, squinting confusedly at the mer. "My father kidnapped my mother from the water?"

Fjord nodded gravely. "We would have gone to her aid, but she ordered us to stay under the sea and keep Telaria hidden. So we obeyed."

Emira's mind continued to reel.

"She was not kidnapped by my father," she countered surely. "She couldn't be. My father was a slave. He was a slave to Vyrion, the king of the Eastern Realm."

The mer's enormous, unsettling black eyes stared at her for a moment, and he tilted his head sympathetically.

"Do you not know, my lady?" he asked. Emira stared back at the mer warrior, waiting. He sighed sadly and lowered his gaze. "Vyrion *is* your father."

Somehow, Emira gasped. She held a hand to her open mouth as her heart dropped and her chest heaved.

"No!" she burst out. "No, no, no."

"It's true, my lady," Fjord said solemnly. "Queen Leilitha sang to him, and when she refused to be his bride, he stole her away. You are a product of that union. When Queen Leilitha refused to divulge the location of Telaria"—Fjord's expression grew hateful—"he slaughtered her."

They treaded water silently as Fjord allowed Emira time to comprehend his words.

"How can you be sure?" she finally asked, looking up once again.

"Our queen siren spoke to her sister and reported."

"Siren spoke?" she questioned, thoughts staggering with the information.

"Before marine species evolved the ability to speak below the surface, we communicated through siren speaking. We spoke mind to mind. It's now a leftover trait that we possess. Your mother was able to communicate with her sister, Lady Calline, while on land," Fjord said, his voice somber, "until our queen's body became too weak to do so."

Emira's mind raced. Vyrion was her father. He was the one to kidnap, torment, and kill her mother. He was the reason that she had never known her true parentage, or her royal lineage. He had suppressed her siren powers and fae strength by keeping her weak and withered. And now, she was to be a queen to a people she did not know, in a kingdom of which she had never heard. Vyrion would pay, not just for her suffering, but for her mother's as well.

"My lady?" Fjord said gently, bringing Emira to the surface of her thoughts.

Emira raised her head high, green eyes alight with anger, and she commanded, "Take me to my kingdom."

CHAPTER

FORTY

Fjord led Emira further and further out to sea. As they dove deeper, signs of life became scarce, and light struggled to penetrate the surface. Her eyes adjusted to the darkness, like a predator in the night. She felt like one too. Rage burned in the pit of her stomach for her mother who had been kidnapped, enslaved, raped, and murdered by Vyrion.

Her father.

Fjord suddenly dove down vertically, aiming for a crevice in a deep, rocky trench. Emira followed, keeping her eyes pinned on the shimmer of blue in the blackening water that was the mer. The trench led them down to a small opening, barely large enough to fit through. Fjord turned his head to Emira, his black orbs piercing through the darkness. Upon the assurance that she was following closely, Fjord slipped through the opening with ease. Emira hesitated momentarily, but an eerie vibration from deeper within the trench forced her body forward and into the cavity. If her curiosity became the cause of her death, Emira would prefer it not to be at the hands of whatever lay in wait at the bottom.

Fjord chuckled ahead of her.

"Wise decision, my lady. You don't want to become caught in the clutches of the Leviathan."

"Leviathan?" Emira questioned, legs kicking faster as her anxiety rose.

"The sea spirit that guards the entrance to Telaria," Fjord answered, continuing ahead. "He is not to harm those with marine blood, but I wouldn't linger and test his patience."

"Would you not kill him if he attacked?"

Fjord glanced back at Emira again, a smirk spreading over his blue lips. "I would certainly try, my lady."

They continued swimming through the tunnel. Despite the rockiness of the entrance, the walls became smooth as they continued further, as if burnished from centuries of use. They swam down, down, down until the channel shifted directions, widening and sending them suddenly upwards into a pocket of air.

Emira sucked in a breath, gasping down air as they surfaced. She wiped away the salty water from her face and rubbed her eyes. Bobbing next to her, Fjord looked on, unscathed and unconcerned.

Emira regained her composure and looked towards the mer. However, her eyes did not remain on him for long, for beyond the mer was a vast city.

Within the pocket of air, Emira saw buildings made from stone, each one crawling with moss. The buildings were held up by massive pillars of rock, spires atop most. Sea glass of blue and green composed the windows. In the sky, the air pocket rose up higher and higher, keeping the sea water out but still allowing the sunlight in.

Fjord's webbed hand swung into her view. He had pulled himself from the water before slithering upright on his tail like a snake, and upon a dock-like platform. There were stone stairs that led from the sea up to him, and Emira accepted his help as she ascended the slippery steps.

"Welcome to Telaria" Fjord said with a smirk.

His voice remained pleasant while within the walls of the Siren Realm, deep and melodic, no longer that of a screeching sea creature. Emira righted herself as she stepped from the sea. She inhaled the surrounding salty air deeply and blew out her last trace of fear.

EMIRA FOLLOWED THE MER THROUGH THE STREETS OF TELARIA, HER eyes wandering to all of the strange and unfamiliar sights around her. The city was mostly made of stone, with tall, moss covered buildings that reached toward the top of the domed air pocket with twists and spirals like conch shells. The path upon which she walked was also made from stone, and littered with sea glass and shells from the ocean beyond. The air was thick with salt and the earthy scent of the moss.

Fjord led her further and further from the entrance of the city, and deeper into the strange realm. Curious eyes began to emerge from the rocky homes, watching them with surprised and shocked expressions. As they continued on, the eyes changed from humanoid to alien, all shapes and colors peering through the frosty sea glass windows. And when the people emerged, whispering to themselves, Emira balked at what she saw.

Many citizens of Telaria resembled Fjord, with blue gray skin, sharp teeth glimmering as they spoke, and black eyes that followed her like a predator. They had long shark-like tails upon which they slithered as Fjord also did. Others walked upon two legs, but that was where Emira's commonality with them ended. Most of those who emerged had gills along their necks or the sides of their faces. Many had golden skin, armored and spiked like a seahorse, while others were covered in a speckling of scales along their arms, legs, and faces.

Emira recognized males, females and children among them, families that lived and thrived here. In that sense, they were no different than those who lived in the Southern Realm.

Suddenly, a low rumble came from beyond, and the underwater city began to gently vibrate. Emira paused, her blood running cold and her mind becoming even more alert than before.

Fjord turned and smiled gently.

"No need to fear," he began. With a webbed hand, he pointed a long black claw past the city and towards the unending blue outside the dome. "Look."

Whales.

The breath left Emira's lungs as she gazed upon the magnificent sight. The low rumble came again, her feet shuddering with the vibration. They were singing, speaking to each other in a language Emira wondered if anyone here could understand.

"That's..." she began, eyes pinned on the silhouette of the creatures. She could not finish her sentence while her attention was so fixed elsewhere.

When the pod passed and was no longer visible, Fjord finally spoke again.

"Let us continue forward, my lady."

Emira's gaze snapped back to the mer, and she stepped quickly, catching up to him, her focus once again on her immediate surroundings.

Gentle steps came from behind her, and Emira turned to see that the Telarian people had been following them. They maintained a respectful distance, their whispers gentle and their curious eyes unblinking.

"What's happening?" Emira asked Fjord, voice low and cautious.

"You are the exact image of your mother," he responded. "There is no hiding your identity here."

Emira listened closely to the whispers that trailed them.

"Our queen!"

"Leilitha, blessed Leilitha!"

"Your blood has returned!"

Voices rang through Emira's head as Fjord calmly led her through the streets. She watched in awe, shaken by the new sights and sounds.

"You'll find no fae here," Fjord said suddenly, his voice taking Emira's eyes away from the crowd. "Only marine species can find Telaria."

"Marine species?" she repeated, careful to not step on the mer's trailing fins.

"Mer, like myself," the warrior started. "Sirens, like you. And marine shifters."

"Oh," Emira replied, unsure who else she had imagined would live here.

"Most of the shifters came during the genocide. Queen Leilitha sent out our armies to lead the endangered shifters to safety. Many have been here for generations since. Before then, all of Telaria was underwater and in the deepest part of the sea. When the war started, your mother erected this space, allowing for air to cradle the new city, so that the shifters may return to their humanoid forms."

"She made Telaria safe for them?" Emira asked, looking around at the many creatures that trailed after them.

"Yes," Fjord responded proudly. "Telaria became a safe haven for those marine species that were being persecuted on land."

They appeared before a large castle, smaller than the one in the Southern Realm but large enough that Emira had to tilt her gaze upwards to see it to the top. It was similarly built to the rest of the town—wet stone made up the tall walls, which were also sprinkled with moss. The wide walkway led them to a set of massive entrance doors, dark wood that was nearly covered in soft, velvet greenery. The stoic guards allowed Fjord to pass but gawked at Emira as she followed.

"I will take you to our Regent, Calline," Fjord said, glancing back at her, "Queen Leilitha's sister; your aunt."

"Calline is alive?" Emira balked. Fjord only nodded in response. "I had presumed…"

Emira had presumed her aunt dead, not living and ruling Telaria in her mother's absence. In *her* absence. Excitement and nervousness fluttered in her belly at the news of a siren relative.

"No king?" Emira asked.

"No," Fjord replied. "Telaria is a matriarchy; has been for thousands of years."

The mer led Emira through a grand entrance, and down a wide hallway. The pearlescent floors shimmered, like the reflection of the moon on the water. The interior stone walls were painted a shade of pale blue, and the tall ceilings were scattered with skylights, allowing streams of ocean tinted rays to peek through.

Emira felt as if she were swimming, not through water but through sunlight.

As they did, they passed a marble statue, elevated upon a grand pedestal, of what appeared to be a woman. She was nude, with sensuous curves making up her hips and breasts. Her hair was long, draped all around her body and ending at the small of her back. Upon her face was a pleasant expression and a kindness that made Emira feel welcome to gaze upon her.

"Who is she?" the siren asked as she stilled, eyes not leaving the woman's kind, unblinking ones.

Fjord slithered alongside her, his eyes also drawn to the statue.

"She is our one and only goddess," he answered, voice as smooth as the marble before them. "She is the moon."

Emira's eyes sliced to the mer, who continued staring at the woman.

"The moon?" Emira repeated.

"She controls the tides," the mer answered melodically, "and gives birth to the sun each new day. She creates life within her womb and keeps the darkness away with her glow. She is our mother."

Emira noticed the mer's black eyes shine with adoration.

"That's beautiful," she said.

Fjord finally turned his head towards Emira. "This statue was erected when your mother became lost to us. It was made in her image as a tribute to her life."

Emira inhaled sharply, moving her sight back to the statue. She looked upon the woman's face, her kind eyes, her full lips, and felt her own eyes well with warm tears. She never thought she would be able to look upon her mother's face, and here she was now, looking upon her entire form, in the most beautiful way possible.

"Come," Fjord finally said. "Not much farther now."

THEY EVENTUALLY MADE THEIR WAY INTO A GRAND ROOM, WHERE A throne made from coral, shells and sea stone was laid before them. Upon the throne sat a woman with the same bold, green eyes as Emira. The woman's auburn hair fell in thick waves around her pale face. She had the same peachy cheeks and full, mauve lips that Emira did too—something she could now confirm came from her mother's side.

"Queen Regent," Fjord greeted, lowering his head in a graceful bow.

Emira's aunt.

Calline stood, holding both heavily jeweled hands over her open mouth, an expression of pure shock and disbelief upon her face.

"Fjord," she mumbled through her fingers. "Is it truly…?"

Fjord nodded his head, smiling in response, and placed a fisted hand across his chest.

"I present," he said, his deep voice singing the words, "Crown Princess Emira, daughter of Queen Leilitha, and heir to the Telarian throne."

Emira startled at the titles said aloud.

Calline leapt forward, her luxurious green gown trailing along the dais behind her, and took Emira into her arms, squeezing tightly and sobbing into her shoulder. Emira awkwardly returned the embrace, unsure what to do or how to respond. When the regent finally pulled away, she wiped tears from her eyes and apologized.

"You just look so much like her! My dear Leilitha."

Emira smiled at the sound of her mother's name upon her aunt's lips.

"My dear niece," the regent whispered, placing a soft hand on Emira's cheek. Finally, she straightened her emerald gown and wiped once more at her face. Turning to Fjord, Calline said, "Report. I want to know everything." She placed a hand on Emira's shoulder and smiled. "We have so much to discuss."

Emira nodded and looked at Fjord.

"You remember our agreement," she stated. "You answer my questions. And you bring me back."

Fjord nodded and followed the sirens for a private meeting.

THE ROOM WAS ELEGANT AND CLUTTERED WITH FINERY. A CHANDElier hung from the center of the domed ceiling, alight with bioluminescent algae and low lit, flickering candles. The light danced off of the spotless, polished stone floors. As Emira made her way through, shelves of treasures caught her attention. Things such as golden coins, conch shells, jars of shark teeth and wet specimens of deep sea fish that looked like the monsters from children's stories lined the walls of the large room. Calline motioned for Emira to sit on one of the plush sofas, made from sea sponge, stone, and coral. She did while her new acquaintances—*subjects*—sat across from her.

Calline reached across one of the fine tables, accented with shells and sand dollars, and plucked a small, brass bell from the surface. With a delicate flick of her wrist, the bell chimed and she set it down again.

"Now," she began, placing her hands on her lap. "Tell me everything and spare not a single detail."

Emira's lips parted to begin, but the doors through which they entered opened swiftly as two shifters appeared. One was male, and in his humanoid form, though he had a speckling of silver scales along his high cheekbones and along the column of his neck. The other, however, was female—a narwhal shifter. She walked upon two legs, but her gray skin was mottled with black specks. Her eyes were nothing but small, black dots upon her humanoid face, and growing from between them was a spiraling horn that was nearly as tall as she was. So tall, in fact, that the shifter had to duck to enter through the doorway.

They entered swiftly and without a word, placing a pitcher of fresh water and a large platter of food before them. Emira noted their nod of departure before glancing down at the food. The silver plate held lightly seasoned crab, small morsels of shrimp and squid, as well as salted rolls of seaweed wrapped firmly against a tuna mash.

"Please," Calline began, reaching for the squid, "begin."

Emira told the regent and the mer guard everything she could possibly remember from her time in the Eastern Realm under

Vyrion's rule. She told them about Tallen, and the Southern Realm, and the power that she was slowly learning to control.

Fjord lowered his head when she finished, placing a webbed hand upon his chest.

"I am sorry for the torment you have endured," he said. Without the ear-piercing screech of his voice on dry land, Emira could hear the sincerity it held. "I would like to offer my assistance in aiding you during training. Your power has been held back for too long."

Emira considered before replying.

"I suppose it would be helpful to learn from a true mer. Although, I'm not sure how Xemile's pride will hold up." She smirked and Fjord chuckled at her acceptance.

They, in turn, told Emira about her mother, Queen Leilitha. Calline confirmed that the queen had been kidnapped, enslaved and murdered. And she confirmed that Emira had been sired by Vyrion.

They explained all they could about Telaria and those who lived there; the sirens—beings that presented similar to fae, both male and female, and were immortal like fae, but also possessing powers of water manipulation and hypnosis, as well as having the ability to swim and live underwater; the shifters that could transform between their land and sea forms, but possessed no power or special ability aside from immortality; and the mer, who spent most of their time in the ocean but could also slither upon land. Their species was agile, long-living and built to be warriors.

Emira sat silently, while the surplus of information filled her mind.

"What is it you plan to do next?" Calline asked cautiously.

"I need to go back to the Southern Realm. I need to see Tallen. I have to tell everyone about this."

Calline's face paled.

"We do not mix with the above world," she said. "Sirens are prizes on land. It is dangerous to be anywhere but the sea."

"I will go back and consult the kings and queens of the fae," Emira countered firmly. "And I will see my Soul Bond."

"Soul Bond?" Calline repeated confusedly. "How is that possible?"

"What do you mean?" Emira asked.

Calline and Fjord exchanged confused glances before she continued.

"Sirens do not have souls," the regent began. "Neither do the mer, or any other water dwelling creature for that matter. When we die, we become the salt and the foam of the sea, to serve the ocean as it served us. How can you be bonded to another without one?"

Her questioning was met with silence. Emira did not have an answer. She knew she felt something for Tallen, something more than plain affection. She was tethered to him; her heart and his heart were two halves of the same.

But doubt wriggled its way into her thoughts at this new information. Could she truly have a soul bond if she, in fact, did not have a soul?

"He can come here!" Calline said excitedly, changing the subject, and cutting through Emira's doubtful train of thought. "Then you would not have to leave."

Emira smiled slightly. "I will think on it." Calline made to argue, but Emira spoke again. "Am I to be queen, or am I not?"

Calline and Fjord lowered their heads in servitude. Emira stood.

"Take me back to shore," she commanded gently to Fjord. Turning to Calline, she said, "Continue as regent in my absence. Tell the people—tell *my* people..." She stopped for a moment to appreciate the confident command in her tone. "Tell my people that I've come home."

CHAPTER
FORTY-ONE

Tallen stood like stone, his boots firmly planted ankle deep in the wet, rocky sand. The tide threatened to spit him from the sea, but he refused to budge as he watched Emira walk deeper into the ocean with a mer warrior that the harpy didn't trust with a sliver of his body. As Fjord dipped into the sea, Emira followed, disappearing below the surface. As their forms beneath the water moved farther from the shoreline, Tallen dropped to his knees and released all of his distress in the form of a guttural scream.

Xemile hauled him upright and back onto shore, echoing his best words of comfort. Tallen's ears rang, and he heard Xemile not, for his attention was too fixed on the unending sea that had swallowed his Soul Bond.

"We should get back," Hallend said urgently.

Xemile nodded his agreement as he planted Tallen's body firmly on shore.

"I'm not leaving," the harpy stated.

"We need to prepare for her return," Xemile pressed. "Who knows what new information she may come back with."

"Then go," Tallen answered, eyes fixed on the sea.

Hallend and Xemile exchanged thoughtful glances as they considered their options.

"I'll stay," Xemile offered. "Tallen and I will wait for Emira's return."

"Then I will return alone. Zuri and Alicus will want to know what has happened." The western ruler transferred back to the south, leaving the two warriors alone in his territory.

Tallen didn't turn his gaze away from the sea as his comrades spoke and planned their next move. The ripples formed by Fjord and Emira were gone as was the sand that had been kicked up by the harpy's boots. There was nothing now but calm waters, frigid cold and a glistening of the sun's reflection as it began to set. All trace of his Soul Bond was gone.

"She'll be back," Xemile's voice said from behind the harpy. He had perched himself on a rocky plateau, out of reach of the tide. Tallen had returned to the water, his boots once again ankle deep in the sea. Even as the sun disappeared behind the horizon, which glimmered with the last bit of light from the day, and the air of the west became glacially cold, he remained on the beach.

Tallen had no plans to leave. He would wait until the end of time for Emira.

His Soul Bond.

He kept his mind open, searching for any sense of her, but the ocean seemed to create a wall, for he felt nothing.

"I should have stopped her," Tallen said, staring out across the endless black ocean. "I never should have let her go."

"You heard her voice before she left," Xemile responded. "There was no stopping her. She's probably getting all of her answers right now."

Tallen heard the doubt in the general's voice, and he knew he couldn't believe a word his friend said.

The harpy stretched his wings and looked back at Xemile. "I'm going to scout again."

Xemile wouldn't argue. The harpy had already searched miles over the ocean since Emira had left earlier that evening.

Tallen beat his wings against the wintry air. As his feet lifted, he spotted a swell of water quickly approaching shore. The harpy slammed his boots back into the sea and rushed forward as Fjord's head and torso emerged from the center of the whirlpool.

"Emira!" he called.

She did not surface. Tallen stomped forward, preemptively pulling his whip from his side and cracking it against the rippling waters, sending a spray of salt in all directions.

"Emira!" he called again.

Finally, he saw a head of the most beautiful, blonde hair emerge from the water behind Fjord. Emira surfaced and gasped as if she had been holding her breath the entire time that she had been gone.

Fjord offered a webbed hand to assist her as she made her way to the rocky shore, finding herself face to face with Tallen.

The mer spoke as his torso lowered into the water, his voice like nails scratching along stone.

"When you are ready, stand in the sea. I will come again." He bowed his head when Emira nodded her understanding, then he vanished.

Emira looked back to Tallen, his massive frame standing mere feet from her.

"I learned so much," she whispered.

Tallen said nothing as his electric blue eyes bore into her. Her gown clung to her curves, and her once beautifully braided hair was soaked and unkempt. He stalked forward rapidly and draped his massive arms around her shivering body, holding her tightly in his grasp. Within seconds, his lips were pressed to hers, his wings sagging behind him in relief. Emira shivered again, and Tallen wrapped his wings around the both of them, shielding her from the tiny flecks of snow that began to fall.

The sound of Xemile's wings beating against the wind sounded behind the harpy and the siren as he departed without a word, leaving them to be alone.

Tallen claimed Emira with another passionate kiss before he finally spoke.

"Never again," Tallen said hoarsely. "We are never separating again." He pulled away to look at her. Her cheeks were pink with chill and her face dripped with water. "I cannot *bear* it, Emira."

She set her head on his shoulder and closed her eyes.

"I have so much to tell you," she murmured against him.

"Later," the harpy answered, stretching his wings and lifting her from the water. "Let's get you home."

"Home..." Emira whispered as exhaustion and bitter cold pulled her into sleep.

CHAPTER
FORTY-TWO

Emira slept in the next morning. She awoke slowly and lazily, her body still heavy with exhaustion from the night before. The smell of fresh cedar and dark chocolate finally roused her. She was in her room.

Their room.

The pillowy mattress cradled her tired body, the soft blankets caressed her skin; and there was Tallen, sitting up in the bed watching her slowly wake.

She rolled into his warmth.

"What time is it?" she mumbled into his side.

He huffed a laugh and turned into her.

"Nearly midday," he answered.

Emira groaned at the late hour, but she had slept so deeply. Tallen must have given her Sarolina's tonic before putting her to bed himself. Her tangled hair smelled of salt, and she wore nothing but one of his black shirts.

"Did you dress me last night?" Emira teased.

Tallen smirked. "I was a gentleman about it."

She tilted her gaze up and planted a kiss on his lips. And she held it as she grasped his hand and guided it down between her legs. He hissed against her mouth when his hand met her core, the heat penetrating through his touch.

"Are you still feeling gentlemanly?" she breathed.

Tallen quickly flipped Emira onto her back and rolled atop her, one muscular arm holding his body in a hover, his other still pressed between her thighs. His fore and middle finger circled her clit lazily as he took his time in building her pleasure. When Emira was grasping the blankets and biting her bottom lip, he plunged two fingers into her slickness. She arched into the pleasure as Tallen kissed along her neck and collarbone, while curling his fingers, caressing that soft spot within her that made her clench around him. She clutched Tallen by the shoulders as she erupted.

Emira reached below his waist, pleased to find him entirely unclothed, and gripped his cock, the throbbing caused by his arousal pulsating in her palm.

"Em," the harpy growled, as she began stroking him base to tip.

Tallen rolled onto his back, wings splayed beneath him as Emira sat upright, still palming his arousal. She shifted her wild hair to the side and slowly pressed her lips to the tip of his cock.

"Gods, Em," Tallen moaned.

His muscles tensed as she teased him, slowly circling her tongue around the head of his erection. As she slowly accepted him into her mouth, leisurely lowering herself down and taking in all of him, Tallen's head rocked back against the pillow, and he let out a guttural moan. He ran both of his hands through Emira's hair as she tightened her lips around him. Pressing her tongue to the underside of his shaft, she slowly brought her mouth back up to the tip, keeping the pressure firm.

Tallen was on the brink of becoming undone. Emira repeated the motion until the harpy was gasping and rocking his hips into her. She cupped his balls in one hand and palmed his length in the other, keeping her lips tightly closed on the tip of him.

Tallen came, his hands still raking through Emira's hair. She lapped up every drop of his orgasm before finally releasing him from her grip.

Emira wiped at the corners of her mouth with her ring finger, smirking and straddling the harpy, whose body had slackened with contentment.

Tallen gently gripped her full thighs, both hugging either side of him, and looked up at her. Her mauve-y lips were swollen with use and her green eyes bore into him with a sultry blink.

"You truly are everything," he finally said.

EMIRA TOLD HER FRIENDS ABOUT TELARIA OVER A PRIVATE LUNCH IN the library while the rulers of the east, north and islands were offered their midday meal in their private quarters. She described the air pocket that held an entire city of marine species. She told them about Calline, her aunt and Telaria's regent. She recounted the memories they had shared of her mother, Queen Leilitha, and the tragic end to which she came after being kidnapped by Vyrion, but not before Emira was sired by him.

They all listened intently, shocked to hear that there was an entire realm under the sea that kept themselves hidden for so long. Alicus barely touched his food as Emira spoke, his curiosity greater than his hunger. Vyla scribbled everything the siren said into her leather notebook, a scowl of concentration upon her face. Xemile and Zuri sat silently, taking in the information calmly while Tallen sat beside Emira stoically.

"So Telaria is not part of the Fae Realms," Vyla stated plainly.

"I suppose not," Emira answered.

"And so they cannot be governed by our laws," the shifter finished.

"They want no contact with land," Emira added. "And they weren't happy to see me leave, either." Tallen's eyes darkened possessively. Emira noticed his building defensiveness and quickly added, "Calline said you could come to Telaria, Tallen."

"How is that possible?" Alicus questioned, a hint of possessiveness in his tone as well.

"I don't know," Emira began.

Alicus sat back in his chair, and Zuri placed a reassuring hand on his arm.

"Will Telaria help us to bring Vyrion down?" Xemile asked.

"It doesn't seem like they want to surface," Emira answered disappointedly.

"But you are their queen," Xemile continued. "They answer to you."

"I can't possibly ask that of them," Emira scoffed. "I've only just shown up after two and a half decades. How can I make my first order to go to war?"

"And what about Tallen?" Zuri cut in. "If his soul is bonded to a queen's, what does that mean for him? What is he to do?"

Calline had said that sirens do not have souls, but Emira kept that information to herself. What she felt for Tallen was unlike anything she could ever describe, and so she kept her friends in the dark about her aunt's words. It would only cause Tallen heartache to hear such a thing, and Emira was unsure that she even found truth to it.

"We need more time," Alicus said. "Perhaps we can convince Calline to surface and meet with us..." His voice trailed off as he looked at his queen. "I need to think on this."

Zuri looked at her husband kindly and nodded.

"Perhaps we can discuss this more at dinner this evening," she suggested to the group. Everyone understood it well enough to be a dismissal of the topic, and so they finished their meal in silence before retreating back to their own quarters.

273

CHAPTER
FORTY-THREE

Training with Fjord began immediately, and the mer did not hold back. From the first day, he trained Emira to within an inch of her consciousness, leaving her exhausted at the end of each session. But only a short period passed before she noticed an increase in her control as well as an increase in her reaction time and speed to conjure the water magic she possessed.

"She's doing very well," Fjord said one day as he lounged near the shore alongside Tallen. Emira was knee deep in the sea of the west, reluctantly allowed there by Hallend, raising and lowering waves at her command. She was soaked head to toe, but the chill of the west remained at bay due to the specially insulated training gear that was brought from the depths of Telaria. It was skin tight, and strong like the thick hide of a seal.

"My Soul Bond has done well in every endeavor she has assumed," the harpy responded, keeping his eyes on the siren. His chest swelled with pride as Emira raised a massive wave above her head, and with a swift pump of her arms outward, split the face of the water in two, before it crashed back onto the surface of the sea.

"Your Soul Bond…" the mer repeated, his voice trailing off slightly. The harpy turned and looked down at Fjord.

"You know," the mer finally continued, feeling Tallen's eyes upon him, "that she will not—*cannot*—love you the way you love her."

The harpy's eyes darkened at Fjord's words. "What do you mean—"

He was suddenly cut off when a colossal wall of saltwater crashed onto shore, soaking him and the mer as it went. Tallen coughed and shook the water from his black curls, and Fjord righted himself from the blast.

When their eyes found the siren, she was sitting in the sea, dark circles beneath her eyes and skin turning pale. She was drained, and her magic had become unwieldy, crashing to shore as her tired body collapsed.

"We're done," Tallen stated to Fjord. Without a glance in the mer's direction, the harpy walked into the ocean, lifted Emira, and shot into the sky.

CHAPTER
FORTY-FOUR

Vyrion's cold hand came around Emira's throat and grasped her windpipe. She felt his hard body pressed against her back as his seething voice rasped into her ear, sending a chill down her spine and forcing her gut to clench painfully.

"So now you know…"

Emira's eyes darted about, her understanding that this was a dream seeping through her initial fear. Tallen and she had fallen asleep together but fatigued from training, she had failed to finish her tonic first and allowed her mind to be open to Vyrion's treachery.

"You killed my mother," Emira stated fiercely, the fae king's grip still holding her throat from behind. "You kidnapped a queen, raped, and murdered her like she was nothing."

"She was no longer useful to me," he answered against her ear.

"You're vile," Emira retorted.

"Oh, dear daughter," he sneered.

"Don't call me that!" she snapped. Hatred dripped from her words, her voice like a viper, cornered, and ready to attack.

"Come now, Emira. Don't be daft. Learn from your dear mother's mistakes." Still holding her throat, Vyrion walked around to stand in front of her. His eyes were angry and evil, and his mouth was set in a hard line. A ripple of fear ran through the siren at the sight of the male who had tortured her, who she had once called master.

"You're going to tell me where Telaria is," he said.

"Over. My. Dead. Body."

Vyrion swiftly slapped Emira across the face. She fell to the ground, clutching at the sting on her skin as the king of the east stood over her.

"I will get what I want, Emira," he promised. "Maybe you don't value your own life, but perhaps you'll want to protect your Soul Bond."

Emira's gaze shot up to him, terror squeezing at her lungs and threatening to strangle her.

Vyrion smirked and continued, "It would not be the first time you caused the death of another."

The demented king manifested an illusion, the same he had used to show her Rocas. Only this time, it was of Tallen. His broken body lay before her. His once beautiful wings of iridescent black and brown were shredded, nearly every feather plucked or torn. He lay upon them, twisted and mangled in the limbs, as if each joint had been snapped in the most unnatural of ways. His face was nearly unrecognizable, blue eyes plucked clean from their sockets, lips cracked and left agape. Blood oozed from his ears and nose, leaking down into his black curls. His armor was marred, ripped as if it had been as thin as paper. And in his hand, he held his whip, but it did not slither or hiss. It was as dead as the harpy who once wielded it.

Emira's stomach churned.

"Stop it," she pleaded through gritted teeth, looking away. Vyrion grinned again, circling the siren who remained on the ground, mere inches away from the illusion.

"Look at what you have done, Emira," he taunted.

Keeping her head turned, Emira sucked in a shuddering breath before shaking her head in defiance.

"Look at what you have done!" Vyrion ordered, this time grabbing the siren by the hair and forcing her head to turn in the direction of Tallen's twisted body.

She released a sob as pain seared through her scalp, and then she wailed at the sight of her Soul Bond. Her cheeks were now stained with tears, her vision blurred.

The eastern king lowered himself to her side, keeping a firm grasp on her hair. "Where is Telaria?"

Nothing but a whimper passed Emira's lips. She refused to speak, refused to allow her mother's sacrifice to be worthless, refused to damn the Telarian people to imminent torture and death.

"The harpy will suffer for your defiance."

A strange sensation flickered across Emira's legs. She looked down to see spiders and millipedes, maggots and worms, crawling from the empty sockets of the harpy onto her skin. She screamed and kicked the vermin away, sobbing at the sight of the remainder of Tallen's face being devoured.

Power rippled under her skin. She couldn't let Vyrion get to Tallen.

The cruel fae king smirked again.

"You think you can defeat me," he stated, sensing her protectiveness. He leaned down, his face now only inches from her own. "I dare you to try."

EMIRA AWOKE QUICKLY, COVERED IN SWEAT, HER FACE STILL STINGING from the blow that Vyrion had delivered. Tallen jolted awake, eyes roaming over her and realization seeping over his features.

His features which, to Emira's relief, were intact.

"He's coming," Emira breathed before Tallen could speak. "He's coming for Telaria. He'll destroy the realms for it."

CHAPTER
FORTY-FIVE

There was no time to alert the others of Vyrion's warning, and ask for transference to the west. Instead, Tallen flew Emira to the sea, his speed to be rivaled by none. Emira swallowed down her queasiness as his feet slammed onto the shore. She stumbled from his grasp and stepped into the water, ignoring the frost that seeped in through her linen gown and the heavy fall of snow upon her skin.

"Go," she ordered Tallen without looking back at him. "You have to tell the others; you have to warn them."

His hesitation pressed in on her back, but it was soon followed by the sound of his wings swiftly pushing himself through the frigid air once more.

He had to be exhausted, Emira knew this. It was a feat to fly as far as he had in as little time as he had, but they had no choice. Vyrion wasn't going to wait any longer. Their time had run out.

Within moments, the surface of the water began to tremble, and Fjord emerged from the sea. He was barely visible against the thick snowfall, but he swam forward, the whirlpool surrounding his body propelling him forward.

"Highness," he screeched, lowering his head and his spear.

"Bring me Calline," Emira ordered quickly.

Fjord tilted his head in that animalistic way and said, "To land, Highness?"

Emira stepped forward slowly, allowing the icy water to reach her waistline. "Yes, she is a siren, she can surface. Telaria is in danger. She must come immediately."

The mer's expression hardened at the threat of danger. His webbed grip tightened on his spear and he bared his pointed teeth.

"Does Telaria have an army? Or a militia of some sort?" Emira added quickly.

"Of course," he answered.

"How many soldiers?"

"Five thousand bodies."

"And who leads them?"

Fjord's expression molded into a vengeful smirk as he answered, "I do, Highness."

"Bring them as well," Emira ordered. "All five thousand."

Fjord nodded once more and asked, "Are we to avenge Queen Leilitha?"

Emira's eyes darkened as she answered, "I will avenge my mother. I will free every slave in the Eastern Realm. I will end this tonight or die trying."

Fjord's smirk widened into a bloodthirsty grin as he dipped below the surface at the order of his queen.

FOUR SETS OF FEET SLAMMED ONTO THE SHORE BEHIND EMIRA. A quick glance back proved it to be Alicus and Zuri, who had been allowed transfer by a quick to retreat Hallend as well as Xemile and Tallen.

"Vyla?" Emira questioned, remaining waist deep in the sea, waiting for Fjord to return with her army.

"In the south, keeping our people safe," Xemile answered from shore. "The others have left as well. Gone back to their own realms to secure their borders."

Tallen walked into the water alongside Emira, placing a hand on the small of her back. She shivered at his touch, fighting the urge to let him scoop her up and take her far, far away. They could go anywhere. They could leave the Fae Realms, fly beyond Harpy Rock or the Mortal Realm to whatever may lie in wait for them. Here, only war and death were certain.

But before her fantasy began to trail too far, the ocean's glassy surface began to ripple violently. Tallen instinctively wrapped an arm around Emira's waist to pull her back, but she rested a hand on his in acknowledgement of what was coming.

Fjord rose, followed by Calline and the five thousand soldiers he'd promised. Many looked similar to their general, with bluish skin, webbed hands, large, black eyes, and rows of teeth. Others were shifters, transformed into their marine counterparts. Some were fish like, with gills at their necks and scales along their bodies. Others had tentacles of six or eight, each arm wielding a sword or spear. Many possessed features of a massive seahorse, their curled tail wrapped around a weapon and their skin transformed into thick, bony plates. The last few were sirens.

Emira's friends gaped at the sight; at the army that no one knew existed.

"Em," Tallen warned cautiously.

She stepped forward, ignoring the harpy, and addressed the soldiers. Fjord and Calline bowed as she approached, and the militia behind them followed.

"My mother," Emira began, her voice projecting loudly and powerfully, "was your queen. She was murdered by King Vyrion of the Eastern Realm."

The armada hissed at the sound of his name, sending skittering sound waves across the water and onto shore. It seemed that this was knowledge they already possessed.

"And now," she continued, "he wants Telaria." The statement was met with another hiss that sent shivers through those waiting on shore.

"We cannot give him what he wants!" Fjord called in response.

The soldiers slapped the water in agreement, forming waves and that forced them to bob chaotically. Emira did not back down as the violence of the waves grew but rather, used her magic to make them even taller. The water around her waist rose, higher and higher into the air, lifting her up above the sea. When she could see the face of each one enlisted in her army, she commanded the waves to still, holding her up above them.

"Look to the east!" she commanded. "Your target is the Eastern Realm! You shall harm no slave who is willing to surrender!"

"Emira!" Alicus called. "Xemile needs time to prepare our armies!"

Emira did not turn to him but continued to order her soldiers.

She looked at her general, speaking directly to him now. "We will bring Vyrion to his knees." Fjord smiled ferociously, his teeth gleaming like lethal gems. She turned to Calline, her aunt. "Go back to Telaria, keep my people safe." Calline's expression screamed concern, but the regent disappeared under the surface of the water silently, following her orders.

Fjord trailed behind her, commanding the army to follow as well. The water shook with the movement, sending the strong tide to crash against the shore. Emira allowed the swell of water to dissipate, and she lowered back to the surface, her body like a boulder against the current. She turned to the shore.

"Are you coming?" She held a hand out to Tallen.

"Emira, you must wait," Zuri urged. "We cannot help with such a hurried response."

"I will not wait for Vyrion to hurt the ones I love," the siren responded coldly.

"We can't go charging into the unknown," Xemile retorted.

Emira's gaze shot to his. "If you continue to wait, Vyrion will destroy the realms. He'll come for the south first."

"We are not going," Alicus responded. "Not like this. Not without a plan."

"Please!" Zuri begged. "Pull back your army."

Still holding her hand out to Tallen, Emira looked at him.

"And you?" she questioned. "Do you feel the same?"

Tallen's eyes searched her face desperately, but he did not answer.

"We are loyal to the Southern Realm!" Xemile hissed at the harpy.

Tallen spun on the general and roared, "You cannot make me choose!"

"Tallen, we aren't ready for battle," Zuri said.

"We must protect the Southern Realm," Alicus added.

"Do you care only for the Southern Realm?" Emira yelled, stepping toward the fae king.

His gray eyes darkened as he answered, "My people and my family are my first priority."

"And what of *my* people?" Emira seethed. "Do you not care for their lives?"

"Your people have hidden under the sea for centuries!" Alicus whirled back. "How can you ask me to place their safety above that of my own people?"

Emira's unblinking eyes pierced into his, and she opened her mouth to retort. Tallen's feathered wing stretched between his king and her as he stepped between them. His eyes met Emira's, pleading. She turned to leave.

"Em, wait," Tallen urged as he grasped her elbow.

She spun on him.

"We are *not* Bonded Souls."

The harpy released his grip on her arm, his icy eyes wide with disbelief.

"Calline said that sirens do not have souls," Emira continued, her green eyes alight with fury. "It is impossible for us to be bonded. I was a fool for believing you. Whatever I thought I felt—"

Tallen remained frozen in place, her words cutting through him like daggers. "None of it was real." She glared past the harpy, throwing one final angry look at the group, before turning and heading back into the sea. "I go alone."

CHAPTER

FORTY-SIX

The ocean before Emira was vast and blue and endless. It was a sickening metaphor—the calm before the storm. She swam alongside Fjord at the front of the armada, heart pounding with every swift kick through the water, and every stroke closer to the Eastern Realm.

"A weapon, my lady," Fjord started, holding a sheathed dagger in her direction. Emira turned to look at the magnificent weapon. Sunlight bounced off the hilt, its pearlescent gleam a stark contrast against the mer warrior's blue skin. They continued forward, no time to stop, as Emira reached out and accepted the gift. She pulled it from its sheath, revealing the magnificent blade and its threatening size. It was the length of her forearm, with intricate carvings from hilt to tip. The sharp point of the blade was like the threatening pointed finger of Death itself.

"Strap it to your leg," Fjord instructed. Emira did so, the sheath and strap fitting comfortably against her skin. "It came from our artillery, made by the mer to be used by royalty."

"Thank you," Emira responded. She swallowed hard and looked out against the vast sea once more. Emira planned to fight alongside her newly found people and die alongside them.

And she knew that Tallen had to be beside himself with grief, but she needed him to choose Alicus and the Southern Realm over her. Vyrion would use him to bend her to his will. It had hurt to be so heartless, and to lie about her love for him, but she couldn't offer him the time to choose wrongly. The vision of Tallen lying lifeless at her feet, mangled and broken, rotting from the inside out, was fuel enough to propel her forward. Bonded Soul or not, she had to leave, and she hoped he wouldn't be foolish enough to follow her.

Emira had always known that Vyrion would kill her. Today would be that day. They would die at each other's hands, with blades at each other's throats. She couldn't let Tallen witness it.

But she had to do this—for her mother, for her people. To keep the Southern Realm and her Soul Bond safe, she would die a thousand deaths at the hands of the monster who ruled the Eastern Realm.

And she was content with her decision to die for them.

"Look," came Fjord's voice. Emira's eyes shifted to where his webbed hand pointed. Two mer scouts that had been sent ahead were swiftly swimming back towards them.

"Report," Fjord commanded when they reached the group.

"They anticipate us," the first one said. "Armies are waiting on the shore."

"How many?" Fjord asked.

"More than us," the second scout answered. "Maybe ten thousand."

"But they look weak," the first scout added. "Frail, even."

"They're slaves," Emira said. "They serve Vyrion, but their loyalty is feeble, and their training is mediocre."

"Then we proceed," Fjord stated.

The scouts fell back in line, and Emira turned to face her army.

"Their numbers are large," she said, her underwater sing-song voice echoing through the sea, "but they do not fight for a leader they love. They fight out of fear. We fight with purpose—to avenge my mother, Leilitha!" Her words were met with the chaotic swishing of fins and yells of agreement. Fists raised above the heads of the warriors as they drove their support upward. She continued, "They wait for us on shore, but we are ready for them. Fight for your queen, fight for Telaria!"

CHAPTER
FORTY-SEVEN

Fjord and Emira surfaced first as they reached the shores of the Eastern Realm. They were barely a hundred meters from land where the army they were expecting stood in wait. The scouts had been correct in estimating the size of Vyrion's army. Standing upon the sandy shore, painted in the red of the setting sun, were thousands of men, their metal armor speckled with water as the waves violently crashed onto land.

Emira had not spent much time outside the castle walls when she had lived in the east. But there was something about the air, a staleness that she knew now only because she had breathed in the fresh air of the south, that permeated through her senses and sent a wave of nausea roiling through her gut. The air was filled with fear and decay and hopelessness. Perhaps she had not noticed before because her senses were weakened in her sickly state, or perhaps it was because she had been a contributor to the stench.

"Surface!" Fjord ordered, his screeching voice riding the violent waves.

The army of sirens and shifters and mer obeyed, dusting the horizon with their menacing presence. Their ratio was roughly two to one, with numbers in favor of the east, but the Telarian fighters were larger, more powerful, and angrier than the slaves who stood on shore. It would be an easy fight for them.

"Vyrion is mine," Emira said to the commander.

He tipped his head in understanding before raising his spear above his head and releasing an ear shattering war cry. The armada followed, crying out as they charged forward. It was a sound unlike anything Emira had ever heard before. The eerie, high-pitched shriek sent skittering waves onto shore. The few human slaves on shore dropped their weapons and brought their hands to their ears—a sad attempt to protect their ear drums from shattering and bleeding out.

Emira kicked her legs, forcing her body through the powerful current and onto land alongside her militia. The rough sand beneath her feet vibrated powerfully as her warriors propelled themselves from the water and onto shore. As the armies clashed, the sound of metal, bodies, and voices grew louder than the waves crashing behind them.

Emira drew her dagger and charged into the chaos, remembering what Xemile had taught her about weak spots in armor. Sadness tugged at her chest as she recalled her time with the fae warrior, their sarcastic banter, and dodging his cheap shots in the arena. But she was quickly pulled from the memory when the glimmer of a blade caught her eye. Before it came down on her, she blocked the blow and kicked the chest of the soldier who had attempted to slit her throat. When he was on the ground, she leapt atop of him and drove her knife into the armor's weak spot near his neck.

Hot blood sprayed her face and hands, mixing with salt water. For a moment, she was brought back to the memory of Rocas, and the feeling of his slaughtered flesh on her skin, but she pushed the memory away and continued on. She did not have the time to process her first kill while Vyrion still lived.

She stood and made her way farther into the throng, heading towards the looming castle that belonged to the king. He would, no doubt, be waiting for her there.

Emira ducked out of the way of a sword that swung toward her face. She sliced at the back of the soldier's ankle before standing and cutting his throat.

Suddenly, a wrench at her hair had Emira careening onto the bloody sand. She arched her body against the pain and rolled quickly to the side, looking for the threat. A blood-spattered eastern warrior reached for her, his eyes black with menace. But before he could grab her again, he was being lifted into the air by a pair of blue, webbed hands.

Fjord was slithering upright and holding the soldier three feet above the ground. With a screeching roar, he snapped the male's neck and tossed his limp body aside.

Emira let out a relieved breath, and Fjord extended his hand to her. She accepted and was pulled back onto her feet.

"Alright?" he screeched.

"Yeah," she answered, looking back towards the castle.

"They're formidable," Fjord added, glancing at the surrounding battle, "but a brainwashed army is easy to defeat. They have no heart. Be safe, my queen. We will make short work of this."

Emira nodded her thanks and continued forward for Vyrion.

EMIRA FOUND HER WAY OFF OF THE BEACH AS SHE MOVED TOWARD Vyrion's castle. She carefully stumbled through the crumbling underbrush that, despite the salty sea air, still clung to life. The castle's silhouette appeared as she pushed back some overhanging branches. The sight made her heart stop, and she recalled the life she had led here. She remembered the constant hunger, fear, and torment that was inflicted at the hands of Vyrion.

Adjusting her grip on her bloody, mer dagger, Emira stepped forward. His reign would end today. It had to.

As she reached the front doors of the castle, she realized that Vyrion had sent his entire army to the shore, even knowing that she would come looking for him. There were no guards posted at the entrance like there usually would be. She could just walk in. It was too easy—a trap, a dare… an arrogant show of confidence.

Just us, Emira thought.

The massive wooden doors creaked as she pushed them forward. They opened into a grand, circular entryway, with high ceilings and moonstone flooring; the same floors that blistered her hands as she had scrubbed them. The alabaster busts of the previous masters decorated the perimeter of the massive room, each of which Emira was all too familiar from the constant dusting that had been required of her.

And on the other side of the room stood Vyrion. Emira's breath caught as his silhouette emerged from a shadowed corner. His thin lips were quirked into a smile, and his wavy, blonde hair was loose around his shoulders. He placed a hand in his pocket and casually leaned against the wall, his emerald eyes roving over her as she stood as still as the busts watching on.

"Quicker than expected," he mocked.

Emira closed the giant door behind her, keeping her eyes locked on the monster that was her father.

Vyrion removed his hand from his pocket and took a step forward, running his fingers through his hair. An evil smile spread across his face, and he pulled a large dagger from his boot.

He spun it skillfully and said, "Shall we begin?"

Before Emira could inhale a breath to respond, Vyrion charged, pinning her against the closed door with the curved dagger held to her throat. A ripple of anger burned through the siren at being so easily targeted. She clutched his bony wrist with one hand, pushing against his strength and barely keeping the dagger's edge off of her skin. With her other hand, she raised her own weapon and plunged the blade into his side.

Vyrion roared, staggering back. Her dagger, still slippery from the bloodshed, remained embedded in his flesh. He ripped it from his body and threw it angrily to the opposite side of the room, and out of Emira's reach.

"You little cunt!" Vyrion seethed.

She made for the blade, but a swift blow from Vyrion's fist had her on the ground. Power rumbled beneath her skin, ready to be released. Vyrion clutched at his wounded ribs as blood gushed between his fingers, but Emira knew it would only be moments before it began to rapidly heal.

"You are so like your mother," he taunted. Emira stood and started to circle around Vyrion towards her knife.

Emira seethed through gritted teeth, "You don't get to talk about her."

"Stubborn," he continued. "Foolish. When you were born"—she cringed at his words—"I thought you would be useful to me."

"Happy to disappoint," she responded.

As he circled closer, Emira circled further away, getting closer and closer to her weapon.

"Leilitha was useless," he said with a wicked grin, "but she gave me a daughter that I had hoped would prove an *equal*."

Emira scoffed at his words. "She gave you nothing. You took everything you wanted."

"Semantics," he responded casually. "But you turned out to be just as weak as she was." Vyrion picked up his pace as the wound in his side closed, and Emira matched his speed.

"Why keep me alive for so long? Why not tell me the truth?" she questioned, eyeing her blade. It was only a few meters away now.

"Why give you a complex?" he answered smoothly. "The daughter of a siren queen and a king of the fae may grow a large head." She scoffed again, baffled and disgusted by him. He stopped abruptly and continued, "But if it's the truth you want, I suppose you can have it. You'll be taking it to your grave tonight, Emira."

Vyrion slowly raised his hands, palms facing upwards towards the high ceilings. Emira stopped and gaped at him. His lips quirked into a menacing half smile as water pooled in his cupped hands, forming spheres that twirled and danced midair. He tossed them about as if they were solid and shot them into the air so quickly that Emira could barely see where they flew before they burst and rained down on both of them.

Water covered the moonstone floor. Her hair and clothes were soaked as were Vyrion's. His eyes glimmered with satisfaction at the confusion and disdain that was smeared across her face.

"You're a siren," Emira breathed.

Vyrion replied with a wicked grin.

"You're a siren!" she exclaimed again, the words sinking into her bones like poison.

Vyrion's green eyes pierced through her as he mocked, "Want to know the rest?"

"What more could there possibly be?" Emira demanded.

Vyrion stood before her, spinning his knife in his hand. The wound she had inflicted on him minutes before had stopped bleeding and was now entirely healed.

"My mother was a common siren," he began, his green eyes still staring threateningly, "and my father was fae, the king of this realm. But the sirens are a matriarchy. And while my birthright is the east, I wanted the mer realm too. I could never rule Telaria, even with royal fae blood in my veins."

"I don't understand," Emira said.

Vyrion smirked. "Why do you think we can communicate tele-pathically? How is it that I can reach you from so far away?" His eyes glistened as realization swept over Emira's features.

"Siren speaking," she muttered.

"A leftover trait," Vyrion continued casually. "Useless, but I quite enjoyed using it to torment you."

Emira's eyes welled remembering the nightmares she had suf-fered; the pain Vyrion had been able to inflict upon her without needing to physically touch her.

He continued, still toying with the weapon in his hand. "If I was ever going to rule Telaria, I needed to gain favor with their queen—your mother."

"So you kidnapped and enslaved her," Emira finished for him.

"She would not be persuaded to disclose the location of Telar-ia, but only female sirens possess the ability of hypnosis. I figured that may be useful to me as well."

"You're fucking sick," Emira said through gritted teeth.

Vyrion huffed a laugh, unphased by the insult. "But like I said, she was a stubborn bitch, and when starvation, torture, and seiz-ing her only child wouldn't break her, I took her to the woods and disposed of her." He tilted his head and smiled maniacally. "You've been to those very woods, remember?"

Bile rose in Emira's throat. The woods—the woods where Vyrion had taken her for stealing an apple, where Tallen and Xe-mile had discovered them. Her mother had been butchered there.

Vyrion's snake-like voice cut off her trailing thoughts. "You'll soon meet the same fate."

"And the contract?" Emira demanded quickly. "You have a contract with the other realms that says you won't—that you can't—keep slaves."

Vyrion took another step forward and answered, "I don't have slaves. I have paid laborers; they just don't know it."

He lunged, dagger raised high over his head. Emira ducked out of the way and made for her weapon. She grabbed the hilt as Vyrion gripped her ankle and pulled her swiftly back to him. He flipped her onto her back with ease and climbed atop her thrashing body.

Laughing murderously, he sneered, "Send my regards to Leilitha."

Vyrion snatched the dagger from her hand, tossing it to the other end of the room, and lifted his blade to strike.

He brought it down swiftly and drove it into Emira's right shoulder. The sting seared through her muscles and into her bones. She let out an ear shattering scream as Vyrion twisted the blade.

He smiled too-widely down at her, crimson blood splattering his demented face. Emira writhed under the weight of his body as he yanked the blade free. She screamed again and arched against the pain, tears running down her face.

"Just deep enough to hurt," he began, "but it will begin to heal soon enough."

Vyrion had not changed since her time in the Southern Realm. He still liked to play with his prey and had likely been planning all the ways he would make her suffer since her rescue.

He grabbed the hair at her scalp and stood, lifting her with him and dragged her across the large entryway, kicking up the spilled water as he went. He flung her body up against the stone wall and glared at her.

"Make this interesting, Emira. Use your power," he dared. "Go on. After all, you have more siren blood than I do."

He released her hair, and swiftly kicked her in the ribs as her body slid to the floor. Emira coughed, and blood filled her mouth.

"Flood the castle," he taunted. "Flood the realm. End this."

Emira's power flickered under her skin like candlelight, but the pain in her bloodied shoulder and shattered ribs was overwhelming. She couldn't move, couldn't think, couldn't take a breath.

Vyrion sighed and tilted his head back boredly.

"You make it too easy, Emira. At least your bitch mother put up a fight."

He crouched down and leaned close to her ear, grasping at her hair again to tilt her head back.

"What shall I do once I kill you?" he asked. Emira sobbed and clutched her shoulder, turning her body away from the male who had enslaved her for decades. "Shall I pay a visit to the Southern Realm? Perhaps I'll look for that harpy you care so deeply for."

Vyrion drove his dagger into her thigh, forcing it down to the hilt, and yanked it free before Emira was able to cry out. Blood gushed from the injury, leaving her femoral artery sliced in two.

Emira's hands went to the wound, instinctively adding the pressure that she knew would do no good. She would bleed out before it could heal.

Still clutching her hair, Vyrion stood and lifted her from the ground, her feet now dangling two feet above the blood and water soaked floor.

"A final chance to cooperate," Vyrion began, "and save those you love from a fate worse than that of mother dearest."

Blood dripped from her shoulder and leg, splattering the opalescent floor, swirling as it mixed with the water. Her scalp burned in Vyrion's grip. Emira forced her watery eyes to focus on his evil face, still smeared with red.

She said nothing. Her energy dwindled as the blood streamed down her body.

"Pity," Vyrion said.

He released her, letting her fall to the hard ground and land in a warm pool of blood. Emira barely moved; she couldn't. Vyrion lifted his blade to strike once more and end her, his daughter's, life.

And Emira, lying in a crumpled heap on the stone, began to hum.

CHAPTER
FORTY-EIGHT

Vyrion stopped, lowered his blade and looked down at Emira.

"A pathetic attempt," he sneered as she continued to hum. "A siren's hypnosis can only enter a weak mind. You have no power over me."

Emira rolled to her side and shifted her eyes up to Vyrion.

You are weak, she said into his subconscious. *You always have been.*

Vyrion blinked rapidly, and shook his head, as if shooing away an annoying insect.

"I am a king!" he argued aloud, leaning down. "I am a conqueror!"

Emira did not move. She kept her green eyes on him and spoke into his mind again, using the same siren telepathy that he had used on her so many times before.

You have conquered nothing. All you have is a realm of slaves. Your army will be defeated by the marine militia before night's end. And then they will come for you.

A ripple of fear shone in his eyes as they clouded over. Emira forced the words from her mind as he blinked the murkiness away, slipping in and out of hypnosis. He knelt down, ignoring the blood that began to seep onto his elegant pants. Vyrion grabbed a fistful of her hair and ripped her up towards him.

Emira winced at the pain but kept her eyes on her father.

You are not respected, she stated into his mind, still humming her hypnotic melody. *You are not an equal to the other kings.*

He growled at her words but was losing his ability to speak freely.

You have no queen, no heir, Emira continued. *You have nothing but the reputation of a liar and a fraud.*

Her humming had grown louder, but Vyrion fought against the hypnotic effect. Still gripping her hair, he held his blade to her slender throat.

"E-enough!" he shouted, blinking and stuttering as the hypnosis clouded his mind. He pressed his blade firmly to her flesh, but Emira reached up and snatched the knife from his trembling grip. With her other hand, she grasped Vyrion's blonde locks and wrenched his head backwards.

A quick swipe of her arm, and Emira slit the king's throat with his own dagger. His grasp on her released, and they both fell to the ground, swimming in blood.

Emira turned her head shakily. Vyrion's mouth was agape, his eyes wide open, and clouded over. Blood oozed from his throat, and his breathing had ceased.

He was dead.

He was dead.

She let out a sigh of relief and set her head back. Her skin and hair were sticky from the bloodbath, and the metallic smell clung to the air. She stared up at the vaulted ceilings as her sight began to narrow. Her leg was warm with the blood that continued to spurt from her severed artery, and her shoulder burned where Vyrion's blade had penetrated her flesh. Slowly, Emira started to feel cold, and numb, and low—as if her very life force was leaving her body. She quietly slipped into darkness, accepting her fate peacefully.

CHAPTER
FORTY-NINE

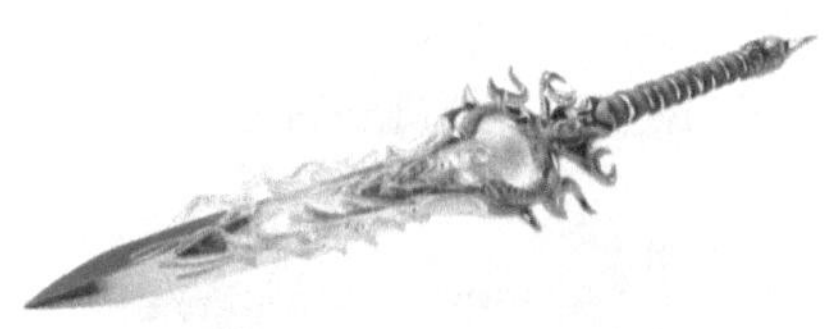

Tallen flew swiftly over the shoreline as the battle unfolded beneath him. Xemile was close behind, followed by the fae armada he commanded. Alicus and Zuri had flown to the east and were already below, both of them skillfully fighting in the throng of blood and flesh. Vyla, unable to swim in her shifted form as quickly as those who flew, remained in the Southern Realm to guard the borders and command the remaining armies in the event of an invasion.

When Emira had left for the east, Alicus remained wary of charging into the unknown. But Tallen refused to stay behind while the Telarians fought, and the loyalty Alicus had for his second in command was unmatched to his doubt of Emira's hasty plan.

It had only taken the harpy moments to shoot into the air and follow the marine armada to the east. With a quick stop to his bedroom to seize more weapons than he'd already had on his person, he was flying over the realms at breakneck speed to find Emira.

And he blocked her hurtful words from his mind; he refused to believe any of it. Emira had a soul. And his was bonded to hers.

There was no doubt, no question in his mind that this was the truth. The draw he felt to her could not be explained any other way. She was his, and he would find her.

Everyone but Tallen landed on the shore to assist the marine army in battle. Tallen continued forward until he reached the stone castle. He knew Emira would have gone straight for Vyrion.

He landed before the doors with a great thud, the weight of his leather armor and weapons pulling him down even harder. He smelled blood. It hung in the air like smog.

The harpy threw open the double doors and entered the massive white entryway. But there, in the center of the floor, drenched in red, lay two lifeless bodies.

Tallen dove for Emira, shoving aside Vyrion's corpse violently and sending it skittering across the blood soaked floor. The harpy lifted Emira's limp figure from the ground and cradled her in his arms. Her blood was still warm. He had only been moments too late.

"Em? Em, please!" he cried, lifting her body closer, and pulling her tightly to his chest. "Emira!"

Tallen sobbed, his knees soaking in the blood that stained the once spotless floors. His wings hung low behind him, feathers dipped in the crimson liquid like paint brushes to paint, and his shoulders shuddered with every weeping breath.

"Gods, Em, I'm so sorry," he admitted into her limp body. "Please, please..."

He drew in a shaking breath and released a powerful scream that shook the very walls. The loud crack of thunder sounded beyond the confines of the castle, and heavy raindrops began to spatter upon the exterior stone. His heart crumbled as he gazed upon Emira, gray pallor in place of her once rosy cheeks.

He gently touched a kiss upon her forehead.

With lips still pressed to her balmy skin, Tallen choked out the words, "I love you, Em. For all of eternity and for everything that comes after, I love you."

CHAPTER

FIFTY

Tallen's heavy feet slammed onto the blood-soaked shore of the beach. His icy eyes penetrated the dusky haze created by the setting sun. The battle was close to won, with less than one hundred eastern soldiers still standing. Upon Tallen's arrival, those around him ceased brawling and turned their gazes to him, the expressions on their faces dropping into those of pure terror.

With his jaw tightly clenched and his mouth set firmly, Tallen looked out across the battlefield. In one arm, he cradled Emira's limp body, keeping her protected from the torrential downpour and bright lightning under the shelter of his wing. In his other hand, he wielded the severed, bloodied head of Vyrion. He had taken it before leaping from the castle and into the sky. The dead master's eyes were frozen into saucers, his mouth agape and tongue protruding.

Xemile ran to Tallen's side, his eyes roaming over the gruesome sight before him. The harpy silently gestured to Emira, entrusting her body to the general. Xemile accepted, gently holding her against his chest, a feeling he remembered from his very first encounter with the siren.

Tallen pulled his whip free, the leather slithering excitedly in his grip. Shock and fear crawled over the faces of the remaining eastern soldiers as Tallen raised their master's head above his own and flung it into the sea with a grievous yell. The swift red tide washed it away within seconds, and Tallen turned his attention back to the enemies before him.

The harpy flicked his wrist, and the whip made a resounding crack that rattled the crimson sand around him. The sky darkened, and as the rain eased, a flash of lightning spider webbed across the sky, casting menacing shadows over the harpy's face. He charged into the throng, his sentient weapon thrashing and flying around him with precision.

A lashing on a throat, splitting it wide open.

A slice at the back of the ankle, severing the tendons, followed by a swift plunge of a dagger in the neck.

A flick of his wrist in the direction of the enemy's eyes, the sting of his whip blinding them and causing the sockets to spurt blood.

With precision and skill, Tallen removed every foreign soldier in his way one by one.

"Tallen!" Xemile yelled over the chaos. The harpy did not hear his comrade as he ripped through his enemies. "Tallen!"

Fjord followed closely behind the harpy, finishing off any soul left to bleed out on the battlefield, a small mercy given to those that Tallen would have seen suffer.

He tore through the last of the Eastern Realm's army, leaving no one alive except the southern and Telarian allies to Emira.

"Tallen!" Alicus shouted next.

His king's voice pulled Tallen from his haze of bloodlust, and he froze, turning his attention in the direction of his friends. Fresh crimson dripped from every inch of the harpy's face, hands and black leather armor. Beneath the flowing crimson, his icy blue eyes were still alight with rage.

Xemile stepped forward, still cradling Emira's limp body. His eyes searched his friend as he said, "Tallen, she's breathing."

Tallen looked down at Emira. Her chest was rising and falling slowly, faintly. The harpy sheathed his weapons and took her swiftly from Xemile's arms, holding her against his bloodied leathers. He turned to his king and queen, who stood alongside Fjord.

"We take her to Sarolina," Tallen stated desperately. "She can heal her."

Zuri balked at the harpy, her raven hair billowing around her blood flecked face. "From broken bones and bruises, but not a severed artery."

"Even if she could," Alicus said, breathing heavily, "we couldn't get to the Southern Realm in time. She'll bleed out too quickly, even with transference."

Tallen's eyes shot to Fjord. "And you?" he breathed. "Do the mer have healers?"

Fjord looked at his queen, and his lips turned downwards at the sight of her labored breathing.

"Not for this," his voice screeched sadly. "The blood flows too quickly."

Tallen tipped his head back to the sky, and looked at the gray, overhanging clouds. He released an angry, desperate, frustrated scream into the wind.

Emira suddenly inhaled a shuddering breath, pulling the harpy's gaze back onto her.

"Tallen," she croaked.

"Gods, Em, don't," he said, clutching her closer and stretching his wings. "I'm taking you home, I'll find Sarolina…" Her eyes fluttered as he spoke, and her body was growing colder and colder.

"Take me… to… the w-water," she managed to say, pausing between words to catch her breath.

Tallen looked at the sea. It was tinged with red from the battle, and the tide was retreating.

"We need to get home," he implored. "You need a healer."

Fjord slithered forward, tilting his head. Tallen growled possessively at the mer and gripped Emira more tightly.

"My queen requests the sea," Fjord stated firmly.

Tallen made to argue, but was cut short when Alicus stepped forward, and motioned the harpy towards the water.

Tallen inhaled a shuddering breath and looked down at Emira. Her skin was gray, and speckled with beading sweat. Blood smeared her face and hair. Her once gushing shoulder was now only trickling while the wound on her leg remained open and flowing with red.

Tallen left his friends and the remaining marine army on the shore as he trudged to the sea. He knelt down into the salty water, scooping up handfuls and washing the blood from Emira's hair. Tears streamed down his cheeks as Emira grew paler and colder with each wave that crashed onto shore.

"I will never forgive myself," he said, pressing his lips to her forehead, "for not protecting you."

The sky darkened further, and the tide pulled at the harpy as he knelt in the sea, cradling Emira as she slipped further and further from life. Rain began to sprinkle from the dark clouds, washing the blood from Tallen's face. Alicus, Zuri, Xemile, and Fjord stood back on shore, watching Tallen hold Emira in her final moments.

"Em," Tallen said, rain water dripping from his black hair and into the sea. "Em, I love you. You are my Soul Bond. I know you are. I don't care what Calline said. I can feel it. Please, please, stay with me."

Emira smiled faintly and forced her eyes open. She brought a shaking hand to his cheek, and Tallen clutched it to his stubbled skin.

"I'm sorry, T-Tallen," she responded shakily. "I love you. You've made… my broken world… whole."

Tallen's shoulders shuddered and he inhaled a shaky breath.

"I can't go on without you," he admitted, his voice breaking. "Em, I'm so sorry."

Behind them, the blood soaked sand started to run clear as the rain fell harder. Xemile's chest heaved, while Zuri cried into Alicus' shoulder. The southern king's jaw ticked helplessly.

Fjord looked back at his remaining soldiers and nodded commandingly. He lowered his head and placed a hand over his heart. The militia followed, a gesture to honor their brave queen.

Back in the sea, Tallen pressed his forehead to Emira's. The water held most of her weight, and she bobbed with the current. Her breathing hitched, and her chest heaved before going still. Her head dropped back against the harpy's grip, blonde hair flowing around them in the sea.

Tallen sobbed, sinking deeper into the water and clutching Emira's lifeless body. She was cold, and her skin was gray. Her once mauve lips were now white and parted. Her wounds had stopped bleeding for there was no more blood left to lose. Her listless body rested in his arms as he wept into her neck. His voice echoed across the beach, and he cried out her name.

"Emira," he cried through gasping breaths. "My Emira…"

"Tallen," came Alicus' voice from behind the harpy. "Let Xemile help."

The general appeared before the harpy, kneeling in the water and reaching his arms out. He gently placed them under Emira's corpse, making to lift her up and away from Tallen's hold. The harpy pulled away from the general, possessively pulling Emira's body from within his reach.

"No," he growled, "No, no, no…"

Alicus and Fjord came up behind the harpy and swiftly gripped him beneath the arms as Xemile made a second attempt to lift Emira from the water. Tallen's grip on the siren slipped, and she was released to the general. Xemile immediately shot into the sky, amber wings beating furiously against the wind, leaving Alicus, Zuri, and Fjord to ready a grief-stricken Tallen for the flight back south.

CHAPTER
FIFTY-ONE

Emira was floating, somewhere between the sea and the sky. Her feet dangled beneath her body as if she were flying, or treading water. The light, fresh air encompassed her body like a cocoon. Looking out over the blue expanse of whatever world she had landed in, she searched for familiarity, but there was none. Images flashed through her mind as she gazed around. She had a memory of Tallen holding her in the sea, his blood-stained face looking down at her, and his warm tears dropping onto her cold skin. Emira looked down at her body, which was clothed in flowing blue fabric that danced around her ankles as if a breeze blew past. Her wounds were gone, and the pain was gone. But so was Tallen.

"Hello?" Emira called out.

Her voice echoed and rang like a song into the vast expanse of blue nothingness. She kicked her legs gracefully, propelling herself through the space as if she were swimming. Her hair flowed like it was underwater, and she moved through the air like a bird. Searching for what, she did not know.

"Hello?" Emira called again.

The silhouette of another appeared far ahead. As it came closer, it appeared to be a woman, wearing similar clothing in various shades of lilac and pink. The woman approached gracefully, her waist length, blonde hair flowing about, and her green eyes fixed on Emira. Atop her head, the woman wore a crown of gold, fashioned in the shape of shells and ocean waves.

Arms reaching toward her, the woman smiled and spoke.

"Hello, Emira."

Recognition swept over Emira's mind and she felt her lip quiver. This woman looked exactly like the marble statue she had seen in Telaria. She was the moon, she was the goddess, she was…

"M-mother?" Emira breathed disbelievingly.

It was undeniable. It was as if Emira was looking into a mirror.

Queen Leilitha responded by quirking her full, pink lips into a smile. She nodded, taking Emira's hands in her own. "You have been so brave."

Tears clouded Emira's vision as her mother squeezed her hands. "How is this possible?" she choked.

"Sirens are immortal, but we become the salt and foam of the sea if our lives are taken," Leilitha answered, her angelic voice barely above a whisper. "But some earn a soul. A gift from the Mother, for a life of selfless servitude to the sea. And you have, my love, done nothing but give your livelihood for the gain of others."

Emira huffed a disbelieving laugh

"I'm dead," she stated with an empty voice.

"I'm afraid," Leilitha answered solemnly, "that your physical body has died."

Emira turned her head, blinking back the tears that threatened to fall.

"Tallen," she whispered to herself.

Her last few words to him had been harsh and untrue. She had torn his heart in two and left him to hope that it had all been a dream. He had cradled her in the sea, respecting her last wishes to be in the water, and he had proclaimed his love for her as she died in his arms. Shame and torment flooded Emira's veins. How could he ever forgive her? How could she ever forgive herself?

Leilitha took Emira's chin in her hands and brought their gazes together.

"You protected Telaria," she began. "And you ended Vyrion's reign. I wish to show my gratitude to a most powerful queen."

CHAPTER
FIFTY-TWO

Xemile landed on the balcony of Tallen and Emira's room. He held the siren's body firmly, ensuring that it remained safe during flight. Vyla met him there, following the fae warrior into the castle when she saw him flying over the Southern Realm's territories.

"What happened?" she demanded as she threw open the balcony doors, allowing Xemile to enter. When her eyes landed on the corpse that Xemile held, her face paled.

"No…" she balked.

"The bed," Xemile replied, nodding in its direction. Vyla obeyed, clearing the unmade sheets and adjusting the pillows. Xemile lay Emira's cold body upon it. Vyla grasped the siren's cold hand and stared down at her blood coated fingers.

"Tallen is coming," the general said, reaching into the drawers for some fresh cloths and holding one out to the shifter. She nodded, understanding their task. She wetted the fabric in the sink of the adjoining bathing room and began wiping at Emira's face and neck as tears welled in her slitted eyes.

Together, Xemile and Vyla cleansed Emira's body, scrubbing away every bit of dirt, blood, and sand. They washed and combed her hair, bandaged her wounds, and dressed her in clean, white linens.

Her skin remained gray, and her lips white, but it was all they could do to give Tallen a serene memory of the siren before she was laid to rest.

Alicus and Zuriel transferred back to the Southern Realm with a thunderous *crack*, landing on the balcony with Tallen in tow. Xemile joined them quickly, helping to hold the harpy upright, keeping his knees from buckling and his body from dropping to the ground.

"Fjord?" Xemile questioned.

"He's taking his militia back to Telaria," Zuri answered quickly as the four of them made their way inside.

Tallen wrenched free at the sight of Emira and flung his arms around her, sobbing into the soft, clean fabric of her dress. Vyla squeezed Xemile's hand while Zuri cried silently beneath the king's arm. Xemile and Alicus lowered their heads, unable to watch the sight before them.

The harpy ran his hands through Emira's freshly washed, blonde waves, and planted kisses along her lackluster cheeks.

"Em," he said through sobs. "Em, please, no, no, no…"

Zuri pressed a hand over her mouth as she began to weep. Xemile wrapped an arm around his queen as he silently prayed to the gods to end Tallen's suffering. Alicus' chest heaved as he too, choked back tears, and Vyla's teary gaze turned numb.

Tallen continued to cry over his Soul Bond's body, begging for her life back.

"I promised you would be safe," he started. "I promised to keep you safe from him. Emira, I'll never forgive myself."

He lifted Emira's torso and cradled her in his arms. He rocked back and forth, her head lolling to the side with the movement.

"Tallen," Alicus said softly.

The harpy's gaze jerked toward his king, as if he had forgotten anyone else was in the room.

"Tallen," Alicus began again, gulping back the crack in his voice. "She shall be laid to rest with the highest honors. A queen's farewell."

"I can't let her go," Tallen sobbed, clutching Emira's body to his own.

"She's already gone," Zuri added quietly.

"No, no, no," Tallen began frantically. "No, it's okay; she'll be okay. We just need Sarolina. It'll be alright."

Xemile took a step forward and placed a hand on the harpy's shoulder. "I'm so sorry, brother."

Zuri gently rested her hands on Emira's body, guiding Tallen to lower the siren's torso back onto the bed. He followed his queen's gesture, hands shaking as he finally let go. Tallen slowly stepped back, creating distance between himself and his dead Soul Bond.

He released a deep, melancholy cry and fell to his knees faster than Xemile could catch him. Tallen remained kneeling over the edge of his bed, sobbing and calling out Emira's name for several minutes while his friends remained close by, mourning the siren alongside him.

CHAPTER
FIFTY-THREE

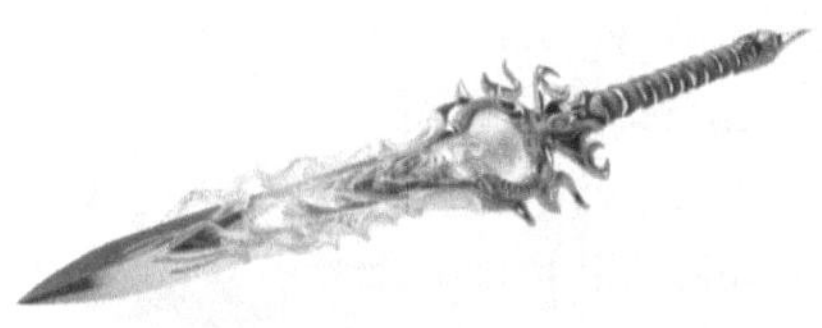

"I don't understand," Emira said to her mother. "Gratitude?"

Leilitha smiled gently, still holding Emira's hands. "You freed the slaves of the Eastern Realm. You kept Telaria safe. Emira, my dear, you have saved *thousands* of lives."

Emira's eyes welled at her mother's words.

"I knew Vyrion would kill me one day," she admitted.

"But, my dear," Leilitha began, "you didn't know this. I, too, earned a soul. And I would die all over again for you." She searched her mother's beautiful face, trying to grasp her meaning.

"I relinquish my soul," Leilitha pledged.

Emira blanched, but Leilitha continued to smile.

"It's alright," Leilitha responded to the silence. "You have so much more life to live."

"What do you mean?" Emira questioned. Leilitha smiled even wider and looked down at the space between them. A translucent mist had swirled from her body and danced in the air like ribbons before fading to nothing. Leilitha reached up and gently lifted the oceanic crown from her head. A small grin curved her lips as she placed it upon her daughter's blonde locks, releasing it and dropping her hands back to her sides.

"Mother!" Emira gasped as she reached up and pulled the crown off. "Mother, no——"

"Keep the soul you have earned," Leilitha started. "I return mine to the Mother, and in exchange, I bid you to go and *live*."

She planted a kiss on Emira's cheek, whispering gently against her skin, "You were always destined for eachother," before floating backwards through the serene air. Her silhouette faded and changed, turning the palest green. In moments, Leilitha had turned to seafoam, slowly falling like raindrops from the mysterious space they occupied.

Emira sobbed at her mother's sacrifice, and she curled her arms around herself, still grasping the Telarian crown. She suddenly felt her body begin to fall within the massive nothingness, as her soul began to awaken on the other side.

CHAPTER
FIFTY-FOUR

Tallen wept upon the floor, his shoulders shaking uncontrollably and his wings hanging low. Fury tugged at his chest. He should have followed Emira to the Eastern Realm. He should have left the south behind and fought alongside his Soul Bond. He would never, *could never*, forgive himself.

Xemile stood behind Tallen, jaw clenched tightly while he tried to remain stoic for his friend. Vyla and Zuri's eyes welled for the harpy's loss, and Alicus finally took a step forward.

"Tallen," the king began. "It's time."

"No," Tallen sobbed, remaining a crumpled heap on the floor. "Not yet, I can't."

Xemile placed a hand on Tallen's shoulder.

"We'll stay with you," he promised.

"Call for Sarolina and her attendants," Alicus said to Vyla, his eyes lowered, unable to face his friend's grief.

"No, please," Tallen begged his king. "You can't take her, not yet."

The harpy sobbed as Xemile lifted him from the floor. He wept and wept and wept, his chest heaving with every desperate inhale. He stepped toward Emira's lifeless, gray body and cradled her one last time, resting his head in the crook of her neck.

"Forever," Tallen sobbed onto her cold skin. "I will love you forever."

He reached down to hold her hand, his lips still touching her skin. But when he felt something cool and sleek in her grasp, his gaze shot to it. In Emira's hand, she suddenly held a golden crown, shaped like the ocean waves and adorned with jewels and shells.

Tallen held the crown, still cradling Emira in his arm. He looked to his friends, who wore the same expression of bewilderment as he did. It was beautiful, but no one had seen where it came from, and Tallen knew that he had never seen it among Emira's possessions before now.

"What is it?" Xemile asked, stepping forward and looking over the harpy's shoulder.

Zuri wiped the tears from her cheeks and questioned, "Where did it come from?"

Tallen looked at his Soul Bond, his brows furrowed, his eyes searching her beautiful face. Her lips were no longer bluish but slowly becoming their stunning mauve color again. Her cheeks pinkened, rosy once more, and her closed eyes seemed to flicker under her lids.

"She's *alive*," Tallen stated sternly, tossing the crown onto the floor and lifting Emira's body upright.

His friends remained still, looking at the harpy solemnly.

"Tallen," Vyla began. "She's not. She's gone."

"Emira," Tallen said desperately, gently patting her cheek. "Em? Emira!"

"Tallen," Alicus said, reaching for the harpy. Tallen shoved his king away and continued grasping at Emira's face.

Emira's chest heaved, and she suddenly gasped loudly, stilling everyone who watched, including Tallen. Her green eyes fluttered open, and her breathing evened. Emira looked around slowly, her gaze finally landing on Tallen, who was cradling her just as he had when she died on the beach.

"Tallen?" she said, her voice barely above a whisper. "My mother…"

Suddenly, there it was. The Soul Bond.

Tallen and Emira felt it at the same time. Their bodies and minds wove together, twisting and tying around each other like threads forming rope. Invisible to their friends surrounding them, the Soul Bond that Tallen and Emira shared made its way through their veins, connecting the two lovers in the most intimate of ways.

Emira now had a soul, and Tallen had been correct in his belief of the bond's existence between them. It was thanks to the late queen of the Telaria that the both of them experienced it fully now.

Tallen cut her off by swiftly pressing his lips to hers. He looped his arms around her body, sobbing her name in between kisses. The others stared in shock as Emira wrapped her arms around her Soul Bond and cried into his shoulder.

"We need Sarolina," Zuri finally said. She gestured for everyone to exit the room immediately, leaving the harpy and the siren to bask in their bonded joy.

CHAPTER
FIFTY-FIVE

Two weeks passed before Emira stepped outside the cottage she now shared with Tallen. The modest home was a gift from Alicus and Zuri—a small haven to heal away from the bustle of the castle. She spent most of her days resting and reading while Tallen remained close. She no longer needed Sarolina's nighttime tonic to sleep. Vyrion wouldn't be haunting her dreams anymore.

Alicus, Zuri, and Fjord cared for those who remained in the Eastern Realm. The enslaved were freed, and given the wages that Vyrion had withheld. They started transforming their lives, starting anew, while awaiting the return of their new queen. With Vyrion's demise, the Eastern Realm became Emira's birthright, as his only heir.

Meanwhile, Calline remained regent to Telaria in Emira's absence. Word had spread that Leilitha had given up her soul for Emira to live, and the Telarian people had wept and grieved to know that their Queen Mother had turned into sea foam.

Emira finally stepped outside the cottage early one morning. The autumn air had given way to winter, and the refreshing chill licked at her skin. The nearby Valeldran River flowed gently. She walked barefoot to the shore's edge and carefully stepped into the frigid water.

The hem of her lilac gown floated on the surface around her ankles, and she briefly recalled the in-between world where she had landed after death. Firmly holding her mother's crown, Emira looked down at the shining gold, and the intricate oceanic detailing that she held in her hands.

"Alright?" came Tallen's voice behind her.

Emira didn't turn to look at him but continued studying the headdress in her hands.

"I had always known that Vyrion would kill me," she began as her gaze lifted from the crown to the surface of the water. It sparkled like diamonds in the early morning sunlight. "And he did," she continued. "But I didn't know I would inherit kingdoms, or find my Soul Bond, or meet my mother, if only for a moment…"

Tallen stepped into the water alongside her, looking down at the crown she held in her hands.

"What am I supposed to do now?" she whispered.

Tallen took the crown into his hand and gripped Emira with the other.

"Do what you want," he responded, kissing her temple. "The weight of this crown is not yours to bear, if you do not want it."

Emira released a breath and relaxed her shoulders, leaning into the harpy.

"But," he continued, "you once told me that you were done hiding, done living in fear." She looked up at Tallen, whose icy blue eyes were fixed on her. "Maybe this has been your destiny all along."

Tallen turned to face her, and brushed her blonde waves back behind her pointed ears. He gently placed the crown atop her head, straightened it and took a step back.

He smiled, and bowed humorously, splaying his wings out wide behind him. Emira laughed at the harpy, and gently brushed her fingers along the ridges of the golden heirloom.

"Your sense of humor has improved," Emira quipped with a smile.

"An honor to please the queen of the east, and the queen of Telaria," he answered back.

"And… you'll be with me?" Emira asked timidly.

Tallen's grin faded as he stepped swiftly towards her. Placing both hands in her hair, he firmly pressed his lips to hers. They stood in the cold river, embracing silently.

Tallen finally pulled away and promised, "Crown or no crown, Em, I will not be parted from you. Until the end of this world and into the next, I am yours. I will not leave unless you order me away."

"You've said that before."

"And I'll say it again."

Emira wrapped her arms around the harpy and put her forehead to his.

"Then take me to my kingdom," she whispered. "I'm ready to rule my people."

Tallen smiled and extended his wings, gripping her at the waist.

"There she is." He smirked, and they shot into the air, ready to face the end of time together.

The End

ACKNOWLEDGMENTS

There are so many people without whom this book would not be possible.

First, to my husband, Jon. Thank you for your encouragement throughout this process. Your positivity helped me to push through when I was feeling uninspired, and your constant, unconditional love has made me feel safe and free to begin my author journey.

To everyone who read my rough drafts and gave me the feedback I needed - Kaitlyn, Sophia, Garrett and Sharmaine - you are all so amazing!

To my cover artist, Victoria Cooper Art, thank you for creating a badass cover that I am absolutely in love with.

To my map artist, Alec McKinley, who made the Fae Realms so visually enticing, and better than I could have imagined.

To my editor, Amy Sjolund, for reading through my entire manuscript and helping me to make it as perfect as possible.

To my book formatter, Brady Moller, for his fantastic work in creating an aesthetically pleasing interior design.

Finally, to everyone who enjoys this book and chooses to write a review, share it with a friend, or recommend it to a family member. Thank you, thank you, thank you!

ABOUT THE AUTHOR

AMBER IS A DAYDREAMER AND HOPELESS ROMANTIC HAPPILY LIVING somewhere in Indiana with her husband, three children, and four cats. When she isn't writing fantasy or reading smut, she can be found cursing the weeds in her garden, trying to befriend wild animals, or perusing the bookstore for the third time this week. Blade of the Siren is her first novel.

Follow Amber on TikTok @authorambergriffey for book related content, dumb humor, and for updates about her next book 'Blade of the Siren Queen'